'I don't unders...

Roslyn looked at Sop... practically had to beg... hands. And how does ...... By implying that I don't appreciate what's being offered here. What does he expect? That I'll just walk away from my life in Chicago because a great-aunt I never even knew existed left me this monstrous home with the condition that I have to live here for a whole year to look after a rosebush. *A rosebush!'*

Roslyn gave a half shrug, palms up in surrender. She sensed the housekeeper was waiting for something more, so she continued.

'The woman obviously didn't give a hoot about my taking the place or she wouldn't have made it so difficult. So when I decide to give it to the other beneficiary, he gets all prickly and accuses me of not caring about any of this.' Roslyn's right hand swept an arc across the room.

'Jack would never—'

'Well, he did.' In fact, Roslyn thought, none of the conversation with Jack had gone the way she'd imagined. She thought he'd beam, offer a humble thank-you for her generosity and maybe even suggest some kind of celebration later.

An unexpected wave of disappointment flowed through her.

Available in April 2004 from Silhouette Superromance

The Inheritance
JANICE CARTER

SILHOUETTE® SUPERROMANCE™

*Silhouette, Silhouette Superromance and Colophon are
registered trademarks of Harlequin Books S.A., used under licence.*

*First published in Great Britain 2004
Silhouette Books, Eton House, 18-24 Paradise Road,
Richmond, Surrey TW9 1SR*

© Janice Hess 2000

ISBN 0 373 70887 4

38-0404

*Printed and bound in Spain
by Litografia Rosés S.A., Barcelona*

Dear Reader,

Writers are often asked the question, 'Where do you get your ideas?' It's a good question, but a difficult one to answer. Because writers are usually storytellers and daydreamers. They absorb anecdotes and snippets of passing conversation like sponges, holding on to them for future use.

When my friends, Jane Baldwin and Paul Christianson, recently married, they received a cutting from Paul's family treasure—an antique rosebush brought to America generations ago by his Scandinavian ancestors. One day, as I admired this plant flourishing in their wonderful cottage garden, they told me the story of their Iowa rose.

I was captivated by the notion of a plant being passed down through generations as reverently as a piece of sterling silver. I could envision blooms from that plant in wedding bouquets, christening posies and funeral arrangements. A celebration of all aspects of life, the rosebush was a living tradition and heirloom.

If the rosebush could speak, it would have hundreds of stories to recount. In this novel, with its imaginary setting and characters, I've constructed one possible tale from the Iowa rose.

I am indebted to Jane and Paul for urging me to spin my own story about their family tradition.

I'd also like to send a big thank-you to my pal Linda Christensen for helping me to develop an investment-fraud scenario for the book.

Janice Carter

For Peter, with love.

A special thank-you to Jane Baldwin and Paul Christianson for the story of their family's Iowa rose.

And to Linda Christensen for the investment information.

CHAPTER ONE

"THAT'S MY INHERITANCE? A rose?"

Randall Taylor, solicitor and executor of the estate of Ida Mae Petersen sighed from the other end of the line.

"Miss Baines, your aunt was concerned about keeping the family home in the family."

"A bit late for family," Roslyn cracked. "I haven't seen nor heard from this Great-Aunt Ida and her side of the family my entire life." She edged forward in her chair, setting her elbows on the desktop. "That's the part I don't understand. Why the contact after all these years? And why me? Can you give me some help here, Mr. Taylor?"

"Please, call me Randall. I've a feeling we'll be having more conversations after today. The Iowa rose has been in the family for generations. Ida didn't want to see it perish from neglect or be uprooted." He paused. "I'm afraid I can't comment on any other family uh…difficulties."

"Randall, then—I don't expect you to comment on the peculiarities of my family, but you have the advantage of knowing my aunt and the rest of the family in Iowa. I don't understand why she's left me anything at all, frankly, since my parents have had nothing to do with the Iowa relatives. Most of all, I'm puzzled by the inheritance itself. I mean, a *rosebush?* Was she some kind of eccentric recluse—or worse?''

Randall chuckled. ''Some considered her eccentric, certainly. But she had all of her faculties, believe me, and a few to spare.''

''And she couldn't get anyone in the whole of Plainsville to take on a *plant?*''

''That wasn't the point. She made it very clear to me when we drew up the will that the rosebush had to stay in the Petersen family. When Ida read your mother's obituary last year in a Chicago newspaper, she decided to change her will. There were no other living relatives more immediate than you. Plus, as she explained to me, she wanted to set the record straight on a few things.''

''Set the record straight?'' Roslyn frowned. ''What does that mean?''

Randall sighed. ''Frankly, I don't know. Ida Mae was a very private person and detested anything that might have been construed as prying. I assumed that she was referring to some family matter.''

''Well, I certainly wouldn't know anything about a family matter. When I was growing up, the only family I had were my parents and grandparents in Chicago. I didn't even know my grandmother had a sister, let alone a twin.''

''To tell you the truth, I never knew myself until I helped Ida make up this new will. My predecessor at our law office here in Des Moines had been her personal lawyer up until the last few years.''

After a moment's pause, Roslyn asked, "Exactly what is the complete estate, then?"

"All right, let's go over it again. Do you have time?"

"Certainly, my next appointment isn't until one-thirty," she said, without mentioning it was for lunch. Her fingers drummed lightly on the wooden desktop.

"Ida was sole owner of the Petersen family home in Plainsville, Iowa. Current market value is about three hundred thousand dollars. That's the value of the house of course, and it stands on five acres of prime land in town with another hundred acres adjoining and stretching into the outskirts. Plainsville's become a kind of distant satellite community to Des Moines, so the eventual value of the land could be quite high."

Roslyn checked the time. "Go on."

"Well, except for some old stock certificates and what's in Ida's savings account, the cash assets of the whole estate come to about thirty thousand, on top of the house. Now, I haven't factored in the land because that part of it is purely speculative at the moment. Someone in your line of work can relate to that."

"Sure," she mumbled. Her fingers settled on the desk. She closed her eyes and massaged her brow. Then she glanced at her watch again. She had about twenty-five minutes. Why was she wasting her time going through all of this again? Why didn't she just say, "Thanks, but no thanks" and get off the phone?

As if reading her mind, Randall said, "I know this is a lot to take in but I'll go over the conditions once more, as well. Then I'll leave you to your appointment.'' He cleared his throat and Roslyn pictured him squinting through his reading glasses at the document. ''So, the main condition to inheriting the entire estate is that you must live in the house and take care of the rosebush. Should you decide not to reside permanently in the house, your share of the inheritance will only be a cutting from the plant.''

Roslyn snorted. Great-Aunt Ida *had* to be some kind of crackpot. ''And may I ask what happens to the estate in that event?''

''The estate will be offered to Jack Jensen of Plainsville, Iowa. Under the same condition.''

''Who's he? Some distant cousin?''

''No relation at all. But the Jensen family is as old and well-known in the community as your aunt's. Apparently young Jack and Ida Mae forged a strong friendship in her latter years.''

''So why didn't she just leave everything to him in the first place?''

''Because they're not family—there's no blood connection. She wanted you to have first refusal.''

''That's a good way to put it.'' She thought for a moment and then added, ''What's to stop me from agreeing and then selling the house once it's legally mine, without permanently moving in?''

''You must actually reside in the house for a year before the deed is officially signed over.''

''A year? In Plainsville?''

''Your aunt explained to me that taking over the home ought to be a true commitment, both to the town and to the family heritage. I suggest you take the weekend or longer to think all of this over. Don't make a decision over the phone.''

Roslyn barely acknowledged his comment. *A year in Plainsville* was all she could focus on. What on earth could this great-aunt have been thinking?

WHEN ROSLYN finished her summary of the telephone conversation with the lawyer, she reached for her wineglass and leaned back into her chair and looked at her boss.

Ed Saunders poured the last of the wine into his own glass and reached into the inner pocket of his pinstripe suit. ''Mind?'' he asked, withdrawing a slender aluminum tube.

''Come on, Ed. That's why we had our luncheon here—so you could light up at the table afterward.''

His grin was sheepish. ''Got me there, I'm afraid. Well, this great-aunt of yours sounds like a real character.'' He shook his head again and chuckled. ''A rosebush! What was that line about a rose garden? Something from the seventies, wasn't it?''

Roslyn shrugged. ''I think it was a song—or a book or something. Anyway, so much for luck, eh? First time an unexpected inheritance falls into my lap and it turns out to be a cutting from an old rosebush.''

Ed rolled the unlit Cuban beneath his nose before moistening the end in his mouth. Roslyn peered down into her glass. She wished he wouldn't light it, but didn't have the nerve to object. They still hadn't got to the heart of their meeting and she wasn't going to jeopardize her chance to be a new junior associate of

Saunders, McIntyre and Associates Investments over a cigar.

She heard the metallic click of a cigarette lighter and looked up as a large smoke ring drifted across the table.

"Thank heavens for my club," Ed murmured, savoring his first puff. "Nothing like a decent Cuban after a fine meal."

"Isn't that 'decent' Cuban illegal?"

Ed winked. "Shhh! Not so loudly. 'Course—" he strained to glance over his shoulder "—I'm sure there are more than a few on the premises as we speak. Illegal, but not impossible to obtain."

"All adding to the enjoyment, of course," Roslyn said.

"That's what I admire in you, my girl."

Roslyn tried not to wince.

"Your quick and very insightful wit. And intelligence," he added. "Which brings me to the purpose of our meeting."

Roslyn gripped the stem of her wineglass. She raised it casually to her lips before responding. Swallowing the slightly fruity wine, she tilted her head in mock interest and raised an eyebrow. "Yes?"

"As I intimated to you several weeks ago, Saunders, McIntyre and Associates Investments are taking advantage of the terrific market of the past year and the board has given the go-ahead to expand our operation. We're setting up a new branch on the south side and want you to be in on it with us. As junior associate, with all the benefits and perks that come with the title."

The tension in Roslyn's stomach melted in a rush of excitement.

"So," Ed continued, taking another drag on his cigar, "you've got to make a decision about this inheritance of yours, I suppose."

"Not really, Ed. I mean, can you see me in Plainsville, Iowa?"

"I take your point," he commented. "But before we leave, there is one more thing."

Catching the ominous tone in his voice, Roslyn had a feeling she was about to hear the string attached to her promotion. After all, it *had* been a day of conditions.

HOURS LATER, on her way home, Roslyn let her forehead rest against the train window. She knew she ought to be feeling jubilant. Wasn't making associate her primary goal since joining the investment firm five years ago?

She sagged against the plastic seat. Her eyes swept across the commuters leaving the heart of the city almost two hours after the peak of the rush hour. They all looked as wrung out as she felt. An inner voice scolded her for yielding to such a dark mood on what ought to have been the best day of her career so far.

She loved the erratic pace of her work days—the frenzy of buying and selling; urgent phone calls and spinning from one monitor to the next, checking stock prices around the world. Everything at her fingertips and everything demanding *now, now!*

Then there were the calm times—the interludes of sanity that Roslyn and her co-workers dubbed the eyes of the hurricanes. Those rare moments gave them time to replenish before the next storm.

You love it, she told herself. The unpredictability of it all. So why the funky mood? Roslyn wondered. Ed Saunders's face floated through her mind. "There's a problem at the firm," he'd said. "Looks as if someone's been skimming from client accounts."

Roslyn's immediate reaction had been simply shock, until Ed had mentioned that he believed that person might be Jim Naismith. Then her disbelief became nausea. She'd dated Jim a few times and liked him.

She thought back to the night almost five weeks before when she'd stayed to finish off the Wallis account and had bumped into Jim at the copy machine. The paper cartridge was empty and he'd shown her where the office receptionist kept a secret supply.

Their easy bantering had led to a late supper together. Although Roslyn had always avoided socializing on a personal level with the staff at the firm, she liked Jim's easygoing manner and had gone out with him a few times. She'd been content to keep their friendship platonic but after she turned down his invitation to accompany him on a Caribbean cruise, their dating had come to an end.

The train squealed into Roslyn's station. She headed for the platform in a daze. Another weekend loomed ahead. There was plenty of work to do, but none of it appealed to Roslyn in her present mood— not even her Saturday morning sleep-in followed by a run around the harbor.

She pushed her way through the turnstile and stood on the pavement outside the El station. The news about her strange inheritance had been sponged from her thoughts. All she could focus on was Ed's request at the end of lunch.

I know you can't—or maybe won't—believe Naismith is our thief, but promise me one thing. If you see or hear him engaged in anything suspicious, let me know immediately, won't you? In complete confidence, of course. Just between partners.

Was there a hint in that message somewhere, implying she'd have more access to Jim's movements than anyone else in the office?

And she couldn't keep back the second question that sprung to mind. What would her previous involvement with a suspected embezzler mean to her new promotion? However the events of the next few weeks played out, Roslyn knew there was no way she'd escape untouched. She couldn't bring herself to spy on a colleague and friend; at the same time, how could she refuse her boss's first big request of her— *partner to partner?*

I'm beat either way, she thought. *All I can do is try to come out of this clean.* She looked up and down the street, hoping to hail a cab for the short distance to her condo. But rush hour had finished and most of the cabs were going farther into the city for evening events.

Roslyn sighed, turned up her trench coat collar against the bite of a brisk April breeze, and, sidestepping puddles from the recent shower, headed home. It seemed an appropriate end to the day.

THE CONGRATULATORY messages were already coming in via phone and e-mail by the time Roslyn walked off the elevator at eight-thirty Monday morning. Her secretary, Judy, looked up in surprise.

"I was beginning to think you weren't coming in today. Too much celebrating on the weekend?"

Roslyn grinned. "I wish. Too much traffic, not to mention too much rain."

"I know," Judy agreed. "Do you believe this weather? I mean, April showers bring May flowers and blah-blah-blah, but this is ridiculous. Anyway, the word is out on your promotion and there's a stack of callbacks waiting for you."

"You're a pal, Jude." Roslyn was halfway into her office when the telephone rang. Judy waved her fingers, mouthed the word *coffee* and turned away. Roslyn shrugged off her coat and tossed it over a chair.

"Hello?" She cradled the receiver against her left ear and sat down in her black leather swivel desk chair. Before the caller could speak, she'd already reached for the stack of messages that Judy had left for her and was shuffling through them. The day's work had just begun.

"Miss Baines? Randall Taylor here."

Randall Taylor? Roslyn closed her eyes. Friday afternoon's revelations had completely erased Great-Aunt Ida and her prized rosebush from her memory.

"Oh yes, Mr. Taylor. Sorry, I wasn't expecting you to call so early."

"Randall," he reminded her. "Well, I have to leave Des Moines on business for a few days and I thought I'd check with you before I left regarding your thoughts on the inheritance.''

Roslyn sighed. ''I'm afraid I haven't made a decision. Something came up at work later on Friday, and I spent most of the weekend reflecting on that. Uh, when will you need a definite yes or no on this?''

There was a slight pause. ''There's no real rush, of course. Although I must admit I'd like to have things settled as soon as possible. Once the will has been probated, I should really move ahead with finalizing things. However,'' his voice shifted to a less businesslike tone, ''may I give you some friendly advice?''

Roslyn pushed aside the phone messages. ''Certainly.''

''I know that to someone who's spent her whole life in a place like Chicago, Plainsville, Iowa isn't much of a draw.'' He chuckled. ''In fact, probably Des Moines itself isn't a grabber.''

Roslyn nodded her head in silent agreement. She wished the man would make his point so she could get to some of her telephone calls.

''But please, take a few days and visit your aunt's house before you decide.''

''Visit Plainsville?''

''It wouldn't be that bad, seriously. Late April isn't the best time of year for Iowa, I'm afraid, but you ought to see your aunt's home before dismissing it.''

Roslyn sighed again. He must have been reading her mind. She'd been about to inform him to call Jackson or Johnson or whoever the other beneficiary was. "Randall, I'm really very busy here. I seldom have time to take a day off, much less a few days."

"The house is very special. Trust me. It's a heritage house, Roslyn, and is well-known in the county."

"I doubt that would be a selling point with me, Randall. Living in a tourist attraction doesn't appeal."

"It's not like that. People here are too respectful of other folks' privacy. But the Petersen name is almost as famous as the house and a visit would be an opportunity to get to know that side of the family."

"There's got to be a good reason why my side of the family chose not to know the other, Randall. I think I'll go with my parents and grandparents' judgment on this." Irritation bristled in her voice.

"I'm really botching this, I'm afraid. But any businessperson will attest that a property should never be turned down sight unseen. As a potential investment for you, the house in Plainsville ought to be given that chance at least."

She admired his strategy, knowing it was one she'd have used with a client herself. "Tell you what, Randall, I'll think about a visit. I believe I have your number in Des Moines—is there an e-mail address on the card?"

"'Fraid not. I personally avoid the computer as much as possible. Should you decide to visit before I return, I'll leave instructions and a key with my secretary."

Roslyn made her goodbyes and gave Randall's suggestion a few seconds of her time until the telephone rang again. Then she retrieved her sheaf of messages and let the day's business take over. Until shortly after lunch, when there was a gentle tap at her door.

It swung open at her "Come in" to reveal Jim Naismith standing in the frame and clutching a dozen red roses. Roslyn's stomach pitched. A crescending drumroll pounded at her left temple. Feeling a rush of heat suffuse into her face, she managed a surprised smile and blurted, "For me?"

ROSLYN DIDN'T get a chance to confer with Ed Saunders until late in the afternoon. For hours, she'd sat in her office staring at Jim's bouquet of roses, stuck somewhat unceremoniously in an empty coffee can. All the while, she kept replaying his gracious congratulations. Something had changed in his manner, she decided.

The old Jim would have hung around longer, teasing her about moving up the corporate ladder. All of the banter would have been delivered with sincerity and pleasure at such a reward of her hard work. The handful of times they'd dated had taught her that about Jim Naismith.

Or had it? she suddenly asked herself. Because this Jim hadn't lingered for small talk and had, after giving her a quick hug, pulled back immediately. He'd been evasive about her general inquiry about his weekend, mumbling that he'd been into the office, and had become defensive at the surprise in her voice. He'd blurted that some people in the office had been dealt a bigger workload than others.

His reaction had startled Roslyn. Jim had never seemed to be the type of workaholic who felt that he was the only one with a heavy load. And when she'd casually asked him what account had kept him in the office all weekend, he'd simply shrugged and left her office. By the time Roslyn closed Ed Saunders's door behind her later that day, she was beginning to think she might have been wrong about Jim.

"I've been thinking about what you said on Friday," she began.

Ed frowned.

"About Jim Naismith."

Her boss placed the pen in his right hand onto the desk. "Go on," was all he said.

Roslyn swallowed. She couldn't go through with it. Even after checking security's sign-in log over the past three weeks and noting that Jim had come into work every weekend, she couldn't ally herself with Ed against Jim. There had to be an explanation, even if it was the standard one—that all the investors were overworked and desperate to earn their commissions and bonuses.

But there was more to her emotional response, she knew. Staring at Ed's florid face, the shock of white hair and rugged good looks that had many younger clerks swooning in his wake, she realized that she was reluctant to voice her thoughts about Jim simply because she feared jeopardizing her promotion. Still, experience had taught her that the truth would always come out in the end.

"I don't think I'm going to be much help to you—about Jim, I mean," she stammered at the question in his face. "You see, Jim and I've...well, dated a few times and although we're just good friends, I thought our socializing might...well..."

"Prejudice your involvement?"

Dry-mouthed, Roslyn nodded.

Ed leaned forward, resting his chin on his right thumb and index finger. He thought long enough to convince Roslyn he might be pondering a way to rescind Friday's promotion offer.

"I appreciate your frankness as well as your ethical integrity here, Roslyn. Of course, I won't expect you to give me information on a colleague whom you've been seeing in a social context."

"A casual social context," she blurted, afraid that this breach of an unspoken office rule would seal her fate.

But Ed smiled. "Whatever. I won't put you in any position of conflict of interest here." He paused, glancing down at the paper lying on his desk. "However, I do have a favor to ask." He raised his head, fixing his watery blue eyes directly on hers.

Roslyn felt her face color. "Yes?"

"Needless to say, I expect you to keep all conversations about this matter in the strictest of confidence."

"Of course."

"The board has decided to conduct its own internal inquiry into Naismith's accounts before calling the Securities Exchange Commission or...the police," he added softly.

The police. The impact of what all of this would mean to Jim suddenly hit her. Roslyn could only nod.

Ed narrowed his eyes at her. "Perhaps, if you've

got nothing immediately pressing on your desk, you might even want to take a few days' holiday. Things might get a bit tense around here. Your...uh, *friendship* with Naismith will place you in an awkward position.''

Roslyn glanced away from the intensity of his stare and the insinuation in his voice. Did he think she might be involved in the fraud as well? *Get a grip on yourself, Roslyn. The man is only trying to be considerate of your feelings.* And she had to admit, he had a point. She'd already felt very conflicted about Jim's gift of roses.

Roses! Her response tumbled out. ''Actually, the lawyer I was speaking to on Friday—the one who called from Des Moines about my inheritance,'' she clarified at the frown on Ed's face. ''He advised me to visit Plainsville to check out the house, before making a decision about taking it.''

''Excellent idea. Take a few days—even a couple of weeks. By then, we'll know whether we have enough to go to the Exchange Commission or not.''

Roslyn backed toward the door. ''Fine,'' she said. ''I'll have Judy arrange for my current files to be monitored by someone else.''

''Not Naismith,'' Ed quipped.

Roslyn smiled, but hated the touch of conspiracy in the gibe. She closed the office door behind her, leaning against it long enough to catch her breath. Ed was right about one thing, she realized. She definitely needed to get away from the office. And right at that moment, Plainsville, Iowa didn't look half-bad.

CHAPTER TWO

ROSLYN HANDED a ten-dollar bill to the cabbie and bent over to pick up her luggage, receiving a wake of puddle spray as the taxi peeled away from the curb. It was the final indignity in a long day of exasperation, irritation and white-knuckle flying. The brief flight from Chicago to Des Moines had been plagued by nonstop turbulence and pitching in the midst of a thunderstorm. On arrival in Des Moines, Roslyn discovered she'd missed her bus connection to Plainsville and would have to wait another two hours.

"There's a crop dusting outfit that uses a local farmer's field for landing and takeoff. I could find out about chartering a plane, if you like. Though—" the information clerk had snapped her chewing gum thoughtfully as she turned to squint out the window "—you might wanna wait for the bus."

But Roslyn had already decided she'd rather walk than get on another plane. *A farmer's field? Only in Iowa.*

The stopover gave her an opportunity to call Randall Taylor's law office to confirm arrangements about getting into Ida Mae's house. His secretary informed her that the key had been left under the front doormat by a clerk who lived nearby. By the time the bus to Plainsville pulled into the station, Roslyn was ready to sign over the deed to the other beneficiary without taking another step into Iowa.

She was soaked before she reached the sweeping veranda of the large house standing in darkness yards away from the rain-slicked pavement. It was almost ten o'clock on Tuesday night, and Roslyn had noted during the short ride from the bus station on the other side of town that Plainsville was quieter than the Exchange after a market dive.

When the taxi had pulled up to her aunt's home— "The Petersen place? No kidding? You a Petersen?"—Roslyn also noticed that the houses on either side of her aunt's were already in darkness.

Between mumbling to the cabbie—"Yes and…uh, no, not really"—and muttering to herself that everything in Plainsville appeared to have shut down for the night, Roslyn had little chance to take in more than the general shape of the house. But from the covered veranda, she paused to look out to the street, observing for the first time a waist-high fence she'd bet was white picket, framing an expanse of property whose borders she couldn't see.

The neighborhood was unlike any she'd seen in the city, where lots were much smaller. Here the homes were scattered like giant building blocks, surrounded by huge trees and sprawling front lawns. Randall hadn't been exaggerating when he'd said the Petersen house was on the outskirts of town. Roslyn couldn't be certain in the rainy night if the road ended less than a mile beyond or not, but she bet it did. In fact, she guessed her aunt's place was probably just a stop sign away from being called a farmhouse.

Roslyn stooped to lift up the edge of the bristle mat at her feet, and her fingers touched a small envelope. She tore it open and shook out a set of keys.

After two attempts, she managed to turn the key and the door swung open, complaining in a low-pitched creak. Roslyn stepped into the dark interior. She felt around the edges of the doorjamb for a light switch and released her breath in a long whoosh when she located and flicked on three lights. The porch, the hallway and the staircase leading from the entry flashed into existence.

Sixty watts, she thought, straining to see beyond the narrow field of illumination. She turned back for her suitcase and briefcase, closing the door behind her. From somewhere within the house she could hear the steady tick of a pendulum clock.

"Hello?" Roslyn's voice cracked slightly, and she tittered. Whom did she expect to answer? All the little critters that inhabit dark places when people aren't around? *Better not go down that path,* she warned herself. *Especially when you're spending the night here alone.*

She stared down at the envelope in her hand, realizing that there was a folded paper inside.

Dear Miss Baines,

Sorry I couldn't meet you at your aunt's but I had to take my son to his karate lesson tonight, and no one else was available. I arranged for Miss Petersen's housekeeper—Mrs. Warshawski—to open the house for you and make up a bed in one of the bedrooms. She also said she'd buy a few provisions—coffee, tea, milk etc.—for you. Mrs. Warshawski worked for your aunt for twenty-five years, and Mr. Taylor asked her to stay on until the will was settled. She lives on the other side of town but will be there to meet you in the morning.

Enjoy your first evening in Plainsville and feel free to call me at Mr. Taylor's office if you need anything else.

Sincerely,

Jane Baldwin

Roslyn picked up her suitcase and headed for the staircase, too exhausted to explore. All she wanted was to find the bed that had been prepared for her, dig out the miniature bottles of airline Bourbon that she'd tucked into her purse and crawl under the covers.

TIME TO TURN OVER, Roslyn thought, and bake the other side. She flung an arm across her eyes, shielding them from the glare of a Caribbean sun that penetrated even through closed lids. Her mouth was so dry. She tried to move her lips but they were stuck together. A tall frosty drink. Had to be somewhere close, she thought. At my elbow. Her eyes blinked open.

Not the Caribbean, she realized at once. Sunlight streamed from the window opposite the bed she was lying in. Roslyn slowly flexed the fingers of her right hand, thick and lifeless from lack of circulation. She rotated her head gently on the pillow, scanning the room and wondering for a brief but scary moment where on earth she was.

The decor of the room helped fix the setting— chintz everywhere and clunky dark wooden furniture. Gilt-framed portraits of people in various periods of dress were arranged on one wall papered with tiny purple violets. Two pastoral landscapes hung on the opposite. The double bed she was sprawled in had once been painted white. A long time ago, she decided, craning round to view the wrought iron headboard, slightly chipped and splashed with dots of rust.

Plainsville, Iowa. Not the Caribbean at all.

Roslyn struggled to raise herself onto the thick feathered pillows beneath her head. Doing so, she knocked the night table with her left elbow and the two empty miniature Bourbon bottles clinked onto the floor. Roslyn winced at the noise, and her head fell back onto the pillows, banging against the iron bed frame.

She raised a hand to rub the tender spot. The travel alarm clock propped against the lamp on the night table indicated nine o'clock. Back in Chicago, she'd have been hard at work for an hour.

Suddenly the complete emptiness of the day loomed before her. She was in a small Midwestern town, a place she'd never even heard of until last week, lying in a strange bed in someone else's house. She'd committed herself to staying five days and didn't have the least idea what she would be doing here.

Roslyn groaned, wondering how she'd gotten herself into such a ridiculous situation. What little she knew about Iowa came from grade school geography. She recalled green undulating hills, flat lands and farms. Lots of farms. She only hoped Plainsville contained a good bookstore and coffee shop.

She groaned again, then stretched, raising her bare arms above her head and wrapping her hands around the curving loops of the headboard behind. The patchwork quilt fell away, exposing the silky top of her sleeveless ice-blue nightgown. No wonder she'd been shivering all night. Flannel was definitely a must for Plainsville, Roslyn decided, even in late April. But the wash of sun spilling over her and onto the hardwood floor was inviting. She flung off the quilt and swung her legs over the side of the bed.

A heavy thud from outside stopped her cold. Roslyn looked over to the window. She hadn't bothered to draw the curtains the night before, guessing there were no neighbors close enough to be spying on her. She padded across the room reaching the long rectangular window just as a man's head popped into view.

Roslyn stepped backward, one hand automatically covering her mouth and the other vainly attempting to sling back the spaghetti strap of her nightgown. The man outside the window grinned and waved a hand. Roslyn noticed then that he was standing on the top rung of a ladder. Suddenly he raised a fist clenched around some kind of tool which he tapped against the window frame.

Roslyn swung round to the bed, grabbed the quilt to wrap around her and ran from the room. She took

the stairs two at a time but when her bare feet
thumped onto the floor at the bottom of the staircase,
she stopped. She didn't know the layout of the house.
God, she didn't even know if there was a telephone.
No. Wait. The note from the secretary mentioned
something about a phone call. But where the heck…?

She pivoted left, then right. The size of the house
daunted her. Better to aim for the front door, straight
ahead. She snapped the dead bolt and pulled hard.
Last night's storm had left behind puddles. Roslyn
shoved her feet into her pumps lying where she'd
kicked them off last night and rushed onto the veranda.

She clipped down the slick cement steps onto the
narrow strip of sidewalk that curved toward the rear
of the house. Roslyn marched along the path, barely
noticing the sunlight bouncing off damp patches of
grass, puffing sprays of mist into the morning air. She
heard voices ahead and as she came around the corner
of the big frame house, she saw two men—one loung-
ing against the bottom portion of a long aluminum
ladder and the other scrambling down the rungs.

"What do you think you're doing?" she snarled at
them.

HE GUESSED right away who she was. Ida's lawyer
had called from Des Moines over the weekend to say
that the niece—great-niece?—might be visiting for a
few days to check the place out before deciding to
move in or not. He hadn't dreamed she'd come so
soon.

All the rain they'd taken over the last four days

had got him to thinking that he hadn't cleaned out the gutters and eaves troughs after the winter. Last fall he'd noticed a few weak spots in the old copper troughs and had dictated a mental note to himself to repair them for Ida. So he'd persuaded Lenny to come along and hold the ladder for him while he cleaned out the troughs. He was still chuckling when he plunked a foot onto the grass at the base of the ladder.

"Should've seen the look—" he said when a vision whirled around the end of the house.

She looked even better in full sunlight, he thought; her hair a swirl of reds and coppers burnishing out from her pale face like an electrified halo. And the face. The white skin translucent enough to reflect hints of spring all around them. He could paint that face! Though, he swiftly amended, not with that particular expression on it.

He held up both palms, dropping his trowel onto the ground. "Sorry about that, Miss. Uh...I was just about to clean out the eaves troughs—"

"The *eaves troughs?*"

Either she'd never heard of an eaves trough or she found his explanation ridiculous.

"I used to work for Miss Ida Mae. Well, we were friends, too. Anyway, I did a lot of odd jobs for her and after the rain this week, I thought I'd better get at those—"

"Eaves troughs."

He stopped then, realizing that the glint in her eyes had more to do with anger than sparkles from the sun. He wondered if his own embarrassment was as obvious as it was starting to feel because she stared at him until he imagined *he'd* been the one caught parading outdoors in a nightie instead of her.

Then her gaze abruptly shifted, zigzagging from a point behind him, to the ladder, to Lenny, back to him and finally, to the tools lying on the grass.

"J.J.'s Landscaping and Garden Center," she muttered. Obviously she'd noticed his truck.

"That's me—Jack Jensen. And this is my nephew Lenny, who's helping me out today. And you must be the niece."

She seemed to be in a daze. "The niece?"

"Ida's niece—or is it great-niece?" Jack turned to Lenny. "Is that what she'd be called? Great or grand?"

Lenny gave him a look as mystified as the niece's, and Jack swore at himself for babbling.

"Jack *Jensen?*"

Jack and Lenny both turned back to the woman. Disbelief was all over her face.

"You mean, *you're* the other beneficiary?"

Jack wasn't certain of the insinuation in her voice but he caught Lenny grinning at it. "Yeah, I guess that's right. And you would be Miss—"

"Baines," she said. "Roslyn Baines." She stuck out her right hand, releasing the quilt she'd been clutching. It dropped to the ground.

The nightgown shimmered in the sunlight, its filmy blue fabric undulating against her long slender legs and body like ripples in a mountain stream. Jack and Lenny looked down at the ground. There was a fluttering sound as Roslyn swooped to retrieve the quilt.

When they both dared to raise their eyes, she was heading toward the front of the house.

"I'll finish this up another time," Jack hollered after her.

She paused, turning around only long enough to say, "Come into the house when you've put your things away," then disappeared around the corner.

There was a moment's silence that Lenny finally broke. "Geez," he said.

Jack nodded, staring at the end of the house. "You can say that again."

THEY TOOK their time putting things away. Roslyn peeked out the bedroom window as she snatched clean clothes from her suitcase and carried them into the bathroom across the hall. A room she figured would be safe from accidental sightings. Then she had to smile. What a sight she must have presented!

Humiliation swept through her. Granted, she'd been startled and perhaps a tad frightened, which came from spending her whole life in Chicago. People who accessed apartments from ladders or fire escapes in the city were usually emergency personnel or cat burglars. Or worse—the stuff of nightmares. But when she'd taken in their smirking faces and the name on the beat-up truck in the drive, the fear had sizzled into anger.

Roslyn knew from personal experience that her temper could be awesome, although its effect was definitely diminished when teamed with a flimsy nightie. Padding across the cool tiles, she slipped a pale lavender shirt off its hanger and buttoned it up, letting it hang loose over her black jeans.

The single window in the bathroom gable telescoped out over the roof. Bending low from the waist, she could just see the front of the truck. The men were leaning against the hood, talking. Part of a ladder extended over the cab of the truck. So they were finished, but not exactly rushing to her front door.

Roslyn sighed. Who could blame them, after such an unfriendly greeting? She closed the last button on her shirt and realized she'd left her makeup bag in the bedroom. If she didn't hurry, they might decide to leave. For some inexplicable reason, she was loath to have her first meeting with Jack Jensen—the other beneficiary—hang on such a sour note.

Abandoning makeup, she fought with her hair, twisting it through an elastic band. A quick brush of her teeth and her toilette was complete. One last glance in the mirror on her way out the door made Roslyn realize that no one in her office would even recognize her at that moment. But for Plainsville, she thought wryly, it would do. She headed for the first floor.

The hesitant tapping at the front door almost made her laugh. Were they afraid of her now? She pulled hard on the heavy door, calling out a hearty "Come in."

A short, plump woman of about sixty stood before her. "Miss Baines?"

"Uh, yes. Sorry," Roslyn stammered. "I—I was expecting someone else."

"You were?" Disbelief echoed in the voice. "Mr.

Taylor's secretary asked me to be here by nine at the latest. And,'' she peered at the tiny watch face on her thick wrist, ''I make it to be five minutes to...on the dot.''

''No, no, you misunderstand. You see—''

''There was no misunderstanding at all, from what I recall.'' She squinted hard at Roslyn. ''Unless you changed the instructions without letting me know.''

Roslyn sighed. ''Please, come in. You must be my aunt's housekeeper. Mrs.—?''

''Warshawski. Folks call me Sophie.''

''Sophie. Nice to meet you. I'm Roslyn.'' She extended her hand, which the other woman ignored. ''Mr. Taylor's secretary mentioned in her note that you'd be coming by this morning.''

''So there *was* a note!'' Vindication rang in her voice.

Roslyn looked past the woman's shoulder to see the men staring up at her from the bottom of the veranda steps. The one who'd introduced himself as Jack had a smile on his face that seemed almost pitying. There was an exchange of glances between the two of them that Roslyn couldn't read. Perhaps telepathic agreement that the woman from Chicago was indeed a major nutbar?

Weary of explanations, Roslyn swung the door open wider and made an ushering motion with her left arm. ''Please! All of you, come on in.''

Mrs. Warshawski frowned, then hesitantly peered round her shoulder. Her face softened. ''Jack! Didn't see you standin' there.''

He nodded. "Mornin', Sophie. Hope you brought some coffee."

The woman beamed. "Sure did. Even a dozen biscuits right out of the oven."

Lenny took the steps two at a time and plucked the canvas bag out of Sophie's hand. "I'm starvin'. Let's go." He crooked an arm through Sophie's and the two squeezed past Roslyn and headed into the house.

Jack paused on the door stoop.

Up close, Roslyn felt dwarfed by his height, a good four or five inches more than her own of five-nine. It was a sensation she hadn't experienced many times in her life and it made her feel strangely vulnerable.

"Sophie's baking is legendary," he explained, giving an apologetic smile for Lenny's rush into the house.

His eyes crinkled in weather-etched lines. Dark as midnight, but kind, Roslyn decided. He swept off the faded baseball cap to reveal a thick head of short, black hair.

"Well? Shall we join them?" He grinned down at her and before she could reply, was halfway down the hall.

Roslyn slowly closed the door. She was beginning to feel like a character in a quirky novel. Not *Alice in Wonderland* exactly, but close enough. She recalled a title from her college days. Yes. More like *Stranger in a Strange Land*.

Their voices led her along the wood-paneled hallway to a kitchen she was seeing for the first time. She watched from the door. The three were bustling about the large, airy room as if they'd spent their whole lives in Ida Mae's house.

They went about the task of making coffee, getting plates and mugs out of tall, wooden cupboards and extracting jam jars and plastic containers from Sophie's canvas bag in a routine that appeared to have been performed many times. All the while, snippets of conversation ricocheted off the walls. Bits of talk beginning with ''Did you hear that…?'' or ''Well, I never…'' and even ''I guess you knew that…'' were followed by occasional lapses into brief silence.

Finally they noticed Roslyn, turning almost as one toward the doorway. Jack placed the cutlery he'd just taken from a drawer onto the rectangular harvest table in the center of the room and took a step toward her.

''Miss Baines—please come and sit down. We…uh, well I suppose we got carried away there. Thinking it was like old times when we'd gather for coffee on a Saturday morning with Miss Ida Mae after we'd done the yard work. Sophie here always made a pan of biscuits or cinnamon buns, and Lenny and I—or Miss Ida, if Lenny wasn't with us—would get the coffee ready.'' He stopped. ''I'm babbling. Please,'' he pulled out a ladder-back chair from the table, ''sit down. We've forgotten our manners. This place is *your* home now.''

Silence doused the energy in the room. Sophie's lips tightened, and Lenny gazed out the window. Roslyn returned Jack's smile and perched stiffly on the edge of the chair. When the coffee was poured and the biscuits set on a platter, the three other chairs were pulled out in unison.

Roslyn sipped carefully on the hot brew. "Since I'm only here a few days, I'd like to visit Plainsville's main attractions," she said to break the silence.

Sophie's face smoothed into a smile. "Not many attractions so to speak, but I'm sure Lenny could drive you around the center of town. We've got some shops and restaurants that some people drive all the way from Des Moines to visit."

Roslyn hastily interjected, "I'm sure Lenny has plans for the day. I can wander into town myself. The ride from the bus station last night didn't take longer than twenty minutes."

"You musta got Morty Hermann," Lenny stated.

Sophie shook her head. "That man. He'd cheat his own mother."

"One of our three cabbies in town," Jack explained. "Unfortunately, he takes advantage of newcomers. The ride here from the station should only have taken five or ten minutes, max."

"Oh, well," sighed Roslyn. "That happens all the time in Chicago, unless you know exactly where you're going."

"You're right. Happened to me a few times," Jack agreed.

"You've spent some time in Chicago?" Roslyn asked.

"A bit," he said. "I lived there for almost ten years."

"Oh," was all that Roslyn could think to say, feeling foolish for assuming he'd spent his whole life in Plainsville.

"Lenny's tied up today," Jack continued, "but I'm

free. How'd you like a guided tour around the Petersen property?''

Roslyn looked across the table at him. His eyes
were bright and smiling. Encouraging eyes, she
thought. ''I'd love to,'' she replied.

''Great. Might want to get a jacket,'' he suggested.
''There's a lot of property to see.''

''Before you leave,'' Sophie interjected. ''I'll need
to know if you'd like me to get in any more supplies
for you—for lunch or dinner tonight.'' There was a
slight pause before she added, ''I'd be happy to pre-
pare something for you.''

''Thank you, Sophie. That's very thoughtful of
you. But I'll be fine. After I've explored here, I'll do
the town. Maybe check out one of those trendy restaurants you mentioned.'' She pushed in her chair and
turned to leave the room. ''I'll meet you on the front
porch then, Jack,'' she said, leaving the kitchen in
three brisk strides.

She felt three pairs of eyes follow her through the
doorway.

''Not much like her aunt,'' she heard Sophie say.

Roslyn stopped, just out of view and heard Jack's
response. ''Not to look at,'' he agreed. He cleared his
throat to add, ''But clearly a family resemblance of
one kind.''

''Yup'' was all Sophie said, along with a very au-
dible sigh.

''IT'S REALLY a branch of the Iowa River,'' Jack explained.

Roslyn stared down the wooded ravine to the expanse of pea-green water. "A very big branch," she commented. Shielding her eyes against the sun, she moved her head from left to right, taking in the whole panorama. Trees everywhere and of every kind for as far as she could see. Some were just budding and some were already in bloom. "How much of my aunt's land extends over there, beyond the river?"

"Oh, I guess another thirty acres or so. The property line extends much farther to the east, behind the house."

"Exactly how much land did Aunt Ida have? We've been walking for about half an hour now and you say we still haven't seen it all."

Jack thought for a moment. "There's about a hundred acres of cultivated fields as well as the river and woods. And the house sits on four or five acres." He paused. "Of course, it's yours now." His eyes bore into hers.

"Well, not exactly," she murmured. "I haven't met the conditions of the will yet." Suddenly uncomfortable, she turned back to the river. The idea of owning such a piece of land was unthinkable. Too much for one person. *Too much for me.* "Anyway, perhaps we should get back to the house. I haven't even had a chance to see more than a couple of rooms so far."

"Would you like to check out the rest later today?"

Roslyn shrugged. "It doesn't matter. I'm here for such a short time, there doesn't seem to be any point."

His face darkened. He seemed about to say something but changed his mind. When he started walking back toward the cultivated fields surrounding the house, Roslyn followed behind feeling like a scolded child. What was he so annoyed about?

His steady, long-legged strides tackled the ridged furrows of the field easily. Roslyn gave up trying to keep pace with him. Her sneakers were caked with clumps of soil, still sodden from last night's rain. By the time they reached the grass that stretched into the lawns encircling the house, Roslyn could hardly raise her feet to walk.

She leaned against a blossoming crab apple tree to take off her shoes and socks. Barefoot, she quickly caught up with Jack. He stopped at the picket fence. Roslyn checked out his boots, noting that they hardly seemed muddy at all. And she couldn't be certain, but she thought she saw a grin shoot across his face.

"Sorry, but there wasn't a faster way back," he said.

He didn't sound *that* sorry. In fact, she suspected he might have purposely led her that way, out of spite. But spite about what? *Don't be so cynical, Baines.* "Nothing a bit of water can't remedy," she said, trying for a lilt in her voice. She stuck out her right hand and said, "Jack, thanks again for all your trouble. I really appreciate it." She paused, then added, "When I'm back in Chicago, I'll have some vivid memories of this day."

The surprise in his face was gratifying somehow. He took her right hand and held on to it a bit longer than she'd expected. Roslyn pulled it away, ostensibly to bend down for her shoes and socks. She'd only taken a few steps up to the veranda when his voice stopped her.

"Let me know when you come back to Plainsville."

Roslyn swung round. "I'm not sure that I'll be coming back," she said.

He opened his mouth to speak, then closed it. A frown appeared on his face, followed by something else that Roslyn couldn't interpret. He twisted the brim of his baseball cap in his big hands. Finally, he gestured with the baseball cap to his right and mumbled something.

Roslyn took a step forward. "Pardon?"

He cleared his throat. "You ought to at least have a look at the rose. Over there."

The baseball cap flipped to his right again.

Roslyn moved down to the step above where he stood. She looked over his shoulder toward the garden bordering the sidewalk. "The rose?"

Impatience surged briefly in his eyes. "The Iowa rose," he clarified. "The reason you're here right now. I think you should at least take a look at it before you go back to Chicago."

He headed for a section of the garden that looped away from the sidewalk in a wide scallop. A bright-pink flowering shrub took center place in the loop, surrounded by other green plants and bushes that Roslyn couldn't identify, although she thought she recognized a row of tulips half-emerged from the ground.

"Which one is it?"

He pointed to what appeared to be a pile of sticks covered in thorns poking out of the ground.

Roslyn wasn't impressed. "That's it?"

"You have to come back in June. Those little greenish-brown things are leaf buds and they'll be out in a few weeks. In June, it'll be covered with blossoms the size of your hand."

"What color?"

"The palest pink you've ever seen, with a streak of deep crimson extending up from lemon-yellow stamens. Not one of those dramatic hybrids, but stunning all the same."

Roslyn heard the admiration in his voice. She glanced at him. He was staring down at the plant and smiling. She looked at the bush again and shook her head. She just didn't see what he was seeing. "Well, it's not what I expected," was all she could think to say.

After a long moment, he raised his head to hers. "Nothing ever is," he remarked. "What we expect, I mean."

Roslyn studied him. Jack obviously wasn't talking about the rosebush. His jawline was set in a forbidding pose. Everything in the rugged, attractive face shouted *How can you give all this up!*

Roslyn looked at the house.

"It *is* a magnificent home," she said. "I'm anxious to poke around inside. My aunt seems to have been quite a collector. The bedroom furnishings looked very old—not that I'm an expert on antiques."

He nodded vigorously. "I don't think Ida's changed anything in the house—except for some wiring and the plumbing—since she inherited it from her folks. A lot of people don't like older things—too big and too dark.''

Roslyn thought of her condo with its airy white-upholstered furniture and minimalist design. ''Hmm,'' she murmured. ''There must be a good market somewhere for all those antiques.'' The devilish side of her relished the horror that crossed his face.

''I—I suppose,'' he sputtered, waving the baseball cap back and forth again. ''But it would take a pretty callous person to—to just sell off their inheritance.''

''I don't think I'd use exactly that word. Unsentimental, perhaps.'' She smiled, turned around and walked up to the top of the veranda.

''Besides,'' he raised his voice, ''the terms of the will don't allow for that. You have to live here for a year before you legally own everything.''

He is after the place! In spite of all his assurances and efforts to get me to like it, he really wants it for himself.

Roslyn pivoted around. ''But I bet a smart Chicago lawyer could chew up that will and spit it out.''

Jack's face flushed. He spoke quietly, clutching the baseball cap tightly at his side. ''I guess so.'' The cap in his right hand came up and aimed directly at Roslyn. ''But I bet,'' he said, his voice low and even, ''that a year of living in this house in this town would guarantee you'd never want to part with a thing.'' He turned on his heel and walked away, heading for the driveway at the side of the house.

Roslyn watched him disappear around the corner. She'd gone too far, she realized. And why, when she already knew she wasn't going to take the house? Why hadn't she simply responded to him with the calm courtesy she'd have used for any stranger? Instead, she'd egged him on, engaging him in some adolescent teasing reminiscent of a high school crush. And in spite of his compelling good looks, there was no way she could possibly be attracted to someone she'd known only two hours.

Still, when she heard the rumble of Jack's truck starting up, Roslyn had to force herself not to look back before stepping inside Ida Mae Petersen's house.

CHAPTER THREE

JACK REVERSED the truck right up to the end of the drive before he remembered he didn't have Lenny with him. Fortunately—meaning, he didn't have to go back into the house and risk seeing Roslyn again—his nephew had heard the engine and was now running down the drive, waving frantically.

Lenny clambered into the passenger side. "Thought
you were leaving without me," he gasped.

Jack roared out onto the street, shifted in an unusually jerky movement, and squealed north on Union Street toward the center of town.

"So...what's up?"

Jack looked across at Lenny. "What do you mean?"

Lenny shrugged. "I don't know. How come you're heading back into town? Aren't we going to the farm?"

"Thought I'd stop in at the post office—see if my catalogues came in."

Lenny nodded, staring silently through the windshield. After a moment, he asked, "So, do you think she's going to take it?"

"She?"

"You know...Roslyn. Isn't that her name?"

"How the hell would I know?"

The air in the cab chilled a few degrees. Jack saw the confusion in his nephew's face and regretted his outburst. "I don't really know, frankly," he added. "Guess she'll take a few days to see the place and make up her mind."

"Sophie and me figure she won't. She's too young to want to settle in Plainsville."

Jack grinned. "Spoken like a true patriot son," he commented.

"Well, you know. Plainsville is for the older generation."

"Like mine?"

"Geez, Uncle Jack, you know I don't think you're old," Lenny protested. "You're six years younger than my Dad."

"Who's already an old geezer of…what? Forty-one?"

"Yeah."

Jack waited in vain for Lenny to respond to the gibe. Finally, he said, "I've no idea how old Roslyn Baines is, but I do know that she must be one heck of a smart businesswoman to get where she is at that investment place in Chicago."

"Too right!" Lenny exclaimed. "And she wouldn't want to give it all up to move to boring old Plainsville is what I'm saying."

"Maybe so, but you never can tell."

"You can't believe that!"

"She's Ida Mae's niece. Great-niece," he corrected himself. "She'll want to keep the house in the family."

Lenny snorted. "Family! Geez, what family? Ida Mae never had anything to do with any family. The only real friend she had was great-grandpa Henry."

"Who knows, Lenny? We don't know everything about the Petersens and almost nothing about Miss Baines. There's no point in second-guessing what she'll do about the house."

Lenny frowned in disbelief. "You act as if you don't care what she decides. As if you almost hope she'll move in."

Jack felt a rush of warmth flow up into his face. He stared straight ahead, avoiding the suspicion in his nephew's face. Of course, he didn't want Roslyn to move in, but he'd hate himself if she turned down the house because of any kind of pressure from him. Ida Mae would have expected more of Jack. No. If the inheritance did fall to him, he wanted no inner qualms about taking it.

"Is THERE anything you'd like, Miss Baines?"

Sophie Warshawski was standing, dish towel in hand, in the archway between the living room and the hall.

Roslyn spun around from the fireplace, where she'd been examining a row of knickknacks on the mantel. "Please," she said, "call me Roslyn."

Sophie nodded, but said nothing in reply.

Roslyn felt as if she'd been caught shoplifting. "I was just looking at some of my aunt's things." Her glance circled the room. "She saved a lot over the years."

Sophie nodded indifferently. "Most of this stuff is

from long ago, when Miss Ida Mae was still a young girl. Far as I know, she never left Plainsville except to shop occasionally in Des Moines.''

Roslyn couldn't imagine a young woman spending her whole life in a town as small as Plainsville. ''She never went anywhere? Not even to college?''

''Nope. Old Mister Petersen apparently didn't take with educating women, especially if they had plenty of money and wouldn't want for anything.''

''We're lucky that kind of thinking's gone the way of the dinosaur.''

''Maybe. Still, an expensive education is no guarantee of happiness, is it?''

Roslyn refused to let the tone in Sophie's voice intimidate her. ''You know, Sophie, I'm completely mystified by all of this.''

Sophie's eyebrows furled together. ''How do you mean?''

Roslyn gestured into the room. ''First of all, I never knew my grandmother even had a sister. I'd always thought she was an only child, like my own mother and like me. So I can't understand why no one ever told me anything about the Petersen family. Then, to have this great-aunt leave me her house...'' Roslyn gave up and turned back to the mantel. After a moment she said, ''Please show me around the house. And whatever you can tell me about my aunt...well, I'd appreciate it very much.''

Sophie flipped the dish towel toward the hall. ''We'll start with the kitchen,'' she said, '''cause that's where I spent most of my time when I worked for your aunt.''

The smile she flashed was quick and tight, but somehow reassuring. Roslyn followed the house-keeper along the corridor and into the kitchen.

"Got a notepad?" Sophie asked when she reached the kitchen counter.

"What do you mean?"

"Don't career women take notes all the time? Case they miss something important?"

Roslyn realized she was teasing her and smiled.

Sophie pursed her lips together and scanned the room. "All this modern stuff was put in about twenty-five years ago, just after I started working for your aunt. She must have been about sixty-five or so when I started. Henry Jensen got me the job. That's young Jack's granddaddy. Henry and Ida Mae were friends for years, and she'd begun to have these dizzy spells. He was afraid she might fall, hit her head on some-thing and lie helpless for days without anyone know-ing about her. So he asked would I come work for her—do meals and light cleaning, laundry—just dur-ing the days like. Ida Mae was a sound sleeper, not the kind to get up and prowl around. Henry figured she'd be okay on her own at night, and I had my sister's kids with me at the time, so it worked out better for me, too." Sophie pulled out a chair and sat down.

Roslyn felt almost as breathless and sat down in a chair opposite her. A notepad would be useless, Ros-lyn thought. I'd never keep up.

"So that's how and why I came here," Sophie be-gan again. "Now, as to this room. The table and chairs are real teak—brought right from Denmark when old Mr. and Mrs. Petersen emigrated to Iowa. I don't mean Ida Mae's parents. Her grandparents," she clarified.

"How long have the Petersens been in Plainsville, then?"

Sophie shrugged. "Ida Mae's grandfather started up the first bank in town and it stayed in the family until after her father passed away. Probably the family came over from Denmark in the eighteen hundreds. Lots of people in town are from Denmark or Norway—Jack's family, too. All the names ending with *en*. That's one way to tell. Later on, people came from Eastern Europe. Like me." There was another glimpse of smile.

She pointed to the wall behind the sinks and counter. "See those blue-and-white tiles? Ida Mae told me her parents got them on their honeymoon in Europe." Sophie shook her head, the smile on her face softening. "Miss Ida loved to tell stories about the things in this house. She was awfully proud. Some folks thought her a snob—and sometimes I thought so, too," she admitted. "But she was always fierce about family and home."

Roslyn averted her eyes from Sophie's and peered down into her lap. Not fierce enough to keep in touch with mine, she thought.

Reading her mind, Sophie lowered her voice to say, "I have to say that you were almost as much of a surprise to me, as Ida Mae to you. First I knew about another branch of the family was in the last year of Miss Ida Mae's life. Henry was over one night for coffee and dessert. I'd stayed a bit late—don't recall why. Anyhow, before leaving I popped by the living room—or front parlor as Miss Ida called it—to say good-night. Henry was telling her she ought to let him contact her niece in Chicago. I remember his exact words because he was normally so mild-mannered. He said, in a very stern tone for him, 'Ida Mae, you've got to put the past behind you. A lifetime of hating is enough. Call your niece.' Then your aunt said in this kind of sad way, 'It's too late, Henry. Lucille is already dead.'"

Roslyn felt her breath catch. "My mother," she whispered. "She died a little more than a year ago."

Sophie nodded her head. "There you go. She knew about your people in Chicago and they surely knew about her, too. Yet not a one came to her funeral!"

Roslyn flushed. "There was only *one* left at the time—me. And believe me, I don't know if we have any relatives in Chicago, much less in Iowa."

Sophie raised her eyebrow again. "No one's blaming you, Miss Baines. I just think it's a shame, is all, that an old lady of ninety has no one at her funeral but a few distant cousins and people like the Jensens, who aren't even related."

Roslyn stared at the woman across from her. For a split second she pictured herself at ninety and wondered if she'd be any better off in terms of family or friends.

This time, Sophie dropped eye contact first. "Well, what's past is past as they say. Best to get on with life. Shall we head into the living room now?"

"If you like," Roslyn murmured. She suddenly felt exhausted, overwhelmed by the peculiar mix of emotions of the day, starting from the first shock of a man on a ladder at her bedroom window.

"You're most likely tired from your trip here and all," Sophie said. "I'll be back tomorrow morning and maybe we can go through your aunt's things. Seems a shame to let all those clothes go to waste when so many people might want them." Sophie placed her palms flat on the table to help herself out of the chair. "I'll bring some apple muffins tomorrow and we'll have another history lesson."

Roslyn looked up into Sophie's face and returned the first genuine smile the woman had given her that day. "Thanks, Sophie. Maybe I'll wander the house myself for a while."

"You do that. And enjoy your two or three days' holiday here." She bustled about the kitchen, retrieving her bags, sweater and purse, then left with a simple goodbye.

Roslyn kept her eyes on the empty doorway a while longer. She couldn't help but be slightly amused that Sophie assumed she'd be heading back to Chicago permanently, leaving Plainsville, Iowa behind in the past. *Right where it belonged.*

AN HOUR of browsing through the house convinced Roslyn that, without knowing the background of the various pieces of china, crystal or furniture, she might as well be wandering through a museum. When she succumbed to a series of yawns, she knew it was time to get out for some fresh air and to grab a late lunch in town.

The house itself had been fascinating. Even Roslyn's inexpert eye could see that no expense had been spared in the structure and interior design. Its remarkable features of rich wood paneling, staircase balustrade and vaulted ceilings edged with swirls of ornate molding reflected not only impeccable taste but meticulous attention to detail. No corner had been overlooked, from floor to ceiling.

It was only on the third floor, arranged in the shape of a T, that Roslyn detected signs of age and neglect. Circular patches of dampness spread across the ceilings in two of the bedrooms and the tiny alcove that made up the third bathroom in the house. Strips of wallpaper hung limply from the walls and, here and there, tendrils of loose paint curled upward. Roslyn guessed this floor had probably once accommodated servants. Out of sight and removed from the rest of the house and its visitors, it had been left to fend for itself over the years. She eyed the ceiling once more.

Must be damage from a leaky roof, she thought, and immediately conjured up Jack Jensen's face. If he'd been looking after the place for the last few years, as he'd suggested, he'd obviously forgotten the roof. But then, perhaps his work had focused on the grounds rather than the house itself. Yet he had *supposedly* come that morning to clean the eaves troughs. Maybe his real purpose all along had been to check out the competition. Namely, her.

Roslyn smiled. He certainly didn't seem like the kind of guy whose motive for helping little old ladies was to inherit their estates.

Roslyn navigated the steep staircase leading to the second floor. After exploring this level, she thought that if she were to move into the house, she'd definitely take the back bedroom across the hall. Twice the size of the other, it featured two gabled alcoves and four windows. The room would always be bright, especially in the summer, and had an unrestricted view of the fields and woods beyond. Roslyn stared out one of the windows and realized all that land could belong to her—if she wanted it.

She shook her head at the image of herself as a landowner. Somehow, it didn't match her Chicago persona. But she'd take a walk through town, if only to see the rest of what she'd be relinquishing when she returned to the city.

As soon as she walked in the door, Roslyn knew the teenager she'd spoken to in the convenience store had been the wrong person to ask about a good place to eat in town. She stood indecisively on the threshold. A quick look around the café told her no one present was over the age of twenty. The pulsing bass of a rock group pumped from a sound system guaranteed to be heard in the next county. Guys and girls in crisp white shirts and blue jeans whizzed about with trays of impossibly tall drinks and enormous desserts. A few heads turned Roslyn's way, but nobody showed more than a fleeting interest in the newcomer. Their dismissal of her presence made her feel twice her thirty-two years. She couldn't leave the place fast enough.

Back on the sidewalk of Plainsville's main drag, Roslyn debated between finding a grocery store and making lunch at home or tackling the other side of the street. The street won, merely because the idea of preparing a meal in an unfamiliar kitchen was more than she could bear.

Jaywalking in Plainsville was a rare occurrence, judging by the number of stares she received as she dodged a few cars to cross. Safely on the other side, Roslyn walked toward the heart of Plainsville—a small grassy roundabout in the center of the street dominated by a bronzed statue of a man astride a horse and with a hawk perched on his shoulder.

Roslyn viewed this centerpiece from the sidewalk. Plainsville's founding father, she wondered, accompanied by his loyal pet hawk? She smiled. Not for Plainsville the lure of modern sculpture! Still, she had to admit the town was pretty, its sidewalks lined with graceful trees and planter boxes filled with plants not yet in bloom. She caught the reflection of light in one of the trees and noticed that its branches were festooned with strings of Christmas bulbs. The streetlights were replicas of gas lamps and arched gracefully over the parking lanes.

"I see you've already managed to find the best diner in Plainsville."

Roslyn whirled to her left. Jack Jensen was standing inches from her shoulder and she brushed against him as she turned. "You startled me," she gasped.

"Sorry, I should have tapped you on the shoulder or something. Either way, guess you would've jumped."

"I—I was just looking at that statue," she said, pointing to the roundabout.

"Oh. I figured you'd just had a bite to eat at Laverne's place." He craned his neck behind him.

Roslyn noticed for the first time the diner with the sign Laverne's Coffee Shop propped against the plate glass window.

"Don't be fooled by the name," he added. "It's not one of those trendy coffeehouses where you pay exorbitant prices for designer coffees and monster-size pastries that have no taste."

Several corners in downtown Chicago popped into Roslyn's mind. "Actually," she said, "I was looking for a place to eat when the guy on the horse caught my eye. Right out of Main Street, U.S.A., isn't it?"

He looked down at her, his eyes narrowing slightly. "The guy represents every pioneer and settler who had the guts to leave a safe home behind and head out for the unknown."

Roslyn felt her face flush.

"And the hawk," he continued, "well, anyone who knows their geography knows that Iowa is the Hawkeye State. Named after one of our famous Native Americans." He waited a beat, then leaned into her face to say, "So much for the history lesson. Care for some lunch?"

"Great," said Roslyn. "Maybe if I put some food into my mouth, I won't be able to fit my second foot in."

He smiled, stepping aside to let her go first. But then she heard him mutter. "Geez, I forgot I'm supposed to be meeting Lenny."

"At Laverne's?"

"Nah. This place is too old-fashioned for Lenny.

He was going to wait for me near the roundabout.'' Jack moved toward the edge of the curb and scanned the parkette surrounding the bronze statue.

His eyes crinkled against the sun and he pushed the tip of his baseball cap back off his forehead to get a better look. It was Roslyn's first chance to get a better look, too. At Jack Jensen. Tall and lean rather than thin, he obviously kept in shape. His profile had strong lines without sharpness. Ordinary features that merged to form an attractive, though very un-Hollywood face. For some reason, that pleased her.

His head swiveled unexpectedly, catching her mid-stare, and Roslyn knew her face was red. ''A dead giveaway,'' he murmured softly.

''Say again?''

''Your skin tones. I bet you can't ever tell a lie convincingly,'' he teased, adding quickly, ''Not that I'm suggesting you ever would!''

She grinned, just as Lenny's shout got his attention.

''Damn!'' he whispered, pulling his eyes from hers and staring down the street. Lenny was running toward them.

Lenny pulled up right in front of Jack. ''Thought you were leavin' me behind again,'' he began, then stopped, catching sight of Roslyn. ''Oh, sorry.'' He looked from one to the other.

''I just bumped into Roslyn here,'' explained Jack, ''and, well, I was thinking of getting a bite to eat with her at Laverne's.''

Lenny frowned. ''Here? I thought we were going to Murphy's!''

Jack stared silently at his nephew.

Willing him to shut up? Roslyn wondered. "You two go ahead with your plans," she said. "Besides, I'm sure you have a lot of work to do today."

"Yeah," said Lenny, brightening at the reminder. "Aren't we supposed to clear some brush for old man Watson?"

Jack flipped the cap off his head and ran his fingers through his hair. Little spikes stood on end, moistened by perspiration. "We can do that any day," he said.

"Not with me, 'cause next week final exams are starting and I won't be available."

Jack sighed loudly and turned to Roslyn. "Look," he began.

She held up a palm. "Another time. Just recommend something at Laverne's for me."

He gave a faint smile. "Anything. For lunch, maybe the club sandwich on whole wheat."

"Sounds good," she said, keeping her eyes on Jack's face but catching the scowl on Lenny's at the same time.

"Okay then," he said, still playing with the cap in his hands.

There was a moment's pause which Lenny broke. "The meter musta run out by now," he grumbled.

Jack shot Lenny a look that silenced him. Roslyn was beginning to feel uncomfortable. "Maybe you could pop around sometime tomorrow," she suggested. "I think we need to talk about...well, things."

"What time?" Jack asked.

She shrugged. "Sophie's coming to help clean and go through some things with me. Maybe around eleven?"

"Good. Eleven." He nodded enthusiastically, then put the cap back onto his head. "Okay, then. Tomorrow at eleven."

"Geez, Uncle Jack," Lenny interjected. "You've already said that a hundred times."

Jack ignored his nephew and held out his right hand. Surprised by the sudden gesture, Roslyn placed hers in his.

"That's good. That we're going to talk, I mean," Jack murmured, staring down into Roslyn's eyes and clasping her hand gently in his.

Lenny sputtered something. Finally, Jack released her hand and, with Lenny tugging at his right elbow, began to move off down the street.

"Good grief," mumbled Roslyn. "What a pair." But her hand was still tingling when she placed it on the door to push it open.

CHAPTER FOUR

ROSLYN COULDN'T remember the last time she'd felt so restless. Or could this gnawing sensation be loneliness?

No, she thought, pushing the suggestion away. More like boredom from midweek in Plainsville, Iowa.

She rose from the wicker rocking chair she'd found in the sunroom off the kitchen and prowled back and forth along the veranda. April was far too soon to be sitting outdoors in the evening, but the silence inside the house was pressing. She wrapped the afghan tighter around her, reluctant to head back inside for her jacket. Once there, she knew she'd simply turn out the lights and go to bed. It was only nine o'clock and she couldn't recall the last time she'd retired so early. Maybe the day after her mother's funeral a year ago, when sleep had been a welcome escape.

Her mother's pretty face flashed before her. Lucille Dutton Baines. Roslyn sighed, trying to conjure up a picture of her mother in which she didn't have a defeated look. If Roslyn went back to the years before her parents divorced, she could almost envision a mother who smiled and laughed. Roslyn had never learned all the reasons for the breakup. She remembered a lot of arguments about money. As the years passed, other issues cropped up, and her father began to stay out at night.

Moving into Grandma and Grandpa Dutton's row house had ruled out any chance of reconciliation. Roslyn shivered at the very memory of Grandma Dutton's hawklike face and thin, brittle body. Not the kind of body that welcomed a child's embrace. Was it any wonder, she asked herself in the center of Ida Mae Petersen's veranda, that her grandmother had never revealed anything about her family? Would *any* family want to claim someone like Grandma Dutton?

That sobering question was unlikely to be answered. For here she was, in the very seat of the Petersen family, and anyone who might know the complete story was dead. The image of herself as sole survivor of the Petersen clan made Roslyn feel even worse than she had moments ago. She headed for the door, pausing to take a last look at the garden Jack had shown her that morning.

The Iowa rose was bathed in the dim light from the front hall. If only the plant could speak, she thought. Then she shook her head. *You're losing it, Baines,* she said to herself. *Next you'll convince yourself that the bush knows all kinds of secrets.*

SOPHIE PURSED HER thin lips together and frowned.

"That rosebush," she enunciated slowly, obviously irked by Roslyn's question, "came to Iowa from Denmark more than one hundred and fifty years ago. They call it an antique rose, because it's from the original stock. Not a hybrid, like most of the ones you get nowadays.'' She smiled, her face softening. "Jack told me all that. Anyway, your Aunt Ida's ancestors carried it with them when they came to America all those years ago. It must have been important to the family even then, because people didn't have the luxury of taking a lot of stuff with them when they traveled on those little boats all the way across the Atlantic.''

Sophie stopped then, her eyes drifting off in a kind of reverie. Imagining the voyage, Roslyn wondered?

The other woman's eyes blinked rapidly, then gazed across the kitchen table at Roslyn. "Sorry, I got to thinking about my own folks coming over, but they traveled in a modern boat, of course.'' She took a deep breath. "As I was saying, the rose was planted in the family homestead—where we're sittin' this minute—and has been looked after by generations of Petersens ever since.''

Roslyn waited for Sophie to continue. "And?'' she prompted.

Sophie raised her broad shoulders in reply. "That's it. You asked what was so special about the rose.''

"So they brought it over from Denmark. I still don't see why Aunt Ida would have been worried enough about it to will it to me.''

Sophie flashed Roslyn a look that questioned her basic intelligence. "The rose has been just as much a part of family life as any person. Every time any Petersen got married, the bride had to have roses in her bouquet. If a Petersen died when the rose was blooming, the flowers would be placed in the funeral wreaths. Whenever a Petersen moved away ·from

Plainsville, a cutting from the rose would go with them.'' She plunked her empty coffee mug down and stared at Roslyn.

''How do you know all this?''

''Oh, your aunt told me many times, over the years. She fussed over that rosebush as if it were her own child.'' She closed her eyes for a second, then shook her head sadly. ''I suppose it was, too. Poor Ida.''

''Why?''

''She never got to use the rose herself, her dying in January....''

''No roses, then,'' Roslyn murmured.

Sophie gave her a sharp look, but went on. ''And of course, the dear soul never married.''

''I wonder if my grandmother had a cutting from the rose in her bridal bouquet.''

Sophie raised an eyebrow. ''Don't you know?''

''I know less than you, apparently. I remember a photograph of my grandma and grandpa all dressed up and arm in arm, standing in front of a building. My mother said it was their wedding picture—they got married in a registry office in Chicago, I think. I don't know if she had a bouquet in her hand or not.''

''Where's the picture now?''

''Probably in a trunk full of stuff from my mother's flat. I—I never had the courage to go through it after Mom died. It's all in storage now.'' Roslyn's voice drifted off.

After a moment's silence, Sophie announced, ''Well, speaking of storage. I guess it's time we got to cleaning out Miss Ida's room.''

Roslyn reluctantly followed Sophie along the hall

and up the stairs. It was a bright, sunny morning. The skeletal tops of trees behind the house were visible through the transom window on the first landing, and Roslyn wondered what they'd look like in full leaf. Then she caught herself. Trees, silly. They'd look like trees.

"When Miss Ida and her sister were young girls, they shared the big back bedroom," Sophie said as they turned at the top of the stairs.

"It's a beautiful bedroom," she murmured. "If I lived here, that's the one I'd have."

"Except you won't be living here," Sophie reminded her gently.

Roslyn's face heated up. She was tempted to say something about not having made a decision yet, but was loath to spoil the easy neutrality that she and Sophie had struck together over morning coffee.

Sophie herself seemed to regret her remark. "Maybe you should move in there for the next couple of nights—just to satisfy your curiosity."

Roslyn's smile was faint. "No," she said. "No point, is there?" She squeezed past Sophie and headed for the master bedroom at the front of the house. On the way, she turned her head to ask, "Why did Aunt Ida move into this bedroom? The other one is so much nicer."

"After her first stroke she said she wanted to be able to see the rose from her bed. Keep an eye on it, she used to say." Sophie snorted. "Jack used to think Miss Ida didn't trust him to give that plant its proper care."

"Well, she could certainly get a good view of it

from her bed,'' Roslyn said, standing at the wooden headboard and peering out the bay window.

"Miss Ida was much shorter than you,'' said Sophie. "She could only see it if she had a lot of pillows behind her. We tried to move the bed, but even Jack and his brother had a hard time getting it to budge.''

Roslyn glanced down at the double bed. "It's huge,'' she said. "I love the way the headboard comes up so high and then curves back like that.''

"It's called a sleigh bed,'' said Sophie. "Handmade right here in Plainsville.'' She lumbered across the room to the mirrored vanity and tall bureau standing next to it. "Might as well start with the drawers,'' she said. "Why don't you take the closet? We may need some help getting this stuff downstairs.''

"Jack will be here about eleven,'' said Roslyn. "I'm sure he'd help.''

"Oh?'' Sophie's only response, but Roslyn sensed the woman was waiting for an explanation. "We have to settle some things,'' she finally told her.

Sophie cast her a knowing glance, but Roslyn ignored her, opening the closet door. "This is so strange,'' she murmured, "to be handling things owned by a person I never even met. It doesn't seem right.'' She stared into the closet. On a shelf above the rack of clothes sat a rectangular wooden box. She pulled it down.

It was a rich mahogany shade, its edges neatly dovetailed and the lid locked with an ornate silver clasp. "How beautiful,'' she murmured, running her hand along its smooth, polished surface.

Sophie looked up from the bureau. "Your auntie

loved that box. It was always by her side. I think she kept a diary or something in it. After she died, I put it in the closet to keep it safe.''

"Is there a key?"

Sophie's face was blank. ''Yes. I've seen it somewhere. Just can't remember where. Would you rather tackle the back bedroom and leave the closet to me?''

Roslyn was grateful for the suggestion. ''Yes, I'd rather do that. Thanks, Sophie.'' She replaced the box on the closet shelf, eager to escape from the task that had brought back too many memories of cleaning out her mother's flat after her death last year.

Although there was now only a double bed in the rear bedroom, Roslyn could see how twin beds might have been tucked into each gabled alcove. And except for the bed, there were two matching sets of everything, all painted white—vanities with attached mirrors, bureaus and, in opposite corners, two identical child-sized rocking chairs. Two scruffy braided rag rugs lay on the hardwood floor.

A perfect bedroom for twin girls, she thought. The gabled alcoves—one jutting out from the rear wall and the other from the side wall—housed small windows trimmed with Swiss eyelet curtains that were no longer crisp and white. Two larger windows between the gables offered spectacular views of the woods and fields behind the house. Roslyn looked out the window closest to the side gable to see the end of the drive and the garage where Jack had parked his truck yesterday.

In spite of the brisk April wind, she opened the window to ventilate the bedroom, then pivoted slowly, deciding where to start. There were two other doors in the room, to the right of the main one. Two walk-in closets for the little princesses? She was beginning to picture a room decorated in pastel accessories and frilly trimmings. Hard to imagine the stern grandmother she'd known growing up in such a room. She bet the closets were jammed with stuffed animals and dolls.

But they yielded only stacks of cardboard boxes. Roslyn began at the top of the pile, expecting to find inside the souvenirs of childhood she'd imagined. Instead, one box after another revealed musty magazines, children's books and even old calendars. No sign of treasured mementos. Someone had mentioned that her aunt had collected things. If so, Roslyn thought, where were they?

Still, she persevered. Some of the boxes contained carefully wrapped vinyl long-playing records; others, neatly folded newspapers. The contents of the second closet were even less interesting: old cookbooks, recipe cards and envelopes of discount coupons that had expired years ago. But at the bottom of the last box in the closet, turned upside down as if to conceal its discovery even longer, was a cardboard-framed black-and-white photograph of two girls. *The little princesses.*

One sat in a rocking chair; the other stood behind to the right, with an arm draped lovingly over her sister's shoulders. They were identical from the tip of their sculpted blond curls to the toes of their shiny patent shoes. Their lacy dresses came to just below the knee. Each girl was holding the stem of a single rose bloom.

Roslyn turned the photo over to ease it out of the cardboard frame. Someone had written, in spidery script, "June Rose and Ida Mae, June 12, 1915, fifth birthday."

"Find something interesting?"

Roslyn craned her neck. Sophie was standing in the doorway with a tray of cold drinks. Roslyn held out the photograph, which Sophie took after placing the tray onto the vanity.

"Oh, my," she said, then flipped the picture over to read the inscription. "Aren't they just the perfect little—"

"Princesses."

Sophie looked down at Roslyn and grinned. "I'd never have thought of Miss Ida as that, but you sure can see it in this picture. Where'd you find it?"

"At the very bottom of a box. You know, Sophie, it's obvious that my aunt was a pack rat, saving a ton of useless stuff. But where are all the things from her childhood? I mean, even my mother, who wasn't at all sentimental, saved some favorite stuffed animals and baby clothes of mine."

Sophie shook her head, handed the photograph back to Roslyn and sank down onto the edge of the bed. "Miss Ida talked a lot about her family and all the antiques and treasures in this house, but she never once said her sister's name aloud. I knew from what other people in town told me over the years that there was a twin sister living in Chicago and that there must have been a falling out between the two."

"Must have been some falling out," murmured Roslyn, "for her to get rid of the memory of that twin so completely."

"I guess it's hard for you to find out all this, seeing as how that twin was your very own grandmother."

Grandma Dutton's solemn face appeared in the room. Hard to reconcile that face with one of those little girls, Roslyn thought. And which one would she have been? She peered closely at the photo.

"Trying to decide who's who?"

Roslyn glanced up at Sophie, whose smile was a mix of humor and sympathy. "Just curious," she said.

"Well, the writing starts off with June Rose, so maybe she's the one standing just to the left. Assuming that the order of the names matches the left to right order of the picture."

"Perhaps, though it hardly matters, does it? They were so identical in looks."

Sophie pursed her lips. "Maybe it mattered to them," she said.

Roslyn studied the picture a moment longer, wondering what it might have been like to grow up as a mirror to another person. Would you feel you could never escape that other face? She almost shuddered at the thought.

The rumble of a truck engine broke the silence. "Jack!" Sophie announced, pleasure ringing in her voice. She heaved herself off the bed and grabbed the tray. "We'll have our snack down in the kitchen," she said, bustling out the door.

Roslyn stared at the picture in her hand, mesmer-

ized by the dimpled faces smiling so expectantly at
the camera. Five years old and so much to look forward to. But something happened to ruin that close-
ness. What had come between two identical twins to
make them virtually renounce each other?

She sighed, pushing herself up from the floor.
Coming to Plainsville had definitely raised a lot of
questions. Unfortunately, they were questions that
seemed destined never to be answered.

JACK WAS comfortable in a kitchen chair, one hand
clutching a glass of orange juice and the other reaching for a muffin when Roslyn came into the room.
He started to get to his feet, but Roslyn smiled and
waved him down.

"Please," she said, "you make me feel I'm at-
tending a board meeting. And work is still a day or
so away."

He had a sudden picture of her then, in one of those
nice-fitting, tailored suits, walking confidently into a
room of executives. The image made him realize how
far apart Chicago and Plainsville really were. Jack
swallowed the lump of muffin in his throat.

"Sophie's been telling me you two have worked
all morning cleaning out closets," he began, as she
sat down in the chair opposite him. "Guess your aunt
saved a lot of stuff."

"Everything but what mattered most, I'm afraid.
For some reason, there's nothing but an old photo-
graph of my grandmother and aunt as five-year-olds.
At least, nothing I've found so far."

"I know Miss Ida kept photo albums. I used to see her poring over them some days," Sophie said.

"There were a few in the boxes. Maybe I'll take them back to Chicago with me," Roslyn said.

Jack avoided Sophie's face, afraid she might wink or something. She hadn't made any bones about who *she* wanted to take over the Petersen home, even though it rightfully belonged to Roslyn. He'd spent a whole day arguing the point with her when they'd first learned the terms of the will.

The house should go to the person who'd taken care of it, Sophie had asserted. The person who'd cherished it. And of course, he couldn't deny that he was that person. He'd always loved the Petersen home, even as a kid when Grandpa Henry brought him to visit and the three would have iced tea on the veranda. He always sat on the swing and pushed it back and forth with the tips of his sneakers.

Still, he'd pointed out, he had no connection by blood to Miss Ida, and family had to count for something. Sophie had snorted at that remark. If Miss Ida loved her family so much, why hadn't she kept in touch? Why leave a house to someone you never even met? And he hadn't been able to think of a damn thing to say to that, except that maybe this great-niece would learn to love Plainsville. Sophie, as usual, got the last word. Or snort.

And now that niece was smiling nicely at him from across the table with eyes that must be the color of a sea somewhere, though not one he'd ever seen. Kind of a blend of blue and green, he decided, but the dominant shade depended on the light. He started to think about what tubes of paint he'd mix to get that shade when he realized she was talking to him.

"Hmm?" he asked, staring first at Roslyn then at Sophie, who was smiling broadly.

"I was saying that we ought to discuss the will. My return ticket's for Sunday and—"

"Maybe I'll go upstairs and finish up that front bedroom," Sophie interrupted and swept out the door quicker than Jack had ever seen the housekeeper move.

He felt uncomfortable, the way Roslyn so bluntly got to the point. No small talk or preamble. Though he doubted she was the small talk kind of woman. Which was another thing that attracted him to her. That and a few other attributes, he had to admit.

"The house is beautiful and I suppose many people would love to live in a place like Plainsville," she said.

He sensed immediately how the conversation was going to go.

"But," she continued, "I've just had a promotion. The one I've been waiting for since I started at the firm. And of course the conditions of the will are preposterous. I mean, did Aunt Ida really think a person could just give up everything and move in? Unless," her voice slowed and she raised her eyes to meet Jack's, "something else was her intention all along."

"Say again?"

She gave a halfhearted shrug. "Perhaps Aunt Ida knew I'd turn the offer down, and the place would go to you. Maybe that's what she wanted all along."

The suggestion really ticked him off, mainly because he'd always thought Ida was a direct kind of person. If she'd wanted him to get the house, she'd have willed it to him. There had to be another reason. He just didn't know what it was. He leaned back in his chair and rocked it impatiently, waiting for her to finish. She was going on about all the things she'd have to give up in Chicago. As if he didn't know a thing or two about giving things up!

Finally, he couldn't listen anymore. "Miss Ida always knew her own mind. She was a real straight player, far as I know. Personally, I think she wanted to make amends. I think that's why she wanted you to have this place."

"Make amends?"

"For whatever caused the split in the family. She was ninety years old and a very proud, stubborn lady. I can see that she might have been afraid of being rebuffed by you, so she left it to you in her will. That way, she'd never have to know if you turned her down or not."

Roslyn's face twisted. He could tell she didn't like what he'd said.

"Well," she gave a nervous little laugh, "I suppose we can use amateur psychology all we like to analyze her motives but what would be the point? We'll never know and frankly, I'm not sure I even care." Roslyn pushed her chair back and stood up. "I'm probably not going to take the house and I should think you'd be happy, rather than acting like I've done something wrong."

Jack scraped his chair back and jumped to his feet.

"It's not that at all. You've misunderstood. I just want you to think everything through. Don't rush your decision."

"Are you worried I'll change my mind later?"

"There is that, of course," he admitted.

"Once I make up my mind," she said, her voice serious, "I seldom change it."

He looked long and hard into her unflinching eyes, now the color of a winter sea, and wondered how he could have lost all of his common sense in the last twenty-four hours. If she was stupid enough to hand over the most magnificent piece of property for maybe counties around, why was he trying to persuade her to keep it?

He plucked his cap off the kitchen table, nodded curtly in her direction, mumbled "So be it, then," and strode out of the room. He knew if he looked back, she'd be watching him with her jaw gaping, but he didn't want to chance her getting the last word.

He almost knocked over Sophie at the foot of the staircase. He mumbled another goodbye and headed straight out of the house.

NONE OF IT had gone the way she'd imagined. She thought he'd beam, offer a humble thank you for her generosity and maybe even suggest some kind of celebration later. And as hard as Roslyn tried, she couldn't figure out at what point in the conversation she had angered him.

"He's gone?" There was a tone of disbelief in the question Sophie posed from the kitchen doorway.

Roslyn gave a half shrug, palms up in surrender.

She sensed the other woman was waiting for something more, but Roslyn's response to Jack's abrupt "So be it, then" had gotten stuck in the realm of stupefaction. Speechless bewilderment led quickly to acute irritation.

"I don't understand that man at all," Roslyn complained.

"Jack?"

Roslyn flashed Sophie a who else? look. "I mean, I had to practically beg him to take this house off my hands. And how does he react? By implying that I don't appreciate what I've been offered here. What does he expect? That I'll just walk away from my life in Chicago? My job? My promotion? My *condo?*"

Sophie shook her head. "You have to know Jack to understand he—"

"Why do I? Why does this whole thing have to be so complicated? I mean, I inherit this monstrous home from a great-aunt I never knew existed and who must have hated my own family, but the catch is I have to live here for a whole year to look after a *rosebush* before I can legally claim it as mine. The woman didn't give a hoot about my taking the place or she wouldn't have made it so difficult. So when I decide to give it to the other beneficiary, he gets all prickly and accuses me of not caring about any of this." Roslyn's right hand swept an arc across the room.

"Young Jack would never—"

"Well," Roslyn continued, ignoring Sophie's efforts, "what do I care? I've made up my mind. Since there's no point in staying until Sunday, I'm going to call the airline and see if I can move up my flight to tomorrow.'' With that, she marched out of the kitchen, catching a last glance of Sophie staring, openmouthed, behind her.

But there was no seat available on a Friday flight to Chicago from Des Moines. When the clerk suggested a charter air service Roslyn said she'd think it over. Then she dialed her office, anxious to find out how things were going and perhaps to pick up some information about the investigation. Sophie had tiptoed upstairs, murmuring something about finishing up and that she'd let herself out. Roslyn was embarrassed by her outburst. What had she expected Sophie to do? Agree with a complete stranger about someone the woman had known for years?

Her office phone rang so many times it was transferred to another extension. Puzzled, Roslyn was about to disconnect and try again when the receiver was picked up on the other end.

''Saunders, McIntyre and Associates Investments,'' Judy intoned from the other end.

Roslyn smiled and felt herself relaxing. At last someone she knew, someone who would be sympathetic. ''Hi, Jude. It's me—Roslyn.''

''Oh. Hi, Roslyn.''

Unsure about Judy's slight pause, Roslyn stammered, ''I…uh…thought I'd better call and see how things are going there. I have a ton of stuff to tell you about Plainsville, Iowa, but I suppose it can wait.''

''Oh, yeah? Well, I can hardly wait to hear about it all.''

The flatness in Judy's voice suggested otherwise, but Roslyn persevered. ''I've tried to move up my flight from Sunday to tomorrow, but there's nothing available. I thought maybe you could try from that end?''

''Well, the thing is, I'm a bit tied up right now. Mr. Saunders has put me in Bob's office to help out because his secretary had to go on sick leave.''

Roslyn frowned. ''Why did he do that? He knew I was only taking a few days.''

''He said you might be gone longer.''

''That's very odd,'' she said, trying to keep her voice calm and neutral. ''I mean, considering he wants me to help set up the new office.''

There was a longer pause. ''Rumor has it that that's been put on hold for a while.''

''What?''

''No one's saying it aloud, but the firm might be in some kind of financial trouble.''

Roslyn closed her eyes. Jim Naismith's face swam before her. ''Umm, has anyone mentioned anything about...about an inquiry?''

''I don't know anything about an inquiry.''

Roslyn relaxed. Okay, she told herself, so not much new on that front. Because Judy would know. ''All right, then. Listen, if I can't get another flight, I just might rent a car or something. I should have done that in the first place. So, I guess I'll see you on Monday morning.''

''Okay, if you're certain. But, you know, I wouldn't rush back if I were you. Things are pretty slow here and it seems like Ed isn't expecting you. Tony says he's managing your cases okay. Take a few more days.''

"I think I've had all I can take of Plainsville, frankly. Bye, Jude. See you on Monday." Roslyn had to force herself to hang up so casually. Something was definitely going on at the office. Her boss was acting as though she didn't exist and the secretary she'd worked with for three years sounded as if she'd been possessed by aliens.

Whatever it is, she thought, it's a good thing I've made my decision about this house. She surveyed the room. The midafternoon sun hadn't yet reached it, but she knew from yesterday that the sunset could be spectacular from the bay window. Probably in the summer, the room would be cool all day until late afternoon. Then the kitchen would get the breezes sweeping up from the river and ravines beyond.

Roslyn drummed her fingertips on the small table where the phone squatted on its lace doily. *What does it matter,* she asked herself, *what this place is like in the summer? It's not yours—let's face it. It belongs to a man who, for some inexplicable reason, goads you into childish rants and peevish moods. And all without apparent effort.*

She thought of Jack's face when he'd hurled his final words at her. *So be it, then.* Roslyn couldn't help but smile at the theatrics of the exit. As if she'd brought down some kind of curse on herself because she didn't want to take care of a silly rosebush. Still, with that flush in his olive skin, the tuft of hair sticking up and the way his eyebrows wrinkled in exasperation, Jack Jensen resembled a little boy who couldn't quite believe someone was saying no.

She admitted to a slight regret though, that they

hadn't met in Chicago. She could picture him in a dark pinstripe suit and crisp white shirt, his lean body, raven hair and big black eyes setting hearts aflutter. Roslyn sighed. *So be it then,* she thought. Truer words were never spoken.

CHAPTER FIVE

WHEN ROSLYN drove the rental car into the drive and saw Jack's pickup truck, she murmured, "Oh no," unhappy at the prospect of a repeat performance of yesterday's quarrel. Not really a quarrel, she told herself, more like a tiff. And of course, Jack had been the one to do the tiffing.

She parked the car to one side, allowing room for the truck to back out, then headed for the front door. She'd left her luggage just inside in the hall and had walked to the car rental place after getting breakfast at a diner on the way. It wasn't Laverne's—which was farther than she needed to go—but had offered a reasonable home-style breakfast, something Roslyn hadn't eaten since she was a kid.

Finding a car rental place—an adjunct of the only car sales lot in town—in the local phone book had been a pleasant surprise. She'd called them last night and arranged to pick up a car after nine. Then she'd called the airline to cancel her return flight. She figured the inconvenience of driving to Chicago was minor compared to spending another day in Plainsville, experiencing all sorts of conflicting emotions about her inheritance. Not to mention getting involved in some ridiculous argument with a man she hadn't even known three days ago. Not worth the aggravation, she told herself for the umpteenth time since last night.

Sophie opened the door, greeting her with a tenuous smile. Yesterday when Roslyn had told her that she'd be leaving in the morning, Sophie's response had been noncommittal. Roslyn wasn't certain what she'd expected—even a wolfish grin of delight that the favored boy would be getting the house might have been understandable.

"Are you leaving right away?" Sophie asked, holding the door.

"I might as well. I'd like to get into the city and return the car before afternoon rush hour. Then I can zip home, shower and pop into work."

"Work! So soon?"

Roslyn smiled. If only the woman knew how many hours a week she logged in at the office. "Back to the grindstone," she said. She stooped to pick up the suitcase.

"Let Jack get that for you," Sophie said. "He's out back just putting something together for you."

"Oh, I can manage." Roslyn had her bags in the trunk by the time Jack appeared from around the side of the house.

He hurried when he saw her. "I didn't hear you drive up," he said when he reached her at the rear of the car. "Sophie called this morning to tell me you were leaving today, instead of tomorrow."

"Oh," said Roslyn. Maybe she'd misread Sophie's reaction. She wondered when the bottle of champagne would be pulled out.

Setting down the plastic shopping bag he'd been

holding, he pulled off his baseball cap and began gesturing with it. "Look," he began, "I hate to have you leave without clearing up things from yesterday."

Roslyn frowned. "Jack," she said, raising an open palm at him, "forget about it. We both have different viewpoints and there's nothing to discuss anymore. I've made a decision I can live with—" she summoned her most sincere smile "—and I'm sure it's one you'll be happy with, too." Even she heard the edge in her voice.

His eyes narrowed ever so slightly. "I'm not the person giving something up here," he continued. "Just remember on your drive home that there's plenty of time to decide. Randall Taylor won't push to close everything for a while. Take a week or two after you get back before you call him."

He looked so earnest, Roslyn felt herself relenting. "All right," she promised, "but I doubt anything will change. Once I return to work, everything will pile up again and I won't have much time to give this matter a lot more thought. You know how it is."

A faint smile appeared. "Sure," he said. Then he reached down for the plastic bag and held it out to Roslyn. "I've taken a cutting of the rose for you. When you get home, give it lots of water every day. You won't have to repot it for awhile. If you don't have a garden—you mentioned your condo—it should do all right on a balcony when the weather warms up, but you may want to bring it in over the winter. Until it gets a good hold."

"Oh," was all Roslyn could think to say. The rosebush. She hadn't given it a second of time in her thoughts in all of her leaving preparations. Still, she was touched by his almost-boyish offer.

Sophie came slowly down the veranda steps and startled Roslyn by wrapping her big arms around her in a goodbye hug. "Come and visit us any time," Sophie said. "Mr. Taylor has my address and phone number—and I'm in the book, too."

Roslyn smiled a thank you, though she suspected they both knew a future visit was unlikely.

She leaned across the driver's seat and placed the plastic bag with potted rose cutting in the center. Just before she climbed in, Jack touched her arm. For a moment she was afraid he was going to hug her too, but instead he extended his right hand.

"I'm not real good at goodbyes," he murmured, "and I've a feeling that you won't be taking Sophie up on a visit. But please give all of this more thought—if you can find the time." He gave a small laugh, lifting his cap slightly in his left hand, all the while clutching Roslyn's hand in the other.

The uncertain smile, the gesturing with the cap and the gentle, warm pressure of his hand was unexpectedly overwhelming for Roslyn. He'd gone out of his way to drive over and cut a piece of the rosebush for her. She knew he'd done it because it was important to him. Part of her wished all of it was important to her, too.

She looked up at Ida Mae Petersen's stately home one more time. It wasn't difficult to imagine children running along that wide veranda and grown-ups sitting on the wicker chairs, chatting idly about their daily lives. Some day Jack Jensen would be living here with his own family, doing the things people in Plainsville, Iowa do. Living simple but contented lives, caring for things like family traditions and rose-bushes.

Tears prickled at the corners of Roslyn's eyes. She pulled her hand from Jack's, whispered a throaty "Thanks" and ducked her head to get into the car. By the time she fiddled with purse and keys, the tears had disappeared and she'd composed herself enough to wave goodbye to Sophie, who was standing in the middle of the sidewalk.

But she couldn't bring herself to look at Jack until the engine turned over and she'd shifted into reverse. She raised her face to his, startled by the intensity of his expression. He gave a quick nod, and feebly waved his baseball cap in her direction.

Roslyn took her foot off the brake and let the car roll back onto the street. When she shifted into drive and edged slowly forward, she turned once more to see the two of them waving. *So be it,* she thought. But surprisingly, there was no surge of joy at leaving Plainsville, Iowa.

IT STARTED to rain about fifteen minutes outside of town. The man in the car rental place had drawn a map for her, asking if she wanted the scenic route to Des Moines or the highway that would bypass the city and take her right to Chicago. Impulsively, she'd requested both. When she'd made the last turn out of Plainsville, she'd hesitated.

The day, which had begun with a pale-lemon sun, was now beginning to cloud over. Reasoning that she'd probably never come back to Iowa, she opted for the picturesque road. In spite of what she'd said to Sophie, she wasn't really in a rush to get back to the office. Besides, office security stayed on duty twenty-four hours, so she could pull into work any time.

The two-lane paved highway meandered around sprawling farms and fields that would soon be planted in corn and grains. This part of Iowa contained the undulating hills Roslyn had learned about in elementary school. She found herself enjoying the ride, hypnotized by the monotonous rhythm of curves, dips and turns. When the drizzle began, the sporadic sweep of the windshield wipers added to this effect, almost putting her to sleep.

Which is why the warning signs of what was about to happen failed to register. The transport trailer appeared out of nowhere, swinging from a graveled side road onto the paved highway about half a mile ahead of her. Roslyn thought trucks that big were supposed to travel on the express highways, and its sudden presence alerted her to pay more attention. The windshield was fogging up and she rolled her window down, at the same time flipping all the buttons on the console until she found the defroster.

Rain, now mixed with hail, slashed across the windshield. Roslyn sped up the wiper mechanism and jacked up the defroster another notch. The windshield wasn't clearing quickly enough. She lowered her head to see through the half-moon of clear window near the dashboard. The truck loomed closer than she expected and her right foot instinctively felt for the brake. Through the passenger window, Roslyn could see that the landscape was grading sharply. They were climbing a hill, which is why the truck had slowed down.

She expelled a mouthful of sour air. Driving in Chicago had made her a good driver, but she'd always hated bad weather conditions. By the time the truck chugged to the crest of the hill, the rain had transformed into sleet. Roslyn swore. Almost the end of April and I'm in the midst of a hailstorm. Only in Iowa, she thought bitterly.

The truck disappeared over the summit and Roslyn cranked up the defroster to the max. It wasn't as effective as the one in her own car and she was beginning to wish she'd waited for her flight the next day.

Her car poised on the verge of the hill, and began to roll down the other side. It began to pick up speed just as Roslyn, squinting through the flying snow, saw the truck jackknife into a skid at the bottom of the hill.

The cab of the truck and its long trailer appeared to travel in opposite directions now, like some deranged beast. The trailer part of the truck slid at a right angle to the highway, snaking erratically. The cab part had swung about and was skidding directly for her car. She tapped the brakes lightly—up and down, up and down—trying to keep calm and not give in to the adrenaline rush that was making her feel light-headed and nauseous. The car was responding well, moving in a jerky but controlled manner toward the base of the hill.

Then Roslyn realized the truck driver wasn't going

to be able to control his vehicle in time. She couldn't move into the other lane because the trailer was still twitching back and forth in it. There was no time to think. She looked left and right, then straight ahead, watching helplessly as the truck and its zigzagging trailer headed straight at her.

Roslyn noticed a flat section to her right—a field maybe. No way to tell if it sloped or not—too much rain and not enough time. She cranked the steering wheel sharply in that direction, gripping on while the car skated sideways. A flash of movement caught her right peripheral vision and she turned to see the bag with the potted rose fly off the seat. Stupidly, she reached out her right hand to catch it and lost control of the car, which began a slow-motion spin farther to the right as the cab of the truck smashed broadside into the back seat. Roslyn's last sensation, before she flew into the void with the car, was the soft crinkle of plastic in her hand.

WHEN THE POLICE cruiser pulled up into the semicircular drive of J.J.'s Landscaping and Garden Center, Jack recognized his friend, Sheriff Mac Christensen, and from the set of the man's face figured something bad had happened. Jack's first thought was that his father had had another stroke.

"Jack," the officer said, taking off his Stetson-style hat and holding it carefully in his big hands. "Got a minute?"

"Sure." Jack pointed toward the shed alongside the store and moved past Mac to lead the way.

"Something wrong?" he asked, keeping his voice as casual as he could physically manage.

"Yeah. But hey," Mac said, stopping in his tracks, "not with your folks or anything. Geez, sorry, man. I should've got to that right off the bat."

Jack's anxiety eased out of him in tiny spurts of exhaled air. He leaned against the backhoe parked at the opened doorway to the shed. "So, what's up?"

"Do you know a Roslyn Baines?"

The unexpected question brought Jack to attention. "Yeah…" Some alarm bell began to vibrate. "What is it? Has something happened to her? She just left town this morning—about ten or so."

Mac held up an index finger. "Hold on, buddy. One thing at a time. She a relation of yours?"

"No. What the hell is it?"

"She have any next of kin here, then? Anyone at all?"

Beads of sweat broke out across Jack's forehead. He wanted to throttle his friend. "Look, Mac, I don't know. She's a Petersen. Guess she's a very distant cousin of old Jacob Petersen down on Walker Line, but goddammit—"

"Anyone you know of in Chicago?"

Jack shook his head. "She's an only child, far as I know. Her mother's dead. I don't know about her father. Would you tell me what's happened before I forget you're wearing a uniform!"

The ghost of a smile flitted across Mac's face. "Good thing we went to school together, buddy, or I'd have to take you in." He peered down at the ground for a moment, then ran his right hand back and forth under the tip of his nose.

"What's happened?" Jack shouted.

Mac raised his eyebrows. "Seems this Roslyn Baines has no one to look after her interests. And...well, the guy at the car rental place said she'd been staying in town and she'd given your name—"

"Get to it, Mac."

Mac shook his head. "Always said you should've gone into law enforcement. Okay, since you know her, guess it's okay to say that she was involved in one hell of an accident between here and Des Moines."

Jack grabbed Mac by his jacket pocket. "Where is she? What's happened to her?"

Mac gently removed Jack's hand. "Relax, buddy. The woman's at Saint Mary's."

Jack tried to control the rush of emotion that overwhelmed him. She was okay. That was the fact he fixed on. "I'm going to the hospital," he said, moving to the store to tell his assistant.

"You want a lift with me?" called Mac.

"Thanks. Then I can leave the truck in case they need to use it here," Jack returned over his shoulder.

When they were in the cruiser, Jack asked, "What happened on the highway?"

"Far as we can guess—"

"You haven't talked to Roslyn?"

"She's unconscious, Jack. That's why I wanted to find a next of kin. In case—"

"How bad is she?"

"Frankly, I don't know," Mac said, as he turned

over the engine and headed out the drive. "I met the paramedics as they were unloading her from the ambulance. I got her ID from them and because it was a rental car, checked in there first."

"Didn't the medics tell you anything?"

"They said the injuries weren't life threatening, her vitals were good but she was still unconscious."

Jack closed his eyes against the nausea creeping up from his gut. "Okay. So how did the accident happen?"

"Don't know yet. Look, buddy, don't get all worked up." He reached out a hand to pat Jack on the shoulder. "There were just the two vehicles involved. The other a transport trailer carrying too heavy a load. I figure that's why he was taking the back roads, to avoid the inspection stations. The paramedics said it looked like she tried to head into the ditch to avoid a head-on with the truck when it jackknifed. The move definitely saved her life, because the truck nailed her broadside, but at the rear end. Then her car flew into the ditch."

Jack closed his eyes again, imagining how scared she must have been.

"So, what exactly is your connection with Miss Roslyn Baines?"

Jack opened his eyes, aware of the innuendo in his friend's question. He sighed, knowing Mac would keep chewing away at it until he was satisfied.

"As I said, she's Ida Mae's niece. The one who inherited the property. She arrived Tuesday night."

"Ah, I thought that's who she might be!" exclaimed Mac, "So she's going to move here?"

Jack knew Mac was curious, but Jack wasn't about to sit and gossip about Roslyn Baines when she was lying unconscious in a hospital bed. "Who knows?" he murmured.

Something in his voice registered with Mac because he dropped the matter. The cruiser turned into the main drive of Saint Mary's Hospital and stopped beneath the reception canopy. Jack was grateful for Mac's presence. It was amazing how quickly questions were answered and doors opened for you when you were with a police officer.

The ward nurse told them Roslyn had regained consciousness, but was still in shock. No, she told Mac firmly, she wasn't yet ready to answer questions about the accident and yes, she smiled sympathetically at Jack, she'd be able to see family for just a few seconds. Not bothering to correct the nurse's assumption, he started to follow her down the hall.

"I'll hang around the waiting room a bit," Mac said, "but if I'm not there when you finish, you'll know I got a call."

"Right, and thanks, Mac." Jack had already overtaken the nurse and was snapping his fingers as he waited for her to catch up.

She smiled. "You're anxious, I suppose. Don't you worry—she's going to be okay. And don't be alarmed at how she looks. She got banged up a bit, but they're just bruises and contusions. Some scraping where her face hit the underside of the dashboard. She was very lucky," she said.

The nurse led the way down the hall to a closed door. Her voice lowered. "We've got her in a private room for now, but we haven't checked her insurance yet so we may have to move her.''

Jack shook his head. ''Never mind. I'm sure she's well covered. If not, I'll make up the difference.''

The nurse smiled. ''Are you her brother?'' A pause. ''Or fiancé?''

He wobbled his head ambiguously. ''Sort of. And thank you.''

She held up five fingers and mouthed the word *minutes*. Jack nodded and waited for her to walk away before he opened the door. He needed to give himself a few seconds to put on the right kind of face. Not to mention catch his breath. When he was ready, he slowly turned the knob and gently pushed the door.

She was lying on her back, her head turned away from the door. He couldn't tell if she was asleep. An intravenous line was feeding something into her right arm, and she was also hooked up to a machine with a small screen that flashed repeating patterns of red and yellow lights. Every few seconds the machine beeped. He didn't want to startle her so he cleared his throat as he closed the door behind him.

There was no response from her. Not even a rustling of sheets. He tried once more and this time her head pivoted slowly on the pillow.

''Jack,'' she whispered.

Her voice had the hoarseness of someone who hadn't spoken for a long time. The face looking up at him was ashen. Jack's eyes took in the coppery hair, now slick with perspiration and clinging in matted hunks to her head. The lump in his throat mushroomed in size. Her eyes looked like someone had circled them with purple magic marker. A wide red swath stretched from the corner of her left eye to her jaw. There was a huge purplish-blue mark on the left side of her neck.

Her left arm was bent at the elbow and wrapped in a cloth sling. She was covered by a sheet and blanket, but he could see bandages beneath the neck of her blue hospital nightgown. Jack felt his jaw working and realized she was waiting for him to speak. He couldn't find his voice.

"That bad, eh?" Her voice cracked, but she managed a wispy smile.

He took a big breath. "They wouldn't know you at the office," he said.

She made a little sound that could have been a laugh or a cough. "Don't make me laugh," she finally gasped. "Ribs." Her right hand, the one hooked up to the intravenous, raised weakly from the blanket and pointed to her left side. "Hurts," she murmured.

"I don't think you should talk too much." Jack craned his head and found a chair tucked into a corner. Pulling it up to her right side, he sat down. Words failed him again. She looked so pathetic. Like a lost waif.

He wanted to lower his head to her and feel her heart beat against his cheek. He wanted to pick up her hand and wrap it inside his. Most of all, he wanted to climb up next to her and cradle her in his arms. And he didn't understand how he could feel this way. He'd barely known the woman forty-eight hours.

"The sheriff—my friend, Mac—came to tell me what had happened."

She was staring up at him, her large eyes magnified by the circles and snow-white skin of her face. He couldn't even tell what color her eyes were now.

When she didn't answer, he went on. "Mac was asking me about next of kin. In case you need surgery, I suppose," he rushed to add, realizing that what he'd blurted might alarm her. But she still didn't respond, just stared across at him as if he were speaking a foreign language.

"Anyway," he heard his voice rise in volume, "I wasn't sure about people in Chicago. I mean, I know about your mother. But wasn't certain about your father or...or..." he faltered under her steady gaze "—any other relatives."

Finally her eyes flickered, moving away from his face to a point somewhere on the opposite wall. "My father," she repeated so quietly he almost missed it.

Her eyes fluttered closed and for a frightening moment Jack thought he'd lost her. Then they opened again, glancing quickly at him and back at the wall. "I've no idea where my father is. We haven't talked since...just after...my mother's funeral." She paused, eyes closed again. "He was in New York...last I heard."

"Don't worry about it, Roslyn. We'll get all that later." He patted her hand.

She turned her head to him. Her eyes glistened. Biting on her lower lip, she summoned a tiny smile. "Pathetic, isn't it?"

He frowned, unsure what she was getting at.

She took a few more breaths, then said, "No one

for people to call. No one there…for me. No…
family.''

Jack felt as if his heart would break. He studied the
drawn, white face with its colorful splotches, the
trembling chin fighting to hold back the tears and
knew, in that very instant, that he was falling in love
with her.

CHAPTER SIX

THE DOOR swung open quietly, and Jack turned his head to see a young, spectacled man in whites beckon to him from the door.

"Hello, I'm Dr. Barnett," he said, extending his hand and ushering Jack into the corridor.

Too cheerful, Jack thought, for someone with bad news. He nodded and returned the handshake. "Jack Jensen."

The doctor frowned, then smiled. "You related to the Jensens on Hutton Side Road?"

"My folks—and my brother and his family, too."

An index finger pointed at him. "Then you must be the Jensen from the landscaping place."

Jack nodded.

"Hey, my wife loves that place. She's always after me to extend the flower beds in the backyard, but I never seem to have the time."

"Someone from my place could do it for you," Jack suggested, willing himself to keep calm at the same time.

"Well, maybe. Though I could use the exercise." Suddenly he seemed to remember why he was standing in front of Roslyn's room and his eyes narrowed. "Are you related to Miss Baines?"

Here we go again, thought Jack. "No, not really—" he started to explain, when the doctor interrupted him.

"Oh yeah, Nurse Hennigar told me. The fiancé, right?"

Before Jack could say a word, the doctor continued, "Say, I gotta tell you. Your fiancée is a pretty lucky woman. Another few inches and—" He shook his head.

Jack wasn't sure if he wanted to grab the guy by the stethoscope—and thus be removed immediately from the hospital—or howl in frustration. "What's the prognosis for Roslyn?"

Something in his tone cued the doctor, for he instantly sobered and said, "Sorry about that. I tend to rave on. Miss Baines sustained two fractured ribs and a dislocated left shoulder which we've reset. Her left foot suffered a hairline fracture when she was unlodged from under the console of her car. She suffered a concussion but there's no indication of serious trauma to the head. Of course, she'll need monitoring for the next forty-eight hours. No internal injuries that we've detected so far. She'll be able to go home in two or three days, but I recommend no work or—" he grinned broadly at Jack "—bed play, if you get my drift."

Jack was grateful for the closed door. He saw his little white lie replicating itself beyond belief. "Actually," he began, but was immediately cut off by the nurse.

"Doctor," she said, holding up a plastic bag. "I've a feeling Miss Baines will be wanting to see this."

The doctor took the bag and peered inside. Then he looked up at Jack. "When the paramedics and fire-fighters were cutting your fiancée out of her car," he explained, "this bag was wrapped so tightly around her fingers they had to take it along with them in the ambulance and cut it away when they got here. Must be real important to her." He held up the bag for Jack to look inside.

He leaned over, though he already knew what he'd see. The potted cutting from the Iowa rose.

"She told the medics that she'd been reaching out to stop this plant from flying through the windshield when she lost control of her car," the doctor was saying. "Oddly enough, that move probably saved her from getting hit directly on the driver's side."

Jack averted his face, waiting for the contraction of jaw muscles to loosen.

The nurse patted him on the arm. "Why don't you go get a coffee?"

Jack was relieved to be alone for a few minutes. Clutching a foam cup of bitter coffee in the hospital cafeteria, he asked himself if he knew what he was getting into—taking on the role of protector.

Not to mention, *fiancé* of Roslyn Baines.

ROSLYN'S MIND kept flitting back to the highway—the horrible screech and crunching of metal just before everything went black. That's where she'd been when Jack had come into her room. On the highway, watching the transport bear down on her and being paralyzed with helpless fear.

He'd been so quiet and gentle, staring at her as if

he didn't know quite what to say. And there had been a moment after she'd admitted that she had no one in the world to turn to, that his eyes had seemed to burn with such luminosity that she'd thought he'd seen a vision. But then someone had come to the door, and he'd disappeared, leaving her to wonder why he'd sat so long at her bedside—like grieving kin. Still, she liked having him there—just sitting, stroking her hand. So soothing was the memory she drifted off to sleep again until she felt something brush against her arm.

The nurse was pulling back the privacy curtain from around her bed. "Remember me? Cathy Hennigar? Look what I have." She held aloft a white plastic bag.

Roslyn tried to sit up but pain ambushed her from all sides.

"Don't be foolish," admonished Nurse Hennigar. "You're to do nothing on your own for at least a week."

Right, thought Roslyn. *Maybe if you let me stay here.* "What's in the bag?" she gasped, waiting for the pain to subside.

"The plant you were holding when you were pulled from the car."

"Plant?"

She brought the bag closer, letting Roslyn crane her neck to see inside. "Oh," was all she said, falling back onto the pillow.

Nurse Hennigar looked disappointed, but insisted on setting the pot on the windowsill. On her way out the door, she paused by Roslyn's side. "Never mind, it's the shock of the accident and your injuries. When you're yourself again, you'll be glad the paramedics didn't leave it behind.'' She moved toward the door. ''By the way, your fiancé is just having a coffee. He'll probably be back soon.''

Fiancé? I don't have— The door closed before Roslyn could give voice to her thoughts. There was a light tap at the door and as it opened again, Jack Jensen's face appeared. *My fiancé.* She'd have laughed at the notion, but that would have hurt too much. Instead, she managed a smile and motioned for him to sit down in the chair next to the bed.

''So,'' he said, ''the doctor says you should be up and about in a few days.''

''Hmm,'' she murmured. He seemed nervous, she thought. He didn't have his baseball cap with him and a couple of fingers drummed against his thighs. She couldn't resist adding to his nervousness. ''The nurse thinks you're my fiancé.''

A stain of color swept up into his face. ''Oh, yeah?'' he commented.

When she didn't reply, he explained with a slight stammer, ''Well, uh, I guess I didn't clarify the assumption. It seemed to open doors more quickly than 'good friend' would have.''

When he paused, she blurted, ''I thought someone I know in Chicago had arrived.'' The flush in his face deepened, and she regretted the remark. So she added, ''I wasn't sure if anyone at my office had been informed. I have a couple of friends there…and my secretary, of course.'' The explanation seemed lame even to her. Besides, how could anyone in Chicago know yet?

"That's what I came back to ask you about," he said. "Is there anyone you'd like me to call right now? Or would you rather do it yourself later?"

Anyone to call? Good question. So, who exactly is there? Her boss? She'd only need to talk to his secretary. Her own secretary? She had a good working relationship with Judy, but they never socialized outside of work. Jim Naismith? The last person she wanted rushing to Plainsville.

"Actually," Roslyn finally said, "I only need to contact my boss and I can do that later." She raised her head to meet his eyes, caught a hint of pity in them and felt herself flush with annoyance. "No need to worry anyone else," she added, knowing there *wasn't* anyone else, "because hopefully I'll be home in a few days."

He nodded, slapped his palms against his thighs and stood up. "Guess I should go now. Let you get some rest." He moved toward the door, opened it and paused. "Thing is," he began, "the doctor told me you'd need someone around to help you out the first couple of weeks. Now, I know you're itching to get to Chicago," he fought to keep his voice light and casual, "but here's a suggestion. I could ask Sophie to stay at the house for a while and you could convalesce at Ida Mae's."

He raised his free hand. "I see the idea doesn't really thrill you, but think about it. Unless of course you've got someone in mind in Chicago who could do that for you." He pulled the door open wider and turned to leave. Suddenly, his head popped back into the room.

"By the way, the doctor told me that that rose cutting—" he pointed to the windowsill "—might have saved your life when you lunged for it in the car." He paused. "Anyway, think about what I was saying. I'll be round tomorrow," he told her and closed the door behind him.

The pulse at Roslyn's temple was throbbing. *Convalesce at Aunt Ida's? Stay in Plainsville another two weeks?* She looked to the window and the thorny twigs sticking out of the plastic planter pot. *The Iowa rose saved my life?* She didn't know whether to laugh or cry.

IT WASN'T until midafternoon Monday—three days after the accident—that Roslyn felt physically up to making a phone call to her office. Even though she'd slept almost constantly, she observed that, while hospitals might be places for treatment, they didn't provide much opportunity for relaxation. There had been a constant stream of people in and out of her room— whether to clean it, bring food and drink, take her temperature, peer at her pupils or simply read her chart. But the nagging headache she'd had since regaining consciousness had finally gone, and she'd worked out a method for raising herself up onto her pillows without collapsing in pain.

She waited until she knew Ed would be back from his customary two-hour lunch and called Chicago. She listened patiently while Ed expressed first shock, then concern over the accident. She knew him well enough to know how very good he was at finding the appropriate words for any situation. But she might have given him the benefit of the doubt if the muted tapping of keys at a computer hadn't told her he wasn't tracking just her conversation, but some business deal or appointment schedule at the same time.

"What's the name of the hospital again?" he asked.

"Saint Mary's. But Ed, there's no need to visit. I'll be back in Chicago in a few days."

"Hmm. Well, I do have a busy week ahead of me. The investigation, you know."

"How's that going?"

"Well, apparently someone's let the cat out of the bag, and the whole office is buzzing." There was a slight pause. "I don't suppose you mentioned it to anyone before you left?"

"Of course not." She suddenly remembered her telephone conversation with Judy and her vague reference to the inquiry. "But you know what the office grapevine is like. Someone overhears a phone conversation…"

"I suppose." He didn't sound convinced. "Getting back to your return. Why are they letting you go so soon? Are you able to work?"

Roslyn hesitated. She'd mulled over that question all morning. In spite of feeling better while she reclined in bed, she knew from trips to the bathroom that walking more than a few feet made her dizzy.

"I could probably do a few things—with some assistance. Judy will be there."

After a long silence Ed spoke again, "Well, that's

the thing, you see. Judy's been seconded to Bob's office for a bit and she won't be finished up until the end of the month."

The throb at her temples rolled into a beat. "Ed, I talked briefly to Judy the day before the accident. Why is she with Bob? Why wasn't I consulted about this?"

A longer silence. "You're absolutely right, I should have called you. It's difficult to break this to you, Roslyn. There are…well…delicate circumstances involved here."

The beat in her head picked up. "What circumstances?"

"Now, don't get upset. You've been in a terrible accident and you're a long way from Chicago right now. I can understand your anxiety, but—"

"Ed!"

A loud sigh erupted from the other end. "All right. I have reason to suspect that Judy has been seeing Jim outside of work and has been passing on information to him."

Roslyn closed her eyes and leaned her forehead against the telephone receiver. "Judy's a happily married woman with a young family…."

"She may be married, but the security log shows that she's been staying late the same nights as Naismith. When I checked, there wasn't any significant reason for her to work late."

"Did you talk to her about it?"

"Of course! She made some excuse about catching up on extra work for you."

Roslyn's mouth was dry. The work she'd left with

Judy could have been completed in a day. And Judy was the type who'd skip lunch in order to be able to leave work on time. Her one-hour commute got her home exactly when her baby-sitter had to leave.

"Roslyn?" Ed's voice was hesitant. "Are you still there?"

Roslyn leaned back against the pillows, too drained to hold herself upright a second longer. "It's okay, Ed. I'm—well—truthfully, I'm puzzled by all of this."

The sound of a throat clearing sputtered along the line. "Yes, well, now that I have you on the phone, Roslyn, I'll level with you. The fact is that this fraud inquiry is picking up. We've found some alarming figures in quite a few of Naismith's accounts and have had to suspend him from duties for the time being. What we're looking at now are his discretionary accounts."

Roslyn used her right hand to pull herself up against the bed rail. Discretionary accounts allowed the financial advisors to invest client money with minimal direction from the client. The accounts belonged to people who wanted the firm to handle all of their investments. No authorizing signatures were needed to move money in the accounts. Because no one was checking the fund, there were plenty of opportunities to siphon off money.

"Do you have definite proof of misuse of funds?" she asked.

"Enough to consider going to the police."

Roslyn couldn't believe what he was saying. "There must be some explanation."

Ed sounded impatient. "Roslyn, believe me we've discussed all of the angles. Take my advice and stay out of this."

When she didn't respond, Ed cleared his throat again and added, "Think about your career, Roslyn."

Roslyn wasn't deaf to his message. When she managed to answer, her voice was hoarse. "I'll—I'll let you know what I've decided. I do have my laptop with me, so perhaps we can work out a linkup if necessary."

"Terrific. And whatever else we can do here to help out—salary advance, hospital costs—you name it"

"Thanks, Ed. Look, don't worry—the office group plan is great. I have to go now. More doctors. Bye for now." The receiver crashed onto its cradle as Roslyn let go of the rail and fell back onto the pillows.

She closed her eyes, wishing she could close off the world. Wishing she'd never have come to Plainsville in the first place. Because then, she reasoned, she wouldn't have been driving along the highway, wouldn't have been away from the office when Judy needed her and where she could fight to keep her own reputation intact. Most of all, wouldn't have met Jack Jensen in person and wouldn't ever have developed any feelings for him at all. Which meant that she could have signed over the house from Chicago and never been sucked into the whole mess to begin with.

A harsh laugh burst from her. She was beginning to sound like a character in a TV sitcom. Except in real life, she thought, bad things can keep on happening and sometimes there is no happy ending.

Jack had been looking at the clock all day. The store was busy for a Monday and one of the clerks had called in sick, so Jack had been forced to spend part of the morning at the cash counter. Then Lenny had phoned to report that the truck had broken down on Goshen Road and had been towed to a garage for repair. By late afternoon, Jack figured things couldn't possibly get any worse until he remembered he still had to visit Roslyn and find out what she'd decided. Yesterday she promised to give him an answer after she called her office.

He wasn't a betting kind of person, but his gut instincts convinced him she'd soon be heading for Chicago. She was just that type—a born and bred city woman—and he might as well save himself a lot of grief by accepting the fact now. That way, he reasoned, he wouldn't have to invest any more thinking time in a woman who'd somehow managed to captivate him in less than a week.

An ugly thought crossed his mind; he could be the loser whatever her decision was. If she returned to Chicago and left him the house, the place would now always remind him of her. He'd never get her out of his mind and he'd never be able to realize his childhood fantasies and really enjoy living in that house.

If she decided to stay and keep the house—which was the way his wish list was going—and he managed to persuade her over time that her life would be more complete with Jack Jensen in it, maybe she'd question whether getting the house was the real objective of his courtship.

You're screwed, buddy. No way is real life going to give it all to you.

By the time the clerk's replacement appeared shortly after three and his father's truck had been seconded to the store, Jack knew he couldn't put off going to the hospital any longer.

He picked up a bunch of tulips and irises from the store on his way. He'd taken Roslyn a fresh bouquet every day. By the time he was strolling down the hospital corridor, feeling more apprehensive with each step, it was almost four o'clock. He reached Roslyn's door as Mac stepped out of her room.

His friend was holding a pen and small notebook in one hand and his hat in the other. His bomber-style tan leather jacket was unzipped, revealing his uniform underneath. His face creased into a smile when he saw Jack.

"Hey, buddy, how's it going? Not working today?"

"Just taking a break to visit Roslyn."

Mac raised his left eyebrow. "Oh, yeah? Well, she's looking a heck of a lot better today than she did on Friday."

Mac hovered near the closed door, eyeing the flowers. Jack knew he wanted to say something else, and his friend's unusual reticence amused him.

"Were you questioning her about the accident?" Jack asked.

"Yeah. Thing is, the truck driver's still in a coma and may not make it. We needed her statement to determine liability. So—" he hesitated a beat "—is your visit business or just friendly?"

Jack grinned. "Subtlety was never your thing, Mac. I guess you could say, a bit of both."

Mac nodded. "Well, she's a pretty amazing woman."

"How do you mean?"

"Went through the whole account without flinching. Mind, her face was dead-white and her voice trembled now and then, but no tears. Good memory for details, too. A lot of people don't recall the little things till days or even weeks later, but she had it all down pat. Maybe she'd been going over and over it in her head."

Jack shrugged for want of a suitable reply, but he knew precisely what Mac was saying. Roslyn Baines *was* an amazing woman. Jack wished she was a bit more the kind of woman who might need a man around.

"Anyhow," Mac added, "I've got all I need for now. Will you let me know when she heads back to Chicago, just in case there's anything to clarify before she leaves? Oh and, uh, good luck." He jerked his head toward the door.

Jack frowned. "Good luck?"

Mac's broad face cracked. "Buddy, I know a lovesick pup when I see one." He patted Jack on the shoulder and headed down the hallway, stopping to hoist up his khaki trousers and plunk his hat on his head. Jack stared after him until he rounded the corner.

A lovesick puppy? Give me a break!

Still, Jack paused with his right hand on the door handle. He could change his mind and simply call her.

That way, the news would be delivered quickly and painlessly. Better still, she wouldn't see his reaction when she told him she was leaving. He removed his hand from the door and took a short step back, bumping into someone.

"Oh, sorry about that. I should have warned you. These hospital shoes are pretty quiet."

Jack lifted his foot off Nurse Hennigar's shoe and wheeled around.

"Oh," she exclaimed, "what a beautiful spring bouquet! Shall I find a container for you?" She was halfway to the nurses' station before Jack could stop her.

The decision made for him, he clutched the door handle and pushed down. Roslyn was half sitting against the raised back of the bed. Mac had underestimated. She didn't look a "heck of a lot better," she looked damn fantastic.

Her hair spilled over the pillow in a rippling coppery waterfall, glossy and vibrant. The purplish rings around her eyes and bruises across the left side of her face were now tinged in sepia, giving her pale face the hues of an old-fashioned photograph. When she turned her head his way, a spectrum of colors bounced from her eyes, reflected by the afternoon sunshine.

"Jack," she said, surprise in her voice and something else too, that he couldn't label.

The whole scene was so different from Friday, he thought, when she'd lain waiflike in the hospital bed, staring up at him with glassy eyes. Even different from yesterday. Now she looked ready for work. *In control.* Disappointment swept through him. Friday he'd been a knight on a charger. Today, he was just Jack the landscaper.

"How're you feeling? I mean, you look great."

Teeth appeared on her lower lip—*ivory and peach.* More colors to remember the dreary winter days to come. If he'd known her more intimately—and he shifted quickly from that idea—he'd have said her voice was husky with desire. *Smoky.* The kind of smoke that curls up from a fire crackling with cedar chips.

Her shoulders, encased in the washed-out blue of a hospital gown, rose and fell. "The miracle of a hot shower," she murmured. Her right hand flicked to the chair in the corner. "Sit down," she invited.

He pulled the chair up to her right side, and sat in it without taking his eyes from her face. His staring must have bothered her because she flushed and turned to the window. He heard himself stammering.

"I...uh...bumped into Mac in the hallway. He said to let him know when you were returning to Chicago. In case he had a few more questions."

The face came back to him, paler than before. Her eyes were a brilliant turquoise now in the brightness from the window. The Caribbean, he decided. That was the color he saw. Some lagoon in the West Indian Ocean. The bosom of her nightgown lifted as she breathed. Jack peered down at his hands, empty and nervous.

"I've thought about your offer," she said.

Jack nodded but didn't dare raise his head.

"Yeah?" he prompted, his tongue heavy and useless for speech.

"And…uh…well, I think you may have a point. Apparently, I'm to be discharged tomorrow. I spoke to my boss today and he…uh…he said they could manage without me."

His mind tried to catch her words, ricocheting about in his head. Finally he put it all together and felt the tension slip out of him. "That's…geez, that's good." He shook his head up and down. "Very sensible." He got to his feet, shifting his weight between right and left, then settling on midstance. "That's excellent, as Lenny would say." Jack barked a laugh that he couldn't believe had come from his own mouth.

Her eyes tracked every movement, her lips forming a smile. "So…could you please call Sophie for me?" she asked.

Jack pointed an index finger at her. "Right. Sophie. I'll get onto her at once." He backed toward the door, reaching it at the very instant that Nurse Hennigar swung into the room, a vase of flowers in her free hand.

Water sloshed down the side of the vase onto the floor. Jack mumbled an apology and kept going, knowing that to stop now would surely cause some other accident to occur. He closed the door behind him and propped himself against it. From inside, he could hear muted giggling. He closed his eyes. *Easy now. One day at a time. Maybe—just maybe—real life will imitate art and we'll all get our happy ending.*

CHAPTER SEVEN

ROSLYN RAISED her head from the paperback mystery she was reading and sniffed the air. The living room was redolent with spices. Sophie was baking again. Cookies, Roslyn wondered, or cinnamon buns? She groaned and rested her head against the back of the reclining chair that Jack had carried down from Ida Mae's bedroom. In the week since she'd been discharged, Roslyn was positive she'd gained a pound each day.

She still blushed when she thought about her homecoming, as Sophie called her return from the hospital. Jack had insisted on helping her up the veranda steps. There was a moment as they'd stood at the front door waiting for Sophie to answer it, when a picture of a groom sweeping his bride over the threshold had flashed into Roslyn's mind. She'd almost mentioned it as a joke, but fortunately had been saved from the embarrassment by Sophie's prompt arrival.

The real suprise had come when Roslyn reached the second floor landing—aided by a crutch and Jack's arm. They'd given the large rear bedroom a "good dustup," Sophie claimed, smiling broadly. Sunlight filled the room. Crisp, new curtains—Sophie's handiwork—had been hung and a quilt thrown across the bed.

She recalled Sophie's words. "Your aunt told me her mother made the quilt for her trousseau. That pattern's called Wedding Ring. Poor Miss Ida never had a chance to use it. Kept it in a trunk in the attic all these years. I only saw it the one time, when she asked me to help her get some albums out of the same trunk and bring them down to her. This was a few months before she died."

Sophie gave a sympathetic tsk-tsk at the end of her story. If Jack hadn't been waiting behind her, a suitcase in his hand, Roslyn would have pressed the housekeeper for more details. But the sight of the room, sparkling brightly that morning the first week of May, had moved Roslyn to tears. She turned to them, unable to speak.

"Sophie's idea," Jack said at once.

The housekeeper glared at him. "C'mon! You said we had to cheer up the place."

He'd simply shrugged, watching Roslyn intently as he had so often the past few days.

He'd been to visit her daily at the hospital and she was beginning to think of him almost as family. The idea startled her. *Starved for affection is what I am,* she told herself. *How else can I explain considering someone I've known less than two weeks as a blood relation?*

Roslyn's face warmed again just at the memory of that afternoon. She still didn't understand why he'd taken such an interest in her welfare. The city cynic inside her teased that his actions were definitely connected to the house and estate. But deeper inside, she wanted to believe that he liked her.

"Roslyn?" Sophie stood in the arch leading from parlor to hall.

Roslyn lay the book down on her lap. "Hi, Sophie. Smells wonderful out there."

"I came to see if you'd like a cup of tea with your cookies."

"Cookies?"

"Gingersnaps."

Her mouth was already watering. "Sounds great. But I'm feeling a bit restless. This book isn't really grabbing me. I thought I might go up to the attic and look through that trunk you were telling me about."

"That's a lot of stairs for someone with a crutch. Besides, those trunks are real heavy and covered in dust."

"Then maybe the next time Jack's over, I can get him to bring them down to the second floor for me."

Sophie shrugged as if unwilling to comment on such foolishness. "So be it," she muttered and left the room.

Roslyn smiled, knowing that was Sophie's way of avoiding an argument. She'd given her opinion on the matter and if Roslyn wasn't sensible enough to follow her advice, so be it. *So be it.* Was it an Iowan phrase, she wondered, recalling Jack's frustrated remark several days ago? Or just a Plainsville one? Either way, she'd wait until Sophie left for the day before she tackled the third floor on her own.

The first four days home, Sophie had stayed overnight, sleeping in the same room Roslyn had had before the accident. When Sophie's sister and her family were expected for a visit, Roslyn insisted she could manage on her own. Both Jack and Sophie had looked skeptical, but finally agreed after Roslyn demonstrated her proficiency with crutches. She was now able to bear some weight on her fractured foot. Her left arm was no longer in a sling, but had a limited range of movement. Bathing was still a complicated procedure, but Jack had appeared her second day home to install safety bars in the upstairs bathroom.

It was only a few days after her return that Roslyn realized all of the attention she'd received thus far had come from people she'd just met. Other than a card from the gang at the office and an enormous bouquet of flowers—which she'd donated to a local church when she left the hospital—there had been no further contact from Chicago.

Roslyn had always taken the fact of friends as a given and had never bothered to count hers, assuming she had many. But during the long hours she'd spent sitting in Ida Mae's reclining chair she'd tallied up a paltry number and most of those were little more than 'work' friends—people she had a drink or a late dinner with during the week. Because her weekends were often spent working, she'd met few people in her condo building.

Though she'd always considered Judy a friend, Roslyn now realized that their status as boss and secretary had maintained a delicate but fixed barricade. She glanced across the room at the huge card from the office, propped against the mantel. Everyone had signed it—even Jim Naismith—and the sight of his familiar scrawl had reminded her anew of the investigation. She wondered what more evidence had been found and if Ed was correct in his assumption that Judy was involved.

Roslyn tossed the paperback onto the floor and sighed in frustration. She felt so helpless and useless. *A prisoner in Plainsville, Iowa!* She reached for her crutches, leaning against the wall behind her chair, and swung her legs toward the floor. Enough of lying around. By the time she reached the end of the hall, Sophie was just leaving the kitchen with a tray of cookies and tea.

"Goodness, you gave me a fright!" she exclaimed. "Were you that starving you couldn't wait for me?"

Roslyn grinned, knowing the sharp question was part of Sophie's cover bluster. "More that I couldn't stand sitting in that room a second longer." She limped toward a kitchen chair.

Sophie carried the tray over to the table and set teacup and cookies in front of Roslyn. "You sound just like your auntie."

"I do?"

"Yep," Sophie said, pulling out another chair and heaving herself onto it. "But the poor soul couldn't do a thing about it because the last few weeks of her life she had to be carried everywhere."

"Tell me about her."

"Not a heck of a lot *to* tell. She was a very private person in many ways. She'd tell me stories about some of the things in this house, but she'd only go so far. Like there was a whole other story she wasn't going to say anything about."

"Like the one about my grandmother and my family in Chicago."

Sophie nodded. "That's right. Who would've guessed? Jack certainly never knew and maybe not even his folks. But—" Sophie leaned forward, her voice hushed "—his Granddaddy Henry knew, that's a given."

"They must have known each other since childhood."

"They did, but the funny thing is, he never talked about Ida's sister, either, as if the subject were taboo." Sophie's voice rose dramatically on the last word.

"If they were close friends, he must have known better than to talk about it."

"Most likely. Though you'd think he'd drop a hint to his own children." Sophie shook her head. "Those two were a strange pair in many ways."

"How do you mean?"

Sophie frowned and thought for a moment. "Hard to find the right words. Lots of times, they hardly talked. Just sat side by side, looking out to the garden. Sometimes when I was passing by, I'd notice one of them kind of look at the other. On the sly, so to speak. Then look away real quick."

Roslyn felt her face warm, thinking of her own surreptitious peeks at Jack.

"When Miss Ida had her first stroke, I thought Mr. Henry was going to have a heart attack himself. Went all white and shaky when I told him the ambulance had taken her to Saint Mary's." She paused, staring hard at Roslyn. "You ask me, I think that man had more than friendly affection for her."

"You mean—"

"Yep. I think he was in love with her."

The image of two people almost in their nineties being in love touched something in Roslyn. "Sweet," she murmured. Then she shook her head. "But what does it matter now?"

Sophie pulled her head back, surprise in her face. "I thought you wanted to know about your auntie."

"Yes, I do. But I really want to know what kind of person she was. What made her tick—that sort of thing."

"Like I said, she was private. Talked some about her family, but always stopped at a certain point. Told me the story of her granddaddy coming to Iowa from Denmark. Brought his young bride whose most prized possession was the rosebush. When they got to Plainsville, one of the first things Miss Ida's grandmother did was to plant that rosebush. They didn't even have a home built then. This house wasn't built until much later. But Miss Ida always said that the rosebush was so important to her grandmother, she made them build the house around it rather than dig the plant up and risk anything happening to it."

Roslyn smiled at the picture of an old lady standing guard over the scrawny plant. "Apparently that obsession about the rosebush carried on through the generations," she remarked dryly.

"Yep," Sophie agreed. "Anyhow, your auntie hated being cooped up in her chair after she had her first stroke. Young Jack had come home from Chicago then and he was a big help. Arranged for a nurse to come in every day. Did all the handiwork around the house. Took Miss Ida and Henry for drives into the countryside. At the end, he even carried her downstairs whenever he came just so she could take a closer look at her rosebush."

"Is Henry still alive?"

Sophie's eyes watered. "That's the tragic part. Everyone was making such a fuss over Miss Ida, thinking she was at death's door, and then poor Mr. Henry ups and has a fatal heart attack. About eight months before Miss Ida passed away."

"What did Jack do?" The question popped out unexpectedly.

Sophie's eyes narrowed in on hers. "What do you mean?"

The protectiveness in her voice irritated Roslyn. "Did he go back to Chicago?"

"No. He'd lost his job there. Worked for the city's engineering department. Jack's always been a builder. He can do and make just about anything."

Roslyn grit her teeth. *Saint Jack on his mighty steed.* "Why didn't he get another job?"

"His father had a stroke himself and needed Jack to come home and work the farm. Plus—" she hesitated, casting Roslyn a cagey look "—Jack had just gotten a divorce from his wife. He never talked about it, but I heard that he was feeling pretty down. When his daddy got sick, Jack came home. See, his older brother was still in the army, posted in Germany at the time. His younger brother had just started college on a scholarship. There wasn't anyone but Jack to come and take charge.''

And he does that so readily. Roslyn bit down on her lower lip, feeling guilty about the thought. Still, the man seemed too good to be true. *And maybe that's what irks you, my girl. He's the kind of guy you used to dream about meeting—years before you stepped onto the investment treadmill.*

''Is his father okay now?'' she managed to ask.

Sophie smiled. ''Fit as a fiddle, though he drags his leg a bit.''

''Why didn't Jack go back to Chicago?''

''No idea.'' She gave Roslyn a sly look. ''You'll have to ask him yourself.''

Roslyn ignored Sophie's not-so-subtle hint that she'd asked too many questions about Jack Jensen. *Ask him myself? Not in a million years.*

JACK LET THE TRUCK idle a few more seconds before turning off the ignition. It was almost seven, and he knew Sophie had left for home at least two hours ago. He couldn't understand why the house was in darkness. Unless Roslyn wasn't feeling well and had gone to bed early. Yet Sophie had promised to call if any kind of problem came up.

Finally he stepped out of the truck's cab and headed up onto the veranda. He palmed the doorknob and it gave slightly under the weight of his hand. He twisted it, opening the big door. He swore. She'd gone to bed leaving the house unlocked. Not a major oversight in Plainsville, but for a woman on crutches and alone, a tad foolish.

"Roslyn?" he called.

Even if she was asleep, he thought he'd better check the back door and lock up for her on his way out. He'd call around in the morning and suggest she be more careful in the future.

He tiptoed along the hall to the kitchen, flicked on the light and walked on to the enclosed porch. The door there was also unlocked and he swore again. *Damn carelessness.* On his way back through the kitchen, he noticed the empty teacups and plate of cookies on the table. He frowned. Not exactly dinner. He pivoted to scan the room and saw the oven light glowing dimly in the shadows. Dinner hadn't been eaten at all.

Maybe she really is sick, he thought. As he returned to the front hall, Jack wondered if he should go up to make sure she was okay. He stood at the foot of the staircase, one leg raised, and froze. A noise drifted down the stairs.

Jack hit the hall light switch and tackled the steps with long, brisk strides. When he got to the second landing, he turned toward Roslyn's room. It was pitch-dark and there was no answer when he hissed her name. He pushed open the door and felt for the switch. Her bed was still made up. Heart pounding in his ears, he took the third flight of stairs two at a time.

The third floor landing extended right and left to two small rooms which Ida Mae had once told him were used by maids when she was a child. The narrow, dark corridor continued its T-shape toward the front of the house. Jack noticed a sliver of light straight ahead.

"Roslyn?" he called out, the echo of his footsteps merged with his voice and bounced off the wooden floor. He made for the light slicing up from the closed door and heard her voice just as his hand found a small metal handle and yanked hard.

"What the—?" He stood inside the attic, momentarily blinded by the naked lightbulb swinging on its chain in the movement of air from the opened door.

Roslyn was on the floor, half reclining against an enormous leather-bound trunk. Books, papers and what seemed to be photo albums were scattered around her like leaves beneath a tree. When he moved farther into the room, he saw her crutches pinned under another massive trunk, upended at her side.

Jack stared at Roslyn's pinched, wan face.

"I thought I'd be spending the night here," she cracked.

But the tone in her voice told him she wasn't joking. She looked ready to burst into tears, he thought, if Roslyn Baines ever did such a thing. Jack heaved the upended trunk aside, kicking away some of the debris that had tumbled out of it...

"What happened?" he asked when he was crouching at her side.

Roslyn straightened up from the trunk that was supporting her. She pushed back the clump of hair that had fallen loose from her hair band and tried to tuck it under. Her fingers trembled at the effort and Jack grasped them.

"Let me," he said, smoothing the thick strands of hair beneath the fabric. Then he took both of her hands in his.

"Your hands are freezing! How long have you been up here?"

"Since Sophie left. I guess this part of the house isn't well insulated. I was thinking I'd have to crawl over to get some of the clothing that fell out of the other trunk to wrap around me."

"What the hell were you doing?"

"That trunk was on top of this one and I decided to pull it down."

"Why?"

"How else could I get into either one? Anyway, it fell forward and knocked me back. The crutches went flying."

"Did you hurt yourself?" His throat felt tight and achy when she nodded.

"Stupidly enough," she murmured hoarsely. "I twisted my other ankle—the good one."

"Geez." He stared at her, willing her to look at him. When she finally did, the light sparkled off the dampness of her eyelashes. Jack took a deep breath, calming himself so he wouldn't tell her what a fool she'd been for even coming up to the attic. "Okay," he said, his voice as level as he could make it. "I'm going to carry you downstairs. Let's hope Sophie's baking hasn't had any serious side effects yet," he teased. "Put your arms around my neck and hold on. Whatever you do, don't use your feet to brace yourself or push up from the floor."

"Okay," she whispered, reaching up to wrap her arms around his neck.

"Not too tight," he warned. "All right, that's good. Now I'm going to lift you up in one go, so don't be alarmed if I move fast. Just relax and have faith that I won't drop you.''

He felt her upper body shake in a giggle. Doing his best to ignore the flowery scent of her hair clustering about his face and the silken skin of her arms against his neck, Jack heaved her up in one swift, strong motion. He shifted her to balance her weight and headed for the door.

"My crutches," she said on the way.

"Later," he muttered, the words lost in the tumble of hair surrounding his face. He could scarcely see where he was going and prayed he didn't slip on the stairs. He made his way down slowly, cautiously feeling for each step before setting his foot squarely onto it. When he reached the second floor, he went into her room. He'd left the light on and was able to make his way easily to the bed. He lay her down and perched on the edge to catch his breath.

"Too many gingersnaps," she said.

He felt himself laugh, but his mind was taking in the white face, its sprinkling of freckles in bas-relief along with the faint swatches of olive and mauve from the car accident. She looked pitiful, he decided, giving into anger now that he'd gotten her safely downstairs. *What had she been thinking?*

"Why—" he began.

She sighed deeply, loudly. "I know. It was incredibly stupid of me to go up there on my own."

"Close enough," he muttered.

"I couldn't sit around doing nothing a minute longer, Jack. I'm sorry to cause you so much... trouble, but—"

He reached out a hand to push back the errant strand of hair again. His fingers slipped onto her forehead and automatically, without any command from him, brushed across the creamy skin, delicately circled her eyes and slid down over the tautness of her cheekbone. Her big eyes—dark as bottomless pools now—fixed on his face. He could feel their brightness as he mindlessly tracked his fingertips down onto the curve of her upper lip, tracing its contours lightly before going on to the lower, fuller lip. Then the tip of his index finger boldly planted itself between the two and slipped along, gently separating the halves. When her lips parted, he suddenly pulled his fingers away and, leaning across her upper body, kissed her.

He placed his palms on either side of the pillow, to keep himself from falling onto her. Though he wanted to. Wanted to stretch out on top of her, press against her softness. He felt himself quicken with desire and opened his lips to hers, separating them farther apart with the tip of his tongue. He paused, waiting for her to close her mouth but she didn't. Instead, her head tilted ever so slightly upward, her mouth opening more for him.

The heat pulsing from his groin intensified and he heard someone—was it him?—moan softly. He shifted forward, raising himself from the bed so that he could lift his leg up and over her. But then he stopped and looked down. Her mouth was locked onto his, but her arms weren't reaching out for him. She lay limply, molded into the mattress by his weight moving down onto the bed.

Jack pulled back clumsily, hating himself for his

adolescent rush. The way he'd totally forgotten about *her,* focusing only on lips, the moistness inside and the waves of desire that had swept him away. Gratifying his own needs, rather than hers.

"Sorry," he said, his voice brusque and foreign to his ears.

She didn't say anything, just watched him, her eyes flickering across his face. He turned away and stood up, keeping his back to her, not daring to reveal how much he still wanted her. But not like this. He swore at himself.

"I'll get your crutches. Then I'm going to call the doctor—get him to take a look at your ankle." He was out of the room before she could reply, dashing up to the third floor again, where he leaned against the attic door for a long moment, feeling as if he'd just run a marathon.

WHEN JACK CLOSED the door behind the doctor, after promising that Roslyn would keep her foot elevated for a couple of days, he headed for the kitchen to turn off the oven. While the doctor was examining Roslyn, Jack had called Sophie, asking her if she could spend the night. But the housekeeper had to give her regrets, unable to leave her niece and nephews alone. Jack placed the chicken potpie, two plates, cutlery and two glasses of wine on a tray and climbed up to the second floor.

Roslyn was propped up in bed, wearing the nightgown that Jack had taken from a bureau for her. He'd caught a glimpse of other lacy objects in the same place and had quickly closed the drawer.

"I can't believe the doctor actually made a house call," she said when he walked into the room. "That would never happen in Chicago."

Jack set the tray on the small oval table he'd carried in from the other bedroom. "Well," he admitted, "I did promise him I'd send Lenny around to dig a new garden for his backyard."

Roslyn smiled. "Ahh! Nice to know that bribery works just as well in Plainsville as any other place." She looked over the tray, "I'm glad you brought the wine."

"The doctor said not with the painkillers, though."

"I'd rather have this than a pill right now."

Jack handed her a tea towel which she placed across her lap, then a plate and cutlery. He set her wineglass onto the child-size bookcase next to the bed. He hesitated, then sat lightly on the edge, juggling his own plate of food and wineglass.

"I'd move over for you," Roslyn said, "if I didn't have that to contend with." She pointed to the mound underneath the covers where her foot rested on two pillows.

"This is fine," he murmured and dug into his dinner with a hunger he'd forgotten entirely about during the last hour. They ate in a silence that felt both comfortable and electric at the same time. Jack rushed through his meal, sensing she should get some sleep.

When she handed him her plate with less than half the dinner eaten, he decided not to argue. Her eyes were glazed with fatigue. He loaded up the tray again and stood up to leave.

"I'm sleeping on the sofa downstairs," he said, "and I'll stay until Sophie gets here in the morning."

"There are plenty of beds upstairs," Roslyn protested.

He felt the corners of his mouth lift slightly. "Don't want to provide any grist for the mill, as they say. Gossip fodder," he explained at the question in her face.

"Sophie would never gossip about you," she said.

"Too true," Jack agreed. "Anyhow, is there anything you want before I go downstairs?" He paused. "Help getting to the bathroom?"

"No, thanks. The doctor helped me already."

When Jack reached the door she murmured, "Thanks, Jack, for everything. I'd resigned myself to a night in the attic, but I'm glad I didn't have to go through with it."

He nodded. "Night, then."

"And Jack," she began.

He turned again, framed by the doorway.

"Don't worry—you know—about the kiss and all. I was feeling a bit scared and vulnerable and you—well—you cheered me up."

Jack was still trying to interpret that last phrase when she added, "It certainly didn't mean anything."

He felt a little whoosh of air squeeze out of his solar plexus. But nodded anyway, backing out the door. He only had himself to blame. Giving in to physical desire when what she obviously needed was simply a hand to hold.

CHAPTER EIGHT

THE LOOK IN SOPHIE'S face said it all. Roslyn figured the tongue clucking and occasional sniff were the icing on the cake, so to speak. When Sophie appeared in the bedroom doorway, breakfast tray in hand, her narrowed eyes and furled brow practically shouted "Foolish girl." But Roslyn already knew the housekeeper well enough to guess that her annoyance would vanish by lunchtime.

The real surprise of the morning was Sophie's announcement that Jack had carried down one of the trunks from the attic and placed it in the bedroom across the hall. Because he didn't want to disturb you, Sophie had said.

Roslyn's cheeks burned at the innocent reminder of last night's parting from Jack. She'd had a restless sleep—not from the throbbing pain in her right foot, but from the embarrassment she felt after Jack's kiss. More to the point, from her response to his kiss. Because she'd seen it coming. The moment his fingertips had begun to trace the outline of her face, she'd known he was going to lean over and kiss her. In fact, to be brutally honest with herself, she acknowledged that part of her had been silently egging him on.

And when he'd *finally* lowered his face close enough to hers that she could smell a faint residue of soap or cologne, she'd tilted her chin upward with such eagerness she'd almost bumped noses with him. The kiss had been no neutral demonstration of sympathy, either. She'd made sure of that, grabbing on to his lower lip and opening her mouth to his with a release of passion she hadn't even known she still had inside her. It had been so long.

That, Roslyn told herself, was the real humiliation. That she could be so starved for passion she'd expose such vulnerability to someone she'd only known a couple of weeks. And that was why she resolved to take extra care in the days ahead not to encourage Jack in any way.

"No appetite this morning?"

Startled, Roslyn looked up.

Sophie motioned to the tray, still sitting on Roslyn's lap.

"Oh, sorry, Sophie. I was daydreaming."

"When you want to go across the hall let me know. Doctor said as little time as possible on your feet today," said Sophie, who removed the tray to the table nearby.

"I'm ready now," Roslyn said quickly, before Sophie could vanish downstairs again. She shifted her legs around to swing off the edge of the bed and waited for Sophie to reach her right side. By using one crutch under her left arm and Sophie on the other, Roslyn was able to make the short distance across the hall without having to bear too much weight on either foot. Although, she thought, wincing as her right foot came down too hard, she wouldn't be tackling the ground floor for a few days.

Someone had placed a sturdy armchair and footrest next to the table where the trunk was sitting.

"Jack set it up like this, so you could reach into the trunk there on the table without having to move around so much."

Roslyn was beginning to feel intimidated by Jack's apparent perfection.

"Now, when you're ready to start on the next trunk, you'll have to wait until Jack comes to move it down for us. I'm not lifting that thing."

"Okay," said Roslyn.

"Mind you listen this time," Sophie warned.

Roslyn gave a sheepish nod, feeling like a scolded child. "What's in the trunk? Can you tell?"

Sophie peered in, wrinkling her nose. "A lotta dust and mildew. What looks like photograph albums. Want me to pick out a couple for you?"

"Please." Roslyn watched as Sophie placed two dusty leather albums on the table.

"Right, then. I'll be up with more coffee in a bit, since you don't seem interested in your breakfast. If you need anything, give a holler. Though," she paused a beat, "I likely won't hear you anyway."

They grinned at one another, and Roslyn knew Sophie had already forgiven her for yesterday. When the housekeeper left, Roslyn picked up the first album and opened it. A yellowed card inscribed in swirling, almost illegible writing was tucked into old-fashioned paper corners. She raised it closer to decipher the inscription. "The Petersen Family, Plainsville, Iowa,

1869.'' The Petersen family history was now going to become hers.

The photographs were dark and shadowy. Still, Roslyn blessed the ancestor who'd meticulously labelled each one. After a few pages, she was accustomed to the handwriting. The main problem was that there was no one to explain the relationships of the people.

Roslyn sighed, frustrated at how little she knew about her family. Her childhood questions had been so vaguely answered that she'd eventually stopped asking them. She began to flip through the pages more quickly, familiarizing herself with people as the same names popped up over and over again. Ilse. Paul. Margaret. Elizabeth.

When Sophie appeared in the doorway, Roslyn was squinting at a picture of a young woman cradling an infant. Its label read: Ilse and Jacob, 1875.

''How's it going?''

Roslyn let the album ease onto her lap and sighed. ''Okay, but I'm only in the eighteen hundreds—too early yet for Ida Mae and my grandmother to appear.''

Sophie placed the coffee tray on the bureau and walked over to look down at the photograph of the woman and baby. ''Jacob,'' she read. ''That was Miss Ida's daddy's name. I bet that's him. I know Miss Ida was born in 1910 because she was going to be ninety this June. That would make her daddy about—''

''Thirty-five when the twins were born.''

''Guess you gotta be a math whiz to be in stocks and bonds.''

Roslyn smiled. "It helps. Anyway, thanks, Sophie. It's really frustrating not knowing who I'm looking at."

Sophie nodded sympathetically. "Maybe you can figure out the main ones, as you go on. So this Ilse was probably Miss Ida's grandmother."

"And I think Ilse and Paul were married because they seem to be together in a lot of the pictures."

Sophie raised her shoulders and smiled. "There you go. You've already figured out who your—what *would* they be?"

Roslyn thought for a minute. "June Rose was my grandmother; her mother, my great-grandmother, which would make Ilse my—"

"Great-great grandmother!" Sophie exclaimed.

They laughed together. "You know, Sophie, this is kind of fun. Like participating in a mystery play."

"It's nice that the mystery you're solving is finding out about your roots."

"Nice, but a bit sad, don't you think? I mean, that I'm only learning about my family now, at the ripe age of thirty-two."

Sophie pursed her lips and patted Roslyn on the shoulder. "Better late than never," she said huskily and, after shifting the coffee tray onto the bed at Roslyn's side, quickly left the room.

Roslyn stared after her, wondering at the unusual display of emotion. Then she reached for the mug of coffee and picked up the album with renewed enthusiasm. By the time she heard Sophie climbing up the stairs, Roslyn had already finished the two albums, ending with photographs of Jacob and his sisters as young children.

When she'd finished lunch, Roslyn was ready to take Sophie's advice and rest. "I'll just nap on the bed here," she insisted, "then I can get back to the albums when I wake up."

"Give me a shout when you want to move to the chair."

But one look at Sophie's flushed face told Roslyn the heavyset woman shouldn't go up and down stairs any more than necessary. "Sure," she lied, knowing she could make the short hop to the chair on her own.

When she awoke an hour later, Roslyn felt refreshed and ready to tackle the rest of the albums. The house below was silent and she wondered if Sophie was resting as well. She struggled off the bed and made the chair in a step-hop-skip movement that left her feeling slightly breathless. She pulled two more albums out of the trunk and sank into the armchair, reveling in a rush of anticipation that she hadn't experienced for many years. Even the expectancy of her promotion hadn't been as thrilling, she suddenly realized, thinking back to a few weeks ago and her luncheon with Ed Saunders. The day she'd learned she'd inherited a rosebush.

Roslyn smiled at the memory, struck by the events that had occurred in the following weeks. Looking back, it seemed as though each one had led inevitably to this moment—studying dusty photograph albums in an upstairs bedroom of a magnificent home that was hers if she would spend a year living in it to look after a rosebush.

You're in charge of your own destiny, she reminded herself. The rosebush. The house. Plainsville. Jack. The kiss. *All of it is in your control.*

Reassured by that thought, Roslyn cracked open another album, puffing dust into the air, and read the delicate inscription inside: The Petersen Family Album, 1900—a new century!

The first photograph featured a young bridal couple in a formal studio pose. Beneath the picture was a sliver of yellowed paper curling up at the ends and bearing the names: Jacob and Gertrude, June 1900.

Roslyn stared at the bridal pair, touching the surface of the glossy photo with almost a reverent touch. Then she noticed the bridal bouquet—roses. There must have been at least a dozen, she guessed, their wide, flat petals so pale Roslyn couldn't determine what shade of pink they'd been. She supposed that Ilse had begun the tradition of using the Danish rose for family occasions.

Two pages of snaps of the happy bridal pair in various poses with other family members followed. Roslyn flipped the pages, stopping at a formal studio pose of Jacob, Gertrude and an infant. The caption read, Rolfe Edward. November, 1901. The parents beamed down proudly at their firstborn. Roslyn frowned. She didn't recall Sophie or Jack mentioning a son.

The rest of the album was devoted to Rolfe's childhood. A visual biography of a boy who appeared to be the center of the Petersen family universe. When Roslyn reached the end, she was exhausted. Delving into the past through photo albums was draining.

Without the emotional connection, it was akin to watching a friend's holiday slides. But she'd yet to come across her grandmother.

Roslyn sighed, blew away the hank of hair that strayed across her forehead, and reached for another album. She began to turn the pages more quickly and almost missed the first photograph of the twins.

A small black-and-white snap of Gertrude, her hair down and hanging loose about her shoulders, sitting in a rocking chair with a wrapped bundle in the crook of each arm. The label read: Twins! June, 1910.

She quickly flipped over the page. In center spot on the other side was a large formal portrait of the new, extended Petersen family. Gertrude sat in a large armchair with one of the twins tucked into her arm. Jacob stood behind, his smiling face framed by a mustache and muttonchop sideburns. On either side of him stood his parents, Ilse and Christian. Seated on the floor in front of his mother and embracing the other twin was Rolfe.

What Roslyn noticed last was the vase of roses perched on the small oval table next to Ilse at the edge of the photograph. How considerate, she thought, of the twins to be born in June so that the tradition of the Iowa rose could carry on.

SOPHIE WAS talking on the phone when Jack came in through the kitchen door from the back porch. He could tell she was deep in conversation because she didn't even hear him close the door. Though she did just about roll off her chair when he tapped her on the shoulder.

"Don't get up. I'm going to see Roslyn. If she's napping I'll bring down that other trunk for her." He didn't wait for her to reply, but headed into the hallway.

He took the stairs two at a time. Not simply because he was anxious to see Roslyn, but because he was afraid he'd lose his courage and leave. All day he'd been kicking himself for not responding to her parting remark last night. Yet the time hadn't been right for what he'd wanted to say. *Don't kid yourself. You enjoyed the kiss as much as I did. I saw it in your face.*

Still, waves of embarrassment washed over him whenever he thought about it. He wasn't going to convince Roslyn to linger in Plainsville if he was drooling like a teenager every time he saw her.

He paused on the second floor landing to catch his breath. Although Roslyn's door was ajar, he heard rustling noises from the guest room across the hall where he'd left the trunk. He stood in the doorway, watching her until she sensed his presence and looked up.

"Jack!"

"I told Sophie I might drop by," he said.

She didn't speak, just stared at him, her face glazed with exhaustion or surprise. He couldn't tell which. "I see you've been at the albums," he continued.

That brought a smile. "I've found pictures of my grandmother as a baby and my great-grandparents."

The enthusiasm in her voice warmed him. "I've never seen those albums," he said.

"Come and have a look." She patted the edge of the bed next to her chair.

The bed sagged as he sat down. For a split second he thought of last night and the bed across the hall. He leaned over her shoulder to get a better look at the album. Her scent, a heady mix of spring violets and lily of the valley swarmed his senses. The photographs blurred.

He struggled to focus while she pointed out each picture, reading the strips of white paper beneath to identify the subject, but he scarcely heard a word. With each arm movement, the V-neck of her dressing gown shifted, sending another flowery waft up into the air. Jack gulped, forcing his eyes to stay on task and his ears to follow the vaguely familiar names she pronounced.

Once she suddenly turned toward him, the tip of her nose almost touching his cheek and he fought the urge to move his own head, meeting her mouth to mouth.

"Did you know," she asked, her question a puff of warmth on his skin, "that Ida Mae and my grandmother had an older brother?"

Startled, he jerked his head toward her and bumped noses. She pulled back, laughing. He grinned but leapt off the bed, adding some distance to their seating arrangement so he wouldn't charge headlong into a replay of last night's blunder.

"No, I didn't." Taking two large paces away from her chair, Jack forked his fingers through his hair. Pivoting around to face her, he asked, "Is there a picture of him?"

She thumbed through to the back of the album. "Here. Just after he was born, I guess."

He moved to a safe place at right angles to her chair and peered down into her lap. "Huh. Wonder what happened to him."

"What do you mean?"

"He must have died or left Plainsville years ago because my grandfather never mentioned him at all— and Grandpa Henry just died a little more than a year ago."

"That's kind of what Sophie implied too—that Rolfe must have died."

"Was that his name? Rolfe?"

Roslyn nodded. She wished he'd come round to sit beside her again. Craning her neck was uncomfortable. But he seemed restless, prowling the room while he talked.

"If he died here, he'd be buried in the Lutheran church cemetery. That's where Ida Mae is and her folks."

"Wouldn't you have noticed his grave when Ida Mae was buried?"

"I suppose I ought to have noticed, but frankly, I didn't. The day was rainy and cold. No one lingered to pay their respects to, well, to the rest of the family. And there weren't a lot of us."

Roslyn imagined that day, wondering who had been left to bury Ida Mae Petersen. She thought back to her mother's funeral. There'd been her father, her mother's best friend and, inexplicably, the man who ran the corner convenience store near her mother's home. A small funeral for a small family.

"What are you thinking about?" he asked. He was standing in front of her, his hand shoved into the pockets of his jeans and concern in his face.

"About my family. Or lack of it, I should say."

"Those photo albums represent a lot of family," Jack pointed out.

"But everyone in them is dead, Jack. *They're all dead.*"

He shook his head. "They're still your family—and a part of you."

She wasn't convinced, but she liked the earnestness in his face. It was an improvement over the wary expression he'd had when he first entered the room. Up close, she noticed that he needed a shave. And a good night's sleep. She wondered about that. Had the kiss kept him awake, too? Or had it been something at work?

Impulsively, she said, "Tell me about your family."

His face lit up and he pulled the chair closer to her, settling back into it with the eagerness of a storyteller. Much later, when Sophie pushed open the door to ask if Jack intended to stay for dinner, Roslyn's head was spinning with names and stories of the Jensen family.

"Dinner?" Jack asked blankly.

"Can you stay?" Roslyn asked, "I'd love the company."

"If you're sure you don't mind," he murmured.

Sophie gave a noisy sound from the doorway. "Well, if you can pull yourself away from all this," she addressed Jack, waving a hand toward the photo albums, "there's a tray set up in the kitchen and the casserole's in the oven." She paused a beat, adding in a meaningful tone, "So you can decide if you're gonna be eating down there or up here."

When Sophie bustled off downstairs, Roslyn caught Jack's eye and laughed with him. "Don't mind Sophie," he said. "She's been trying to match me up with someone ever since I returned to Plainsville."

The comment begged the question Roslyn didn't want to ask. *So there's no one in your life right now?* Instead, she leaned forward and said, "It must have been hard coming back home from the big city. Weren't you leaving a lot behind?"

His eyes locked onto hers. "Nothing I wanted to keep," he murmured.

And that simple statement, Roslyn realized, underlined the gap between them. All that she had and wanted in the world was back in Chicago. As attractive and charming as she found Jack Jensen, there was no getting round that fact.

"Shall we eat up here?" she suggested, changing the direction of her thoughts.

The gleam in his eyes set her heart racing. She was on the verge of changing her mind when he scrambled to his feet.

"I'll get the tray."

And he was out the door before Roslyn could call him back.

JACK CONTINUED with his family history while they enjoyed the casserole and salad Sophie had prepared. Roslyn hung on every word, reveling in his humor and envying the warmth in his voice whenever he referred to a specific family member. The Jensens were a big clan, she learned, with relatives spread all over the Midwest. Every five years there was an enormous reunion with family coming from all parts of the country.

"Next year the event's supposed to be held here," he said, forking the last scrap of rice and chicken into his mouth.

"In Plainsville?"

"You sound surprised. Think this place isn't racy enough for my city relatives?"

She shrugged, embarrassed at her unintended slight. "It doesn't seem big enough. Where will they all stay?"

"You're right about that. We're working on it. If the weather's good, a lot can camp on our property. Dad's looked into renting portable toilets, showers and big tents. 'Course the older ones may have to commute from Cedar Rapids or some place closer. Anyway, we've still got a year to finalize details."

"You plan this for a whole year?"

"Actually, my folks started planning when their name was drawn to host this one, about four years ago."

"I can't imagine planning for something five years away."

"Don't you do that in your job? You know, plan for people's investments and retirements and stuff. Isn't that what you do?"

"True," Roslyn admitted. "Though most of my clients are now corporations and some smaller businesses. I meant organizing your personal life. How did you even know you'd be in Plainsville for the reunion?"

"Jensens have always been in Plainsville. And probably always will be. Most of them, anyway." He paused. "I'm not sure about my younger brother. He's at college this year and I've a feeling he's not going to want to farm."

"You said your older brother runs the farm now."

"Yeah. After his stint in Germany he decided not to make a career out of the army. He missed the land too much. Besides, his wife and kids were getting tired of not having a permanent home."

Missed the land. It was an expression she'd never heard before, but she knew right away what he meant by it, even if she couldn't relate to it. The only land she'd ever been connected to was the tiny backyard behind her grandparents' row house.

"What about you?"

"Me?"

"I know you left Chicago to take care of things here—while your father recuperated from his stroke. Didn't you want to stay on the farm? Or even go back to the city when your brother came home?"

He seemed to think about what she'd said for a moment. Then he replied, "I didn't want to work the farm. It's a hard life and—for me—not a very rewarding one. There's…well, a lot of stuff I like to do in my spare time that I'd never be able to do if I worked the farm. Besides, my brother's the best choice for that job."

"And going back to Chicago?" she prompted.

He stared at her, shaking his head. "Like I said, there was nothing I wanted to return to in Chicago." He picked up the tray he'd loaded and headed to the door, where he stopped long enough to add, "If you stayed in Plainsville long enough, you just might find that out, too."

"What do you mean?" she said.

"This is where your family came from and this is where most of them are buried. In good old Plainsville, Iowa. You're just as connected to the land here as my brothers and I are. Only you don't know it yet." With that he left the room.

SOPHIE WASN'T HAPPY. Her body language and furtive looks at Roslyn all morning had conveyed that message loud and clear. She'd raised her eyebrows at Roslyn's explanation that Jack had washed up the dinner dishes and left early.

"I would've done those dishes this morning," she complained.

"He was saving you some work," Roslyn pointed out.

"Work! I'm used to that kinda work. He wasn't *supposed* to do the dishes. He was supposed to—"

"What?"

Sophie averted her face. "Nothin'," she mumbled.

"Keep me company?" Roslyn persisted.

"Whatever," the housekeeper murmured, picking up Roslyn's breakfast tray and heading for the bedroom door.

"I don't need looking after. I'm not a child," Roslyn asserted, spurred on by peevishness and a poor night's sleep.

Sophie turned around from the doorway. "'Course you're not a child. And neither is Jack." She walked out of the room, leaving Roslyn to sort out the cryptic remark on her own.

Roslyn eyed the trunk sitting near the door. Before he'd left last night, Jack had insisted on packing away the albums she'd finished with and bringing down the second trunk. He'd pushed it into her bedroom, then given a brief good-night from the safety of the doorway.

She knew when he'd said good-night that the evening's magic had worn away. More like been blown away, she admitted. *By none other than myself.* But she hadn't been able to come up with a way to salvage it. Overwhelmed by fatigue and her own conflicting emotions, she'd muttered a curt farewell herself and watched helplessly as he disappeared out the door.

Roslyn sighed. In the last twenty-four hours she'd managed to irritate the only two people she knew in Plainsville. Yet she remained completely dependent on those very people. Her eyes filled. Homesickness for Chicago and familiar faces at the office overwhelmed her. She decided to call Judy. Maybe even Ed, to see how things were going.

Descending the staircase wasn't as difficult as she'd imagined. By holding on to the banister with her right hand and bearing most of her weight on her right foot, she could use the crutch under her left arm to support that side of her body. Reaching the ground floor, she hobbled into the living room.

Ed's secretary announced that he'd left for the weekend.

"But it's only Thursday," Roslyn said.

"He's gone to the Caribbean," the secretary explained.

Roslyn frowned. Ed hadn't mentioned a holiday when she'd been talking to him. And why would he go so far for a weekend? "On business?"

"Mr. Saunders didn't discuss the purpose of his trip with me, Roslyn. Is there someone else here who could help you?"

"Well, I just called to see how things were going." She hesitated, then asked, "Could you connect me to Judy?"

There was a brief silence. "Uh, I thought you knew, Roslyn. Judy's not here anymore."

"What do you mean?"

"She quit."

"I don't understand. I was just talking to Ed a few days ago and he said Judy was filling in for Bob's secretary."

"She was."

"Then what happened?"

The secretary lowered her voice. "I don't like to gossip, Roslyn, especially about Judy. But there've been a lot of rumors flying around here. Some people think that Judy has been involved with Jim Naismith, in more ways than one. If you get my drift."

Roslyn shook her head, hoping to clear some of the

cotton batting out of it. "Actually, I don't get your drift. Can you be a little more specific?"

"Well, Ed had a long talk with her last week and when she left his office I could tell that she'd been crying. The next day she phoned in sick and the day after that, she faxed us her resignation."

Roslyn closed her eyes. She thanked Ed's secretary and hung up, too upset to talk any longer. Everything seemed to be falling apart miles away, and she was helpless to do anything about it. Suddenly, she wasn't certain about anything. The people she'd known for years were all behaving unpredictably and those she'd known only a couple of weeks were acting as though they'd always been her close friends.

CHAPTER NINE

ROSLYN SAT in the living room until dusk. Sophie found her there and had known that something was amiss. She tiptoed about, switching on lamps and bringing in Roslyn's dinner tray without comment.

"I'll stay till you've finished," she said, "so's I can help you upstairs."

But Roslyn wanted to be alone. On Sophie's instructions, she left the tray in the living room, then went upstairs. She'd crawled under the covers, eager for escape from the day. Hours later and still wide awake, she heard the telephone ringing downstairs. At first she considered trying to reach it, but decided rushing the stairs wouldn't be smart. Besides, what if it was Jack? And what would she say to him?

By midmorning the next day, showered and fed a huge breakfast by Sophie, Roslyn was ready to tackle the other trunk that Jack had retrieved from the attic. Sophie had removed some of the albums and deposited them on the night table in the guest room.

"Holler when you want more," she said.

"Sophie, I can manage. Really."

Still, the housekeeper had lingered, fussing with the dishes. Finally, she glanced at Roslyn and said, "I noticed you didn't need the crutch at all when you came in here. If you're getting about better now, would you mind if I took the afternoon off? I've got some family business to attend to in Des Moines," she added quickly.

Something in Sophie's voice suggested a problem. "Of course I don't mind. Is it something serious? Anything I can do?"

"Nope, more's the pity. Ain't nothin' anyone can do, except me. The other thing is, I was wondering if I could have my week's pay before I go."

"Of course! I'm so sorry I didn't think of it."

Jack had alluded to Sophie's family troubles a couple of times and Sophie herself had mentioned that she was helping look after her sister's children. Yet Roslyn hadn't registered any of these remarks, assuming that Sophie's personal life was as free of personal troubles or financial constraints as her own.

What a precious little princess I must seem to both Sophie and Jack. Embarrassed by her own self-absorption, Roslyn added a bonus to the amount agreed on for Sophie's weekly services. She folded the check into an envelope, sealed it and left it on the edge of the bed. Then she took the first of the three albums on the night table and delved into the past.

When Sophie returned an hour later, Roslyn said, "I've gone through those three albums and the twins are just into their teens. Their parents must have spent a fortune taking photographs."

"Well, I guess their daddy had lots of money, being the president of the bank and all. I've left casseroles in the freezer and there's a fresh loaf in the bread box on the counter. Also a dozen cookies from yesterday. I made a nice salad and there's some homemade chicken vegetable soup for lunch. When would you like it brought up?''

''Thank you, Sophie, I'll get it myself. I haven't been this well fed and taken care of since I was a kid. Maybe not even then,'' she said, thinking of her Grandma Dutton's no-nonsense approach to child rearing. She held out the check. ''Thanks again, for everything, Sophie. Will you be in on Monday?''

Sophie shrugged. ''If you'll be wanting me.''

''I have a doctor's appointment on Tuesday and I'm sure he'll give me the okay to go back to work, but I'd love to have you come in. I'll be calling Randall Taylor to find out if I'll be entitled to any of Ida Mae's personal things, like the albums.'' She paused, catching the frown on Sophie's face. ''If I give up my claim to her estate.''

Sophie nodded. She started to say something, but obviously changed her mind. Then stopping in the doorway, she mumbled, ''Maybe you'll stay on anyway'' and departed with a quick goodbye.

Nobody seems to believe I'm not going to stay in Plainsville, Roslyn thought. *Maybe I should quit fighting and just give in.* But when she peered down into the trunk and saw only two albums left, she wondered how she could possibly fill her time beyond Monday. Besides, things at the office were getting very bizarre. As soon as Ed returned from his weekend in the Caribbean, she'd call and tell him she was coming back to work.

By early afternoon, she'd finished the last two albums, taking her grandmother and Ida Mae up to the ripe age of twenty. The year was 1930 and the last photograph was of the twins, arm in arm and standing in front of their home. Off to one side of the sisters and cut off by the photographer, was a trousered pant leg. Their father? Roslyn wondered.

1930. The year after the great stock market crash. The sisters were only twenty in the last photo and, judging by the smiles on their young faces, eager to tackle the world. When and how did it all go wrong for them?

Roslyn closed the last album and dropped it on the bed. She'd never know the answer to those questions and that rankled. Unresolved issues were messy and tended to lead to trouble—or so she'd learned in the money trade. *Yet you never seem to apply that dictum to your own personal life, Baines. Relationships left to hang and wither from apathy; resentments and hurt feelings buried instead of resolved. That's been your life.* Not a reassuring picture, Roslyn decided. She sighed and headed for lunch, sensing the irony of the moment.

Roslyn lingered over lunch, savoring every bite and knowing that everyday eating in Chicago would never measure up to Sophie's deft hand. Besides, there was only a long afternoon ahead of her and a wet one, ruling out even a taxi ride into Plainsville. Rain slashed at the kitchen windows and thunder rolled from miles away. Roslyn wandered around the ground floor, ending up in the living room again.

The room was gloomy and cold, even for early May. Roslyn eyed the fireplace and wondered when it had last been lit. A roaring blaze would certainly cheer the place up, but there didn't appear to be any logs or kindling. She puttered about the room, reexamining objects that she'd fingered a dozen times since the accident. The repetitiveness of the past couple of weeks was another acute reminder how different her life in Plainsville was from her life in Chicago.

There, every moment had been packed with work. Any downtime had been filled with punishing visits to the gym or jogging or, on occasion, theatre or art galleries. She'd never allowed herself idle time and now she knew why. Too much thinking could occur. Especially thinking about personal problems or dallying with fantasies of romance. Both of which, Roslyn had always suspected, were futile pursuits.

She stood in the curve of the bay window to gaze out at the front garden. It was difficult to imagine the scene in full bloom. The only plants and flowers she was familiar with were the standard varieties sold by florists. She squinted through the streaked window. Which one was the Iowa rose again? She rubbed away the fog patch she'd made on the glass and stretched her neck to see above the cedar branch that bobbed up and down in her line of vision. There. The clump of canes arching out from the ground. She could just make out tiny buds on the canes. Perhaps leaves would appear before she left Plainsville.

Roslyn frowned. But not likely. Maybe she'd get Sophie—or even Jack, if she had the nerve to ask— to take a photograph of the bush in bloom. She could tape the picture to her computer, the way the secretaries posted snaps of their children, and tell others the story of the Iowa rose. Roslyn smiled at the idea although an inner voice taunted, *You're pathetic, Baines. Substituting a plant for family.*

She turned away from the window, surveying the room and its old-fashioned decor. How many long hours had Aunt Ida devoted to this room and its view? She had a sudden vision of herself sitting in Ida Mae's armchair in front of the window, her feet propped on the same needleworked ottoman with the crocheted afghan draped over her shoulders. The focal point of the whole scene was the Iowa rose, standing alone on the periphery of the garden. Aunt Ida's sole remaining connection to family. And Roslyn's.

She shivered.

JACK PULLED into the driveway just as Roslyn rushed out the front door. He wondered what she was doing until he noticed the waft of smoke billowing out after her. He jammed his foot on the brake, cranked the gearshift into park and sprinted across the lawn.

She was coughing, but managed to gasp, "The fireplace." And he knew as he sprinted onto the veranda that he'd forgotten to warn her about the damper. The hall was filled with smoke. Hand over his mouth, he headed for the living room and crouched down in front of the fireplace. He knew exactly where to place his hand and pulled hard. The rusting iron damper resisted, then opened.

Jack dashed back outside to wait for the smoke to clear. He found Roslyn sitting in one of the wicker chairs. "I'm sorry about that," he said. "I forgot to tell you that the damper doesn't open all the way unless you give it a good yank."

"I'm sure you didn't expect me to be lighting any fires."

Jack grinned. "True enough. It is May—although a damp and chilly day. I guess I timed my impromptu visit right."

"Your timing is always right. I haven't forgotten that you saved me from a night on the attic floor."

"I'm a regular knight in shining armor," he quipped, then he stared down at her, taking in the dark circles under her eyes and her pinched lips. "The place wouldn't have burned down," he said, wanting to reassure her. "The fire didn't catch properly anyway. Looks like you just used newspaper. It would've smouldered for a few more minutes then died out."

"Thank heavens for that. Maybe I should've gone to Girl Scouts."

He had to laugh, trying to imagine a young Roslyn in uniform. "I actually came by to see if I could get you any supplies for the weekend and also, to… well…" He found himself stammering under the intensity of her scrutiny. "To invite you to dinner at my folks' place tomorrow night. That is, if you feel up to a houseful of Jensens."

Her smile was transforming. "I'd love to come. I've spent most of the day so far wondering what I could do until Monday."

"Great," he said. He raked his fingers through his hair and continued to look at her.

Until he noticed her rubbing her arms. "You should get inside," he suggested.

She nodded, but didn't move. After a moment, she said, "Strange things have been happening at work.

My secretary quit and didn't even call me to tell me. My boss has left the country for the weekend, and no one else is there to explain anything." She paused, then added, "I should be getting back. Dealing with these things by phone isn't working."

Jack held his breath, waiting for her to continue. He shifted his gaze to a point beyond where she was sitting, but he could feel her eyes on him. Waiting for a response? he wondered. Problem was, he didn't know exactly how to respond. He felt sick at the idea of her leaving Plainsville. Yet she was obviously worried and looked terrible, as if she'd lain awake all night.

When he finally came up with a reply, she was already standing, ready to go back into the house. "Do you feel ready to return?"

Half a smile flit across her face. "I was ready physically days ago. It's the mental part that kept me here."

"How so?"

"Hard to explain, really. I have to admit I've been fascinated by the photograph albums. Looking at a lot of dusty old pictures means more when you know all the people are related to you. The puzzle of the split between my grandmother and Ida Mae is one I'd like to solve, of course. And as much as I complain about the dullness of life here in Plainsville, I know I've never been this relaxed."

Jack winced at the image of a dull Plainsville. "You have to stay in a place longer than a few weeks to know it," he murmured.

"You're right. Absolutely. And it's been great for

me to be able to unwind. If I'd simply taken those albums back to Chicago, I'm sure they'd still be packed in their trunks.''

''Learning about your family and the interior of this house is only part of what Plainsville is all about. There's the town, the people. And the land. *Your* land.''

She smiled. ''You sound like one of those salesmen pitching a product on television.''

''I know. According to Lenny, I'm unbelievably idealistic about what Plainsville has to offer. It's just that I've been on the other side, too. I've been trapped in the whole frenetic game that goes on in big cities like Chicago. I know how the life there can suck you dry.'' He turned away to look out across the lawn and garden. After a moment, he said, ''The thing is, what really nourishes the soul are the basics. And they're right here. Right out there,'' he said, swinging his arm in a wide sweep.

When he turned around, she was staring in the direction of the Iowa rose. ''What will it look like when it blooms?'' she asked.

''Beautiful. Uncomplicated. No dramatic colors or petal configurations that hybrid roses have. Just a large, uncluttered bloom of a pink so subtle that its hues change with sunlight and shade. And a fragrance you can never pin down, because it moves with the wind, the heat of the day or the night dew.'' He stopped, fearing he was beginning to sound more like a TV evangelist than a pitchman.

She didn't speak for a long time. Jack felt his blood pressure rise. If only he knew when to shut up.

Then she whispered, "Will you send me a photograph of it?" and his stomach lurched.

"Sure," he mumbled and peered down at his feet. All he could focus on was the fact that tomorrow might be his last chance to convince her to stay on. When he glanced up again, he said, "I'll pick you up about three. We can take a little drive around your property."

Her shrug seemed dismissive. "Okay," was all she said.

He left then, for once timing his exit right. Even if everything else was miserably unchanged.

HE WAS PUNCTUAL, and Roslyn liked that in a man. It was a virtue that went arm in arm with reliability. And he'd thoughtfully driven a car, solving the problem of climbing into the truck in pumps and a short, tight skirt. She'd spent most of the day trying on various combinations of the few clothes she'd brought with her. A visit to a working farm probably indicated casual wear. Yet she also realized that she'd never worn anything but jeans or nightgowns in Jack's presence. Wanting to look as attractive as possible was her goal, although she stopped herself several times during the morning to question her sanity.

What does it matter? You're leaving in a few days anyway. Why do you care? But she did care and when she opened the door, the rush of pleasure in his face was all she needed. "You look fantastic," he said.

"So do you." He too had abandoned the jeans, choosing olive-green chinos, a pale-green striped shirt and tan sport jacket.

He rubbed a forefinger thoughtfully across his upper lip. "I'm beginning to feel a tad underdressed," he said.

Roslyn laughed. "I'm only wearing a skirt and sweater," she protested.

He made an exaggerated survey of her from head to toe. "Yes, but that's no ordinary sweater. I mean, it clings…uh…very nicely and that skirt…" His eyes traveled downward, pausing at the hemline above her knees. He shook his head. "All I can say is, it's a good thing today isn't Sunday because the good citizens of dull old Plainsville would be shocked."

Roslyn gave him a playful punch on the shoulder. "As long as I meet with your family's approval, that's all that counts. Just a sec—I'll get my purse and coat."

When they were pulling out of the drive, he turned to her to ask, "Did you mean what you said? About getting my parents' approval?"

Roslyn fidgeted with her seat belt. She didn't want the talk to get serious. Light and easy was safer. "Isn't that what this is all about? I mean, you want me to meet your family, and I want them to like me because…well, why not?"

He smiled back. "Why not, indeed. Okay, ready for the tour?"

"Plainsville here we come!"

Twenty minutes later, they'd reached the outskirts of town, backtracking along Goshen Road to Ida Mae's house. "Has anyone ever got lost here?"

"Only hapless tourists and big-city folk who are certain they've made a wrong turn and missed something. Seriously, the size of the town isn't important. What's important is—''

''The size of people's hearts?''

''God, do I sound that preachy?''

''Just about.''

He nodded. ''Okay, let's strike a deal. Every time I get on my bandwagon, you just—''

''Poke you in the ribs? Say something snarly?'' .

''I guess a poke will do.'' He pointed to his right. ''See that grove of trees? That's where we walked to the first day you came.''

Roslyn followed his finger. ''It looks a lot bigger from here.''

''You get the full panorama. I wasn't exaggerating when I said Ida Mae's property extends for almost a hundred acres. Past this ravine to the north and east from here another fifty or so. Picture a long rectangle, with the house at the short end.''

''You said she rented most of the land. Does that arrangement still hold?''

He glanced across at her. ''Yeah, I think so. Guy by the name of McDougall uses it. I don't know the particulars, but I'm sure there's some kind of written agreement that Ida Mae's lawyer might have. Although most people here do business on a hand-shake.''

''That wouldn't do in Chicago.''

''Nope. You're dead right about that.'' He paused. ''Do you think you might want to extend the lease agreement?''

Roslyn turned her head to look out the window. ''It won't be my decision, I'm sure. Just curious.''

Roslyn sensed she'd dampened Jack's enthusiasm but didn't know how to retrieve the lighthearted tone. So she took in the scenery, breaking the silence once in a while to ask polite questions. Twenty minutes of winding roads later, they turned into a long tree-lined drive. The flatness of the surrounding fields gave way to a two-storey russet brick farmhouse trimmed in white frame gingerbread.

"It's lovely!" she exclaimed.

"And old," Jack said. "My great-grandfather built the original one-storey two-room cabin and it's been added onto over the years, as you'll see when you get the grand tour. My grandfather was quite the carpenter and he put on the fancy trim."

"What do your parents farm? Do they have animals?"

He held up a palm. "Hang on, I'll get you there in two minutes."

Up close, Roslyn noticed a large, gray aluminum-sided barn and two other buildings. There were a couple of pieces of machinery parked off to one side and, in the section of driveway that curved in a semicircle in front of the house, were Jack's red pickup and a van. Three dogs bounded out from behind the house at their approach.

"Stay in the car until I calm the dogs. They're a bit too friendly." Jack parked the car. As soon as he stepped out, he was mobbed by the dogs. Roslyn laughed. By the time he reached her side, the dogs were sitting politely, wagging their tails.

Roslyn swung her right leg out, took Jack's hand

and extended her left leg, revealing a lot more thigh than she'd expected. "Thanks."

"My pleasure."

Roslyn turned from his enthusiastic grin to the dogs. "They're beautiful animals. What breed?"

"Two of them are golden retrievers and the goofy one ogling you on the far right is a Lab."

"Is he yours?" she asked, patting the Lab and craning her head back to Jack.

"Yeah, that one is. Why?"

"Oh, just noticed a resemblance," she murmured and headed for the front door of the house, where a man and woman were waiting to greet them.

Jack hurried after her, arriving, face flushed, a second behind her, to make the introductions. "Roslyn, my Dad, Pete, and my mother, Marion."

They both smiled. Pete pumped Roslyn's hand while Marion's eyes, glinting with amusement, went from Jack to Roslyn and back again. Roslyn was struck by the physical similarity between Jack and his father. He had his mother's dark hair and eyes, but his father's build and facial features.

Dinner was as hectic and noisy as Jack had warned. Initially, Roslyn felt overwhelmed by the confusion. She learned that Jack's older brother, Bill, and his wife Jeanette lived at the farmhouse with their three children. Lenny, the oldest, was there, grinning amiably, and his girlfriend whose name Roslyn didn't catch. The two others were girls—one a lively eleven-year-old who was constantly at Jack's side and the other seemed about sixteen. Jack's younger brother,

Mike, had arrived home from college and had brought his roommate with him.

From the way everyone deferred to her, showing her about the house and then around the yard and the outbuildings, Roslyn gathered that Jack hadn't brought home many women friends. As they collectively exited the barn, after Roslyn oohed and aahed at the spring lambs and two calves, Jack's youngest niece—was it Sarah?—blurted out, "You're the first girlfriend of Jack's we've ever seen. Except for his ex, of course, and she doesn't count. Right, Uncle Jack?"

Everyone laughed, including Roslyn who didn't bother to correct the girl's use of the term *girlfriend*. In spite of Jack's embarrassment, the remark set the tone for the rest of the visit.

Roslyn watched while Jack's mother single-handedly orchestrated the entire meal, delegating jobs with the ease and precision of a career army officer. She also put up with a lot of teasing along the way, tossing back quips of her own. Roslyn decided that Jack had a lot of his mother's calm, relaxed manner and her quick humor. His father was more reserved, content to sit back and watch the commotion with a solemn face that occasionally broke into a fleeting grin or a fast wink.

Over a simple but delicious pot roast dinner, Roslyn learned that the farm had been in the family for more than a hundred years. The original cabin, which now was part of the family room and kitchen, was considered a heritage home.

"Just like your place, Roslyn," Bill pointed out.

"My place?"

Faces turned her way. Across the table, Jack raised an eyebrow. "Well, your place now. Ida Mae's."

Roslyn nodded. "Right. Aunt Ida's house."

The conversation shifted in another direction as Marion appeared with two large pies. Roslyn felt herself uncoil from the spring of tension that had unexpectedly shot through her at Bill's innocent comment.

As soon as the dessert dishes were cleared, people began to scatter. Marion, still stacking dishes in the dishwasher, refused Roslyn's offer of help.

"I never have guests clear up their first time here," she said. Then she smiled broadly. "The next time, for sure."

Jack and his father were discussing something in the family room when Roslyn returned. Pete stood up, placed a hand on Jack's shoulder and patted it reassuringly. Leaving the room, he clasped Roslyn's hand and said, "I hope you'll come back real soon. Next time if your footwear is more appropriate, I'll take you round the acreage and show you where we plant the corn and soybeans."

Roslyn laughed. He'd teased her earlier over her delicate pumps. Now Jack was bringing her trench coat and purse from the hall closet. "I don't mean to rush you but I see you're favoring your foot a bit and probably you should get home."

She nodded, grateful for his thoughtfulness. They said good-night and stepped out into the crisp, starry night. Roslyn paused on the veranda, gazing up at the sky. "It's so clear out in the country."

"You'd love the meteor showers in August. The

Perseids. We often get blankets and lawn chairs, a bottle of wine or two, and sit out for hours.''

"It sounds wonderful.''

"Then come,'' he urged.

She turned toward him, not realizing he was standing inches away. The warmth of his breath fanned across her cheek. She recalled the way he'd described the Iowa rose yesterday. The fervent ardor in his voice had made her wonder what it would be like to have him speak about her in that same manner.

Roslyn glanced away, back to the night sky. "It's tempting, believe me.''

He moved closer, his hushed voice at her right ear. "Let me tempt you. The rose in June, the family reunion in July and the Perseids in August. What more could a person want?''

Roslyn tittered like a nervous schoolgirl. Jack placed his hands on her shoulders, gently turning her his way. His right hand ran down the short French braid she'd rolled her hair into and snapped the hair band. He cupped the back of her neck under the tumble of hair and drew her head to his.

"You are so beautiful,'' he whispered. He lowered his face and kissed her.

Her body folded into his, swaying with the heat of his kiss while his hands slipped beneath her sweater and unclasped her bra. Roslyn's breath caught in the back of her throat and rolled into a low purr of contentment as he cupped her breasts in both hands.

"I want you so badly,'' he moaned into her hair, his lips moving from her lips to the crown of her head, to her cheek and down the column of her neck.

"My house," she breathed into his ear, not realizing until hours later that it was the very first time she'd said those words. *My house.*

She melded her body against his inside the car, keeping the embers burning, she told herself. Her hands boldly strayed, distracting him until he pleaded for time out. The dark countryside flew by in anonymity. She wished they could drive forever like that. Never having to face the real world of daylight. Or to have to make decisions.

The car swung into the drive of Ida Mae's house. Jack braked sharply. There was another vehicle parked in the drive.

"What the—" he swore as a figure stood up from the front steps. "Who the hell is that?"

Roslyn straightened up, dazed. Had she fallen asleep? Was she dreaming?

"Were you expecting someone?" Jack asked, his voice thick with disappointment.

"No," she murmured, watching the shape lurch toward them, its vague, undefined outline sharpening as it moved closer. A *man,* she registered suddenly, panic welling up from deep inside. Jim Naismith.

"Oh, no," she whispered.

CHAPTER TEN

JACK'S FACE turned from the windshield to her. "Friend of yours?"

"Well, not exactly. Jim works with me."

"Long way to come at this time of night. Must be important." He turned off the ignition and moved his hand to open the door.

"Wait." Roslyn swallowed, silenced by the cool question in his eyes. Finally she said, "I'm not sure why he's here. It's a long story and—"

"And it's late, Roslyn. I have to get up early in the morning." He pushed open the door just as Jim reached the front of the car.

"Roslyn?" Jim peered through the windshield, caught sight of her sitting on the passenger side and rushed to open her door.

"Jim! What are you doing here?" Roslyn took the hand he extended and winced as she set her left foot down hard. She stumbled slightly, caught up in his arms in an awkward embrace. He held on a long moment. Roslyn looked past his shoulder to where Jack stood, arms folded, watching.

She pushed herself gently away from Jim. "I don't understand. Why—"

"I have to talk to you, Roslyn. I know this is bad timing, but we have to clear the air."

Jack cleared his throat. "I've got to go now, Roslyn."

"Jack, wait! Will you call me tomorrow?"

He held on to the car door long enough to say, "Tomorrow? Sure, if you won't be too busy." The door slammed shut and the engine turned over.

Roslyn watched silently as the car slowly reversed and headed toward the center of town. She fought to keep the resentment out of her voice when she turned back to Jim and said, "You'd better come inside."

HE TALKED LONG into the night. In the beginning, Roslyn was wary. She told him right away that he shouldn't have come. That it was inappropriate for her to be discussing the inquiry with him.

"But that's the problem, Roslyn. The whole thing is that I started my own inquiry weeks ago. No, no, please. Hear me out." He was pacing from counter to table in the kitchen, where they'd been sitting since she'd brought him inside. Roslyn toyed with her empty coffee mug and watched him. But all she saw was the detachment in Jack's face when he'd taken one last look at her as he'd climbed into the car.

"It started shortly after I got back from my holiday. There was a query for me from one of my clients, a widow who lives in Florida. She said her son-in-law wanted some information about one of her funds. I assured her everything was in order, but when I double-checked, I saw that money had been diverted from one fund into another. It wasn't a fund I recognized."

Roslyn stifled a yawn and rubbed her face. She wanted to go to bed. She wanted to fantasize about what might have been if Jim Naismith hadn't been sitting on her front porch when she'd arrived home. *Home.* There, she'd used that word again. Her eyes wandered from Jim's anxious face to the corners of the kitchen. Its familiarity was unexpectedly comfortable.

"Roslyn?" He stopped pacing to peer down at her. "Are you with me here?"

"Yes, yes. But, Jim, please, don't tell me any more. It's not appropriate. The inquiry. What if—?"

"I still think of you as a friend, Roslyn. You and Judy."

That got her attention. "What happened to Judy? Why did she quit? Why didn't she call me?"

"Judy didn't quit. Not really. Saunders gave her the choice of quitting and taking a severance package or being investigated along with me." He pulled out a chair and slumped into it. "You know Judy's financial situation. Her husband's been out of work for two months. She didn't have any choice."

Roslyn shook her head in disbelief. "I didn't know her husband wasn't working. Why didn't she tell me?"

"I don't know. Probably you were busy. Maybe she just didn't get around to it."

Roslyn thought back to the daily routine at work. She saw herself breezing into the office early every day. Always friendly, she knew, but preoccupied. The picture wasn't very flattering. Obviously, Judy hadn't mentioned her own problems because Roslyn never took the time for personal talk. Their chatter always centered on business, broken occasionally by a laugh over some office gossip.

The recollection depressed her. "What's Judy doing now?"

He shrugged. "I don't know. She won't return my calls. The thing is, Judy tried to help me. She believed me when I told her someone was setting me up."

Roslyn raised her head to confront him. "How could someone set you up, Jim? We all have our own passwords. No one could access those accounts without your knowledge."

"But someone did."

"Bruce is the only one with the passwords. And he's—"

They stared at one another, the rest of the sentence already known. Bruce McIntyre, the senior partner, had been in a nursing home since his stroke a year ago.

"Out of the picture," Jim finally said. "The thing is, the amounts moved aren't large. I checked my other accounts and in every case that involved discretionary accounts, money has been transferred to this new fund."

"What is the fund?"

"People seem to know something about it, but not enough to give me any hard information. Tony said a couple of his clients have invested in it, too."

"So it must be legit or Tony wouldn't be using it."

"Yeah, but everyone is really vague about it."

"How so?"

"They know about it because it appears in their

files. But when I ask for specific details, they can't give me any. It's as if the fund got started by word of mouth. Like one of those old pyramid schemes. Everyone has a fuzzy idea how it works but no one knows who's really running it.''

Roslyn considered what Jim said. None of it really made sense. No matter how objective she tried to be, she kept ending up at the same place. The password. "Jim, I have to get some sleep. You take the couch and we'll talk some more tomorrow. Okay?"

"You don't believe me, do you?"

"I—I want to believe you, Jim. But I don't understand how anyone can get at your files. And why would someone use *your* files? Why wouldn't they just skim from their own clients? We all know how it could be done."

"To frame me! Dammit, Roslyn. That's what I've been trying to tell you."

He stood up, his slight frame stiff with anger. There was a fierceness in his eyes she'd never seen before.

"Jim—please." She held up a palm, trying to calm him. "Tomorrow. Okay?"

He turned away. "Sure," he mumbled. "I'm sorry. You're still recovering from the accident. Thanks for the loan of your couch."

"Jim—my mind will work better after a night's sleep. Don't worry—we'll sort everything out."

He didn't answer. She waited a few seconds and then headed upstairs. In spite of her exhaustion, Roslyn didn't sleep well. She couldn't get Jim's face out of her mind and his hurt voice thundered in her ears all night long, shutting out even the memory of Jack's lips on hers.

WHEN SHE AWOKE, Roslyn resolved to have Jim go over the whole story again. She wanted to believe him. But when she negotiated the last few stairs and called his name, there was no answer. He was gone.

She paced around the living room, as if expecting him to pop out from behind a chair. The afghan lay in a bundle on the floor next to the sofa. Roslyn wondered if he'd even attempted to sleep, or whether he'd left as soon as she'd headed upstairs. She opened the curtains. The driveway was empty. She stood a long moment, staring blankly out the bay window. Tears pricked at her eyes. She knew why Jim had left. He'd given up trying to convince her. She'd shown little sympathy when he'd come to talk. Perhaps she'd done the same to Judy, which would explain why Judy had avoided her. Both Roslyn's colleagues sensed that Roslyn wouldn't—or couldn't—provide the support or advice they needed.

She turned from the window, catching as she did a glimpse of the Iowa rose. More leaf buds had appeared overnight, stringing the stalky canes. A surge of resentment for the rosebush took hold of her. If she hadn't come to Plainsville....

Roslyn sighed. *Too late for all of that. Besides, who are you kidding? Would you have been any more open to Jim if you'd stayed at the office?* She reached for Ida Mae's armchair and sat down. Plonked her feet on the needlepoint ottoman and craned her neck to take one more look out the window at the rose.

How had Ida Mae filled the time, she wondered? There weren't enough books in the house to suggest she'd been an avid reader. The few needlepoint pieces might have been made by her aunt. Even so, after her stroke, she wouldn't have been able to work on them.

Roslyn drummed her fingertips on the table at her side. She rested her head against the back of the chair and closed her eyes, piecing together the scene from last night. Before Jim. Before driving down the long, dark road away from the farm. She imagined Jack's hands on her. Stroking and caressing. Awakening parts of her she'd shut down years ago.

She felt the eagerness of his desire all over again and shivered. Her mind hadn't been in control at all last night, but every nerve in her body had craved his touch. Wanting more. And, at the same time, wanting to give herself. That was how Jack's kiss had been so different from all of the other kisses she'd exchanged with various dates over the years. She'd always been content to stay on the receiving end.

Roslyn forced herself upright in the chair. Reliving the kiss was only going to make the day more difficult. She picked up the telephone receiver and set it back down. She didn't know Jack's number and she couldn't call Jim. Besides, he might not be back in Chicago yet. She fiddled with the knickknacks on the table, noticing them for the first time.

Roslyn knew little about porcelain or glassware or any of the objects that littered her aunt's house, but she did know that her grandmother owned an identical amber glass dish. She picked it up, turning it around in her hands. It was actually a widemouthed goblet, topped by a small lid with a gracefully rounded knob. She took the lid off to find a ball of cotton wrapped around a small tarnished key. Roslyn held the key in her palm until she remembered the wooden box in Ida Mae's bedroom closet.

ROSLYN TOOK THE BOX into her own room. Well, her grandmother's childhood room. The sun had finally broken through the cloud layer and the room was cheery and bright. Roslyn sprawled on the bed. The lock was tight but patient wriggling of the key back and forth finally opened the box. It was lined with a deep burgundy velvet and filled with hard-covered leather-bound books. Roslyn picked one up and carefully opened it. The sweeping curves of handwriting inside the flyleaf announced that the journal was the property of Ida Mae Petersen. The year—1930. Roslyn began to read.

Henry Jensen has just brought me a beautiful hand-carved wooden jewel box for a wedding present. He blushed when he gave it to me and stammered out his best wishes. I thought it strange that he chose to present it to me almost a month before the wedding. And he seemed to intend it for me, rather than as a gift for the both of us. But when I mentioned it to June, she laughed and said, hadn't I ever noticed that Henry had a crush on me? Of course, that made me feel sad rather than comforted. I went to bed wondering why I hadn't noticed.

Roslyn set the journal down in her lap. Reading the journal was like invading her aunt's thoughts. On the other hand, she reasoned, it was her only tangible link to the past and just might reveal what had happened in the Petersen family. She sat up, rearranged the pillows behind her back and checked the time. Almost eleven and Jack still hadn't phoned. Maybe the store opened on Sunday, she thought. Or maybe he simply didn't want to talk to her.

Roslyn took a deep breath. Right now, she had more important things on her mind. She read the first entry again. So, Aunt Ida had been engaged to be married once. Who was the lucky guy? she wondered, as she turned the page. And why hadn't there been a wedding?

June 1, 1930

Today Papa was angry with me. He said I didn't need to invite quite so many people. But I've dreamed about this wedding for years. Even before I fell in love! Perhaps I am being selfish. I asked June if she thought I should cut back on the numbers and she was snappy with me, too. The only one who's cheerful is Mama and of course, she's in her element. A big wedding is what she's always wanted to plan, it seems. The buds on the rose are getting bigger every day. I know they'll be in full bloom by the fifteenth.

Roslyn thought Ida Mae sounded like someone accustomed to getting her way. Remind you of anyone? she asked herself.

She tossed the journal onto the bed and left the room. The phone call to Jim couldn't be postponed any longer.

He wasn't home. The answering service came on, and Roslyn left her message. "Jim, I'm sorry about last night. Please call."

She sat by the phone longer, toying with the idea of calling Jack. Surely even Plainsville would have an information directory. She touched the receiver once more, her hand hovering over it. No, she decided and headed into the kitchen to make a sandwich, relieved that common sense had stopped her from making a fool of herself. She took her lunch upstairs with her, eager to read more of the past.

June 6, 1930

Nine days to go! The arrangements proceed nicely, thanks to Mama's diligence—and Papa's check! Papa has shown me his wedding gift to Richard and me. Bearer bonds he purchased on our engagement a year ago. He assured June that when she marries, she'll receive the same. I must say, he was very generous!!

June is very quiet these days. Mama says it's because we've always been together—just the two of us since poor Rolfie died—and that June really can't bear the thought of my leaving. But somehow I think there's more to it than that. She's so much more serious than I am! Especially these last few months. Since my engagement, really. Richard says I'm imagining things. One more week. I can hardly wait.

Roslyn put the journal down and reached for the second half of her sandwich. She craned her neck to check the time again. Past noon. Still no phone calls. It was going to be a long day.

She swung her legs off the bed, noticing there was no stab of pain when she put weight on her foot. *I'm on the mend,* she thought. No more reason to linger in Plainsville. She thought back to the other night and knew that leaving Plainsville a second time was going to be more difficult. Unless Jack didn't call back.

She rubbed her eyes and moved about the bedroom, unkinking the knots. Pausing in front of one of the vanities, she picked up the photograph she'd propped there. The twins, aged five. Long before life or love separated them. Maybe even before Rolfe died. She imagined they'd been more pampered and protected after his death. Roslyn sighed and replaced the photograph. Another journal entry beckoned.

June 8, 1930

Mama's in a tizz because the caterer's charging so much money for the strawberries. Papa's complaining loudly as usual. The only quiet one is June. Yesterday I found her sitting on her bed in our room just staring into space. I tried to talk to her, but she brushed me off. That night she slipped out of the house after Papa had locked up. I never heard her leave or come in, so thank goodness I didn't have to lie when Papa asked me what time June got home. She's as closed as a clam these days. Nothing seems to cheer her up. And positively nothing about the wedding. Perhaps she is jealous, after all. Anyway, in one week's time I'll be Mrs. Richard Dutton. What more could I want?

Roslyn dropped the journal. *Mrs. Richard Dutton?* She picked it up, fumbling to locate the page. She hadn't misread it. Surely Ida Mae wasn't going to marry someone with the same name as Grandpa? Roslyn shook her head. *No, you dolt. She was going to marry your grandfather.*

June 9, 1930

Had the last fitting for my wedding dress today. June looks gorgeous in her gown, too. She and Rachel are my only attendants as Mama and I thought big bridal parties too extravagant these days. I bought them each a lovely pressed glass candy dish in a rich amber color. I was so excited, I showed June hers before I wrapped it and we had a giggle together. The first bit of laughter we've shared in many weeks. The moment affected both of us, for we soon had tears in our eyes. Then June said a very odd thing. She said, "I just want you to know, I will always love you. No matter what happens." I suppose it was her way of telling me that marriage wouldn't separate us. I hugged her tight and reassured her that Richard and I would always welcome her in our home. She turned away then and abruptly left the room. I guess the emotion of it all was just too much.

I guess so! Roslyn leaned her head back onto the wooden bed frame. Knowing what she was going to do, June Rose must have been feeling just a touch guilty. It was impossible to imagine June—her grand-mother—running off with her sister's fiancé. But that's exactly what must have happened, Roslyn thought. She closed her eyes to conjure up a memory of her grandparents. Ordinary people. One quiet but tender; the other, solemn and stern. Not the type of people to cheat or deceive others.

She opened the journal again, almost afraid to keep reading. Could her family history get any worse?

June 10, 1930

The impossible has happened. June has dis-appeared! She hasn't been home since after din-ner last night. Mama and Papa are beside them-selves with worry. The police have been called, but they say that, considering June's age, they need to wait twenty-four hours before they post her as missing. I can't believe such ridiculous bureaucracy. Of course she's missing. We know that already. She's never stayed out all night be-fore. But the sheriff says there's always a first time and maybe she ran off with a young man. Papa almost burst a blood vessel when he said that. She hasn't even had a boyfriend since the year before high school graduation. If she's done something silly, I'll never forgive her. What nerve to jeopardize my wedding. I called Richard to tell him but his landlady said he hasn't returned from Chicago yet. He promised he'd finish his visit with his aunt and uncle to be back for the Andersens' dinner party tonight. I'm sure Mama and Papa won't be going now. I don't want to go alone, but will have to. It's in our honor, after all. But I don't want to be peevish toward Richard just five days before our marriage, so no matter when he arrives, I vow to bite my tongue.

Well, I can guess why Richard hasn't returned from Chicago! Roslyn reflected. How could the grandfather she remembered do something so sleazy? Her stomach was beginning to churn. She took a deep breath. When was Ida Mae going to figure it all out?

June 11, 1930

My life is over. An hour ago, we got a telegram from Chicago. June has eloped with Richard. I fainted when Papa read it. I've been in my room for hours. There are no more tears left inside me now. I can hardly write this because my eyes are so swollen I can't see the page. I've heard nothing from Richard. How could he do this? Be so cruel? I don't think I can ever get over the hurt.

Roslyn flipped the page. Whatever Ida had written there, she'd ripped it out, leaving behind only a zigzag margin. The next entry was dated more than a week later.

June 18, 1930

Hard to believe so much can happen in a
week. Papa hasn't spoken to anyone. Mama is
still weeping in her room. Poor Rachel has been
on the telephone all morning. I wouldn't let her
pay for her gown—it was hardly her fault the
wedding didn't go through. Then she had a peculiar look in her face and finally she confessed
that June had hinted months ago that she was in
love with Richard. Said she'd had a crush on him
from the start. Rachel insisted she never dreamed
the crush was so serious or she'd have done
something. What? Made them not love each
other?

Anyway, what does any of it matter now? Tonight I took a walk around the garden. It's a
perfect June evening. The rose is in full bloom
as Mama said it would be. What does that matter
now, too? I don't know who to hate more. My
sister or Richard.

There were only two more entries in the journal.

June 25, 1930

Today we would be returning from our honeymoon in New York City. So much for plans.
So much for dreams. Instead, we received a
newspaper clipping announcing the marriage of
June Rose and Richard Dutton. They wed at city
hall in Chicago. No picture. No Iowa rose, either.
There was a note for me inside the envelope. I

read it in the privacy of our room. My room,
now I suppose. June said she'd never forgive
herself. That she couldn't get over her feelings
for Richard and that once he'd proclaimed his
love for her, they planned to elope.

I want to know when he knew he was in love
with her. And how? What did she say or do that
was so different from me? I'll never know, because I plan never to have anything to do with
either of them again. That was the vow I made
to myself the night we found out. And I'm determined never to break it.

But at some point in time, Roslyn thought, Ida softened. Too late for June. Too late for the niece she
never knew—my mother. Even too late for me. Then,
when meeting was impossible, she changed her will
to bring me to Plainsville. Why, when it was so obviously too late to bring the family together? Unless,
she mused, Ida Mae had other reasons. She opened
the journal to the last page.

June 30, 1930

The roses are just finishing. I picked a bouquet
for the parlor, but Mama asked me to take them
away. She said their perfume gave her a headache but I think it was the reminder of the so-
ciety wedding that was never to be. And I suspect she knows I shall never marry now. How
could I trust another man? The only male friend
I have is Henry Jensen and he's been wonderful.
Sometimes I think he'd have me if I said the

word. But I've vowed not to.

Papa isn't looking so well these days. The bank might have to close. He's been borrowing from everywhere, but can't cover all the debts. I know I could help out by just confessing something. But it's too late for that now. June and Richard deserve to be cut off from all of us here in Plainsville. They showed no mercy or sympathy to me or Mama and Papa. Why should they get any from me?

Confessing something? Roslyn frowned. What could Ida Mae have meant by that cryptic remark? Pushing the journal aside, Roslyn lay back against the pillows and stretched. She was exhausted. And no wonder. It wasn't every day you learned that your own grandparents betrayed their family. She thought of all the years that she and her mother had lived with Richard and June.

What dreams had been fulfilled by that elopement? Her grandfather worked his whole life as a butcher, and her grandmother took in sewing jobs. They'd had one child, whom they adored. They'd taken Roslyn and her mother in on a moment's notice during the divorce and fed and sheltered them both for almost five years. But life had been a bit of a struggle for all of them, Roslyn thought. From the little she'd learned about Ida Mae's life in Plainsville, it had been a hundred times more luxurious.

She set the journal on the floor. It was after three, and Jack hadn't called. She pulled the quilt up around her and lay down to have a nap. She'd call Jim again when she woke up. And maybe—if she was feeling brave enough—she'd call Jack, too. The memory of Ida Mae's vow never to forgive had struck a chord.

IT WAS DARK. Roslyn sat up from a strange dream, moistening dry lips and shivering. She reached out to click on the bedside lamp. Ten o'clock. Not in the morning, she told herself, but at night. She pushed the quilt away, thinking that she hadn't slept through a meal since she was a kid, sick in bed. *And now that you've just had a solid seven hours' sleep, what the heck are you going to do until it's morning?* Roslyn eyed the wooden box on the bureau. No. There'd been enough revelations for one day.

She climbed out of bed, refreshed herself in the bathroom and headed downstairs to heat up one of Sophie's casseroles. While the oven preheated, she walked around the ground floor, turning on all the lights. She opened the big front door and stepped out onto the porch. The night was balmy, so she decided to eat outdoors.

Tray in hand, she set up the wicker table and sat in Ida Mae's rocker to enjoy her dinner. How many times had Ida Mae done just this? And by herself? Roslyn shied away from the image. It was too easy to insert herself into that picture.

She finished her meal and enjoyed the tranquility of a spring evening in Plainsville. Roslyn knew she'd never find such a perfect starry night back in Chicago. In fact, she sighed, there would be many things she wouldn't find back in the Windy City. Jack's face floated across her mind. She shivered. Which would be worse, she wondered? Alone and unloved here in Plainsville or in Chicago?

CHAPTER ELEVEN

JACK DRUMMED his fingers on the armrest of the
cruiser. He didn't know why Mac had to drive so
slowly at this time of night. The streets were deserted,
for God's sake. On the other hand, he didn't exactly
want to rush over to Roslyn's house with the news.
He glanced at Mac, his profile outlined by the glow
of the traffic light.

"Do you have to stop when there's no one
around?" he asked.

"Does a tree falling in the woods make a noise if
there's no one to hear it?"

"What kind of answer is that?"

"You get my drift, buddy. S'pose a car wings out
of nowhere and plows into us. Everyone points the
finger at everyone else, but I'd be the one that went
through the red light."

"This is Plainsville on Sunday night for crying out
loud. It's after midnight. Geez." Jack set his elbow
on the opened window.

"Look, I know you're concerned about Roslyn
Baines. Thing is…" He paused to take a quick look
at Jack. "Do you know the nature of her relationship
with this Naismith guy?"

"What's that supposed to mean?"

Mac rubbed the side of his nose with his forefinger. "Just wondering is all," he said. "Calm down. I told you the Chicago cops picked up a message from her on Naismith's answering machine."

"And?" Jack blew out a mouthful of sour air. Did he really want to hear all of this? Why didn't he simply get Mac to drop him at the next corner and suggest he take Sophie instead? The housekeeper would probably be a heck of a lot more comforting to Roslyn right now than he would be. Especially after last night. Especially after what Mac was hinting at. The guy could sniff out gossip like a pig after truffles.

Mac tapped lightly on the brake pedal and turned his way again. "Look, I gotta tell you, since you're a buddy of mine and all."

"Geez, Mac, spit it out."

"Okay. So Miss Baines left a message asking Naismith to call her back. Then—"

"Mac!"

"Well, then she said she was sorry about last night."

"Oh." Jack couldn't think of a response. He wasn't sure what the comment meant. Wasn't sure he wanted to *know* what it meant. He looked away and mumbled, "So?"

"Sounds to me like they might have had a quarrel or something. Maybe a…you know…a lover's tiff."

Jack was grateful for the dark interior of the cruiser. Humiliation rushed into his face, pounded at his temples and bellowed in his ears. Storming the nice little barricade he'd erected around himself since his disappointment last night. The wall of not caring,

he called it. He'd be naive to think that even a workaholic like Roslyn wouldn't have had a love life. He
just didn't want to ponder it with Mac sitting beside
him.

"Well, what do you think?"

Jack sputtered impatiently. "Who knows, Mac?
She told me he was a friend from work. End of information."

Mac gave the cruiser some gas and turned onto the
Goshen Road. Roslyn's house was less than a minute
away and Jack started to sweat. Now was his last
chance to get out and let Sophie be the support team.
But he couldn't talk. He kept repeating Mac's words.
Or rather, Roslyn's. *Sorry about last night.* That could
mean anything.

Sorry I said no and slammed the door in your face?
Sorry I was preoccupied, having just enjoyed a first
kiss with my new friend, Jack? Sorry I wasn't very
responsive when we made love because I had other
things on my mind? Like, my first kiss with Jack.

Jack's stomach churned. There was no point in trying to second-guess what Roslyn had meant. The one
thing Jack was positive about, was that she'd enjoyed
that kiss. Then they'd pulled into her driveway and
this Jim Naismith appeared out of nowhere like a bad
dream.

The cruiser's headlights swept across Ida Mae's
front lawn, catching Roslyn as the beam settled on
the veranda. Jack blinked. She was sitting in Ida
Mae's rocker.

"There she is," Mac was saying. "You coming?"
He'd already opened his door.

Jack took a breath. "Yup," and got out his side.

She stood up as they approached. Jack dropped behind Mac, staying on a lower step.

"Miss Baines." Mac's big voice boomed in the still spring evening. "How ya doing?"

Her face was pale. "Fine, thank you," she said.

Mac moved up onto the veranda, leaned against the stone balustrade and removed his hat. "Miss Baines, I understand you're a friend of Jim Naismith."

She looked over Mac's shoulder at Jack before answering. "Yes, he works with me. In Chicago. Why?"

"I'm sorry to have to tell you that Mr. Naismith was killed early this evening in an accident just outside of O'Hare Airport."

Roslyn swayed, shock reshaping her face. Jack was on the veranda now, helping Mac lead her back to the rocker. When he stood behind her, she tilted her head slightly, leaning against him. "Oh, God," she whispered.

Jack crouched at her side, wrapping an arm across her shoulders. She seemed to shrink into him. Finally, when she'd caught her breath, she asked, "What happened?"

"Far as we know, his car left the road and went over an embankment. It happened just past an off-ramp of the expressway from the airport."

"He must have been on his way home," she murmured.

Mac waited a moment, then said, "The police went to his apartment to inquire about next of kin. The super let them in. Guess they noticed a message on his answering machine and that's how they got your name. Did some checking and traced the call here. As a courtesy, they phoned me to ask me to break the news to you. I brought Jack along, in case you needed a friend.''

Jack felt Roslyn craning to look at him when Mac mentioned the message. But he avoided her glance, afraid of what he might see in her eyes. Afraid that Mac might be right after all, with his hints about Roslyn and Naismith.

''Do they know what caused the accident?'' Her voice quavered.

''Not yet. At least, they haven't advised me. I think they were hoping you might know if—''

''If?''

Mac let the word hover in the silence a bit longer before finishing his sentence. ''If you'd know the next of kin. Or, if you'd be taking charge of the arrangements.''

''Why would I do that?''

''Well, if you and Mr. Naismith…you know…had a special relationship.''

Roslyn slipped out of the chair, letting it swing back against Jack's shoulder. She wrapped her arms about her, standing in the center of the veranda, facing the two of them. Jack had to restrain himself from reaching out to her. He thought he could hear her teeth chattering.

''Jim and I dated for a few weeks,'' she said, the words jerked from her lips in tiny breathless spurts. ''That was the extent of…of our relationship.'' The last word was spat out.

"Miss Baines," Mac said, softening his voice, "if you can let me know who the Chicago police can contact about Mr. Naismith, I'll give them a buzz right away. As I was saying, because they picked up your message, they just made an assumption about you and Mr. Naismith. It's not a big deal."

"I—I know that he had a cousin in Chicago. Same last name. I...can't remember the first name. Someone at the office will know." She passed a hand across her face. "I can't believe he's dead."

"Roslyn, sit down. Please." Jack spoke for the first time, stepping forward to coax her back to the chair.

"I just can't believe it," she kept saying, while she rocked back and forth, clutching her arms about her.

"Can I get you something?" Jack asked. "Do you have any whiskey or brandy?"

She stared blankly. "I'm okay," she mumbled. "Just stunned. That's all. It's a shock. He...he was just here last night. He left before I even saw him this morning. I didn't even get a chance to say goodbye."

Jack clenched his jaw. He flushed and avoided Mac's eyes, knowing his friend would have some expression of interest in his face.

Finally Mac said, "Okay, then. Guess I'd better call Chicago and let them know there's a cousin around." He picked up his hat. "You coming, Jack, or staying?"

Jack looked at Roslyn's bent head and hunched shoulders. "I'll stay."

"Right, then." Mac started down the veranda stairs, then paused midstep. "By the way, Miss Baines..."

She glanced up.

"The police in Chicago asked me to find out some-thing else. They, uh, they wanted to know why Mr. Naismith was here to see you."

Roslyn stared vacantly at him a long moment be-fore whispering, "I—I really can't say. It didn't have anything to do with the accident. It was personal."

Mac caught Jack's eye, raising both eyebrows at him as he said, "Right, then. Talk to you later." Then he left.

After the cruiser pulled out of the drive, Roslyn finally looked at Jack. "Thank you for coming."

He could only shrug. He wanted to wrap his arms around her, but Jim Naismith's presence filled the air, holding him back. He couldn't get that blasted phone message out of his head.

"I do have some whiskey," she continued. "A couple of airline bottles." Then, in a hesitant voice she added, "Will you come in?"

"Sure," he said.

"THAT'S PRETTY MUCH IT," Roslyn said, finishing up her explanation of Jim's visit the night before. She stared across the kitchen table at Jack, willing him to look her way, but he kept his gaze fixed on his empty coffee mug. He'd been kind and considerate for sev-eral hours, but remote. Not that she blamed him his detachment. Playing back the events of the past two nights, Roslyn figured Jack had probably jumped to a number of logical conclusions.

Eventually he raised his head, sighing loudly as he

did. "So, in spite of what Naismith told you, the facts still point in his direction."

"Unfortunately. All of us have our own passwords, which even Ed Saunders doesn't have access to."

"Except for?"

"Bruce McIntyre, the senior partner. The thing is, Bruce had a stroke more than a year ago and has been in a chronic care hospital."

"Well, he must have stored the passwords somewhere. What happened to them when he had his stroke? Surely someone would need to have access."

"They're kept in a safe in his home where his wife still lives. We never removed them because everyone at the firm felt that, unless the need arose, they should stay where they were. I guess no one wanted to take them while Bruce was still alive."

"You mean everyone's going around acting as though he'll be coming back to work?"

Roslyn rubbed at her eyes. She was exhausted. It was well after two already. "I know it sounds crazy, but things are always hectic at the firm. The storage of the passwords never came up as an issue. We didn't even think about them until—"

"Until money went missing from Naismith's accounts."

"Right."

"And it seems reasonable to assume that Naismith—like the other employees—did not have access to anyone else's password."

"Yeeesss," she slowly agreed, not sure where he was going with the question.

"And I suppose the audit team ensured that the passwords are still locked up in McIntyre's safe?"

"Ed told me that was the first place they checked. Mrs. McIntyre insisted that the keys have never left her possession."

Jack stared at her a long moment before he said, "Then I don't see how Naismith could have been framed. Unless he was careless about his password."

Roslyn dabbed at her eyes again with the soggy wad of tissue. "If only I'd taken the time to hear him out last night—"

Jack pushed his chair back and stood up. "Don't beat yourself up about it, Roslyn. Accidents happen. There's no connection between what he came here for and what happened to him. Just as you told Mac. Look, you need to get some sleep. Do you want some help getting upstairs?"

Roslyn shook her head. "No, I'm fine. But…could you stay?"

He didn't hesitate. "I was going to, anyway. The living room sofa and I are getting used to each other."

"The guest room is all made up. Jim used the sofa." Roslyn knew the tagged comment sounded lame, but she wanted to put to rest any speculation about her and Jim.

When he came around the table to her side, she took his hand and let him lead her upstairs. She had a sudden flashback to her childhood, being taken to bed by her mother, and felt comforted by the memory. At the second floor landing, she turned to him to say good-night, but didn't get the chance.

His hands came up to her hair, sweeping it back.

When he lowered his head to her, she was ready, raising her face to his. "Jack," she whispered as his mouth found hers. She closed her eyes, falling into the warm haven of lips and arms folding around her. She'd have been willing to stay right there, locked into his embrace all night, but he pulled away.

"Get some sleep," he ordered and turned toward the guest room.

Roslyn watched him close the door quietly behind him, sensing that one word from her would have him rushing out to the landing. But he was right, she thought. She needed sleep. Needed the dark and stillness to lose herself and her thoughts.

Except she couldn't. She kept replaying Jim's story, torturing herself with an endless game of what if. Sometime in the early hours, Roslyn confronted her guilt. If only she'd paid more attention to what Jim was saying, if only she hadn't been too distracted by Jack's leaving, maybe Jim would still be alive.

Roslyn switched on her bedside lamp. There was no point in berating herself any further. Jack was right. Changing any part of last night wouldn't have prevented the accident. But she couldn't bear lying alone in the dark a second longer. She knew where she wanted to go. She crossed over to the door and opened it. A streak of moonlight ribboned the hall. She tiptoed across and reached out a hand to the guest room door, turned the knob and pushed lightly against the door.

"Jack?" Her whisper reverberated into the silence. Unnerved by the echo as well as her own boldness, she started to withdraw when Jack's voice, drowsy with sleep, replied, "Uhh? Roslyn?"

She stepped into the room. He hadn't closed the bedroom curtains and there was enough moonlight to find the side of the bed. She stood there, knowing that it was already too late to leave. "I can't sleep," she murmured. "I—I don't want to be alone. I can't stop thinking about Jim and how he might have stayed longer if I'd—"

"Come here." His arm emerged from rustling sheets, and she took his hand, sliding with it under the thin quilt. He pulled her against him. He was naked and only the thin cotton of her long T-shirt separated his skin from hers. She shivered.

"Cold?" he whispered against her hair.

"Not any more," she said, burrowing her face into the V of his neck and shoulder. So good to feel another person against her. Life flowing through her and him, his warmth and strength protection against the night. Against her thoughts.

"You're still shivering," he murmured.

"Your hands—"

"Should I move them?"

"Nooo."

"You sound unsure." He tugged his arm out from around her and propped himself up on his elbow, looking down at her. His eyes glimmered in the moonlight. "Because if you're going to stay, Roslyn, I can't guarantee that I'm going to be able to just lie here next to you."

"I don't want you to just lie beside me," she whispered. "I want you to make me feel alive." She clasped the back of his neck with her hands and gently lowered his head to hers.

It was a long kiss. When their lips finally broke apart, their hushed breathing filled the room. Roslyn was content to cradle into him, letting the rush of adrenaline ease.

"I've something to confess," Jack said in the silence.

She held her breath.

"Since my divorce a few years ago, I haven't really had a heck of a lot of practice at this."

Roslyn stifled a laugh, pressing her mouth against the smooth warmth of his chest. She lifted her head just enough to say, "And neither have I, I assure you."

"That's good. So we're both going to be on an equal footing here."

She ran a fingertip down the middle of his chest, stopping at the edge of the thick tufts of hair springing below his navel. He gasped.

"They say," he added, his voice huskier now, "that it's like riding a bicycle. You never forget." The last word pitched on a low moan as Roslyn's tongue probed gently on a nipple, then traced a narrow moist line downward. His hands reached out blindly, grabbing at her hair. "Here... Come here," he groaned as he tugged her up toward him. She lay on top of him, her shirt rucked up around her armpits. She felt him pulse against the damp heat between her legs. Wanting him consumed her.

"Slow down," he urged, his lips brushing across her forehead. He gently shifted her to the hollowed sag of mattress alongside him. "Let's make it last. Savor every moment of this night."

And he began with his fingertips, arousing nerve endings Roslyn never knew she had, graduating on to lips and tongue as time crept by, until she cried out his name over and over in the graying light of dawn. Spent, they lay spooned into one another. Jack's lips prowled across her shoulders and the knobby tip of her backbone.

"You were right," she murmured. "Like riding a bicycle. It all comes back."

"But, oh, so different," he said. Jack rested his head back onto the pillow and tucked her hair under his chin. "Everyone knows *how* to do it, but it's the *who* that makes the act pure pleasure."

"You definitely have a flair for words," Roslyn said. Then she sighed contentedly. "And for other things."

He laughed, rolling her to face him. "If it wasn't so late, I'd put that statement to the test."

Roslyn closed her eyes. Morning already. "I wish the night could go on forever."

Jack followed the curve of her eyebrows with his finger, slid it down the length of her nose and leaned over to kiss its tip. "So do I. But I suppose Sophie will be coming."

Roslyn moaned. "Oh, God! Sophie. I—I—"

He tapped her on the lips with his finger. "It's okay, I don't want to be here either when she arrives. I don't think I'm up to Sophie's raised eyebrows this early in the day."

A laugh burst from Roslyn's mouth. "Nor I. Is my T-shirt over there? Behind you?"

Without taking his eyes from her, he craned an arm around and tossed it to her. He watched while she sat up, the blanket falling away to expose her breasts.

"Titian would have wanted to paint you," he said in a hushed voice.

Roslyn stuck her head into the neck of the shirt and pulled it down. "I don't think I have enough curves for him, do I?" She grinned.

"Enough for me." He started to reach for her, but she swung her legs to the side and hopped out of bed. "I'll take the first shower and make the coffee while you have yours."

She hesitated in the doorway, unsure suddenly what to say. Or whether to say anything at all. She was content just to look at him a moment longer. The way his hair spiked out around his head from sleep—or lack of sleep, she amended to herself. The perfection of his body. The way he knew how to use it, in spite of his claims that he'd been out of practice. Roslyn shivered at the anticipation of future training sessions.

"Changing your mind?" he asked.

"Huh?" She felt her face flush. "Don't tempt me."

His grin was cocky and lopsided. He patted the mattress. "We still have ten minutes," he whispered.

She smiled and went to him.

OVER COFFEE AND microwaved muffins from the freezer, Roslyn told Jack about her discovery of Ida Mae's journals.

"No kidding," he commented. "I'd be interested

in reading them myself.'' His brow wrinkled. ''I vaguely recall seeing her sit in her armchair writing away at something.''

''There are at least eight or nine left in this beautiful wooden box.''

''I remember that box. She told me once my grandfather made it for her. What I can't believe is that your grandfather was once engaged to Ida Mae.''

''He was! The whole story's in the journal.''

''God, that must have really stirred up the family.''

''I think it explains why my grandmother never came back or why she basically blotted this side of the family from her life.''

''But why? Couldn't she have simply made up some story for your benefit? Besides, wouldn't her parents have gotten over it themselves, eventually? I know my folks would forgive us kids just about anything.'' He thought for a moment. ''Well, my Dad still grumbles about the time I drove his new Buick through the barn and out the other side.'' When her laughter subsided, he continued, ''Seriously, I can't understand why Ida's folks didn't visit you and your family in Chicago without Ida Mae.''

Roslyn shrugged. ''No idea. Feelings must have been pretty intense and from what I've read, Ida Mae became very embittered.''

''I have to admit, I don't recall that side of her. The Ida Mae I knew was generous and thoughtful. Always giving me a treat—when I was a kid—or slipping me a twenty-dollar bill when I was a teenager and used to mow her lawn. Later, when I came back to live in Plainsville and started my business, she co-signed a bank loan for me. Otherwise, I'd have had a heck of a time getting the money." He paused a moment. "I owe a lot to Ida Mae, including meeting you."

Roslyn held his gaze for a second longer before averting her own. Sipping coffee in Ida Mae's kitchen in the pink dawn of a May morning was far removed from last night's passion. A small voice inside reminded her that, in spite of that lovemaking, nothing much in the everyday world was likely to change.

Jack cleared his throat. "Guess I should move along, then." He got up to clear his dishes. Roslyn joined him in the doorway. She felt shy all of a sudden and said lightly, "I feel just like I did when I was in college. After...well, after the first time."

Jack placed his hands on her shoulders and drew her close. "I feel fantastic," he murmured, bending down to kiss her cheek. "I feel like coming over again tonight and—"

Roslyn placed a fingertip on his lips. "Shhh! I still have the whole day to get through."

"Okay, okay. But about tonight..."

"Dinner?" she suggested.

"Sounds great. At my place, okay?"

"A deal." Roslyn followed him to the front door. He hesitated before stepping out onto the veranda.

"You okay now? About this Jim Naismith and everything?"

"I'm okay. You?"

His grin set her pulse rate soaring. "Like I said— I feel like a million bucks. Tonight then?"

"Tonight." She closed the door behind him and leaned against it a long time, basking in the afterglow of Jack Jensen's incredible self.

CHAPTER TWELVE

SOPHIE WAS solicitous over Roslyn's story about Jim Naismith. They sat together at the kitchen table all morning, drinking coffee while Roslyn talked and Sophie listened. Roslyn also mentioned Ida Mae's journals.

"I ought to have remembered about that key!" Sophie exclaimed. "Your aunt had told me that Henry Jensen made that box for her, but never that it had been intended as a wedding gift. Who would've thought! So your grandmother never breathed a word about all of this?"

"How could she? Admit to eloping with her own sister's fiancé? That's not exactly a tale to reveal to your grandchild."

"True," Sophie agreed, "but surely your own mother would have known."

Roslyn thought for a moment, then shook her head. "I doubt it. You'd have to know my family, Sophie. Nobody talked about unpleasant things."

"Well, I can't say my own family has a better record of communicating," Sophie admitted.

"Are things okay with your sister and her kids?"

Sophie closed her eyes and sighed. Then she looked across the table at Roslyn and said, "My sister's youngest boy—Frankie—has been in trouble with the law all his life it seems. We went to Des Moines on Friday to talk to a judge and the lawyers. If I agree to put up the family for a few months till they get settled, Frankie will be released into his mother's care.''

"How old is he?"

"Seventeen. If he gets in trouble again, he'll be sent to the penitentiary. My sister is beside herself with worry about him."

"What have you decided?"

Sophie raised an eyebrow. "What can I do? Family is family. You got to stand by them. Right?"

Roslyn thought of Jack leaving Chicago to care for his father and the family farm. Then she thought of her own family—her father's attempt to mend the break at her mother's funeral. His card was still inside her wallet, untouched since he'd pressed it into her hand and urged her to visit him and his second family.

"You okay?" Sophie was frowning at her.

Roslyn shook herself. "Yes. Just thinking of my family."

Sophie gave an empathetic nod. "The Petersens do have a peculiar history all right. Now the Jensens— they seem to be the model family. Very close."

"Yes. Although if Henry Jensen was in love with Ida Mae, what about his own wife?"

"Mr. Henry and Miss Ida Mae were from a different generation. My guess is that after Henry married, he remained completely loyal to his wife."

"In spite of loving my aunt?"

"They enjoyed a wonderful friendship. Maybe

Mrs. Jensen was the kind of person who could accept that without feeling jealous.''

"If she was, she must have been pretty amazing. I doubt I could be so magnanimous.''

"You're far too hard on yourself,'' Sophie said.

Roslyn stared at the older woman for a long moment, realizing she'd never had such a long and open conversation with any member of her own family. "Thanks for the vote of confidence,'' she finally said. "You know, Sophie, if you ever need any financial help—''

Sophie waved a hand. "Your aunt helped me invest some of my money and thanks to that, I have a decent pension for myself. As to my sister and her family, I'll do what I can for them within reason. The rest will be up to them. Now—'' she pushed her chair back from the table and struggled to her feet "—time to get at some chores.''

As she picked up the empty coffee mugs and turned toward the sink, Roslyn said, "I hope you'll come to visit me in Chicago, Sophie. I'd love to show you around.''

Sophie smiled down at her. "That's very generous of you, Roslyn. But cities aren't for me. I can hardly tolerate Des Moines. Anyway,'' she gave Roslyn a coy look, "I'm hoping you'll be here in Plainsville. Where you belong.''

Roslyn stared at the woman's broad back as she bustled about the room. *Where you belong.* It had been a long time, she realized, since she'd felt as though she belonged anywhere.

ROSLYN SPENT MOST of the next hour on the telephone. Ed Saunders's secretary reiterated that Ed hadn't shown up at the office and yes, she'd have him call as soon as he did.

She called Judy again and left a message. Five minutes later, Judy called back. "You heard about Jim," she said without preamble.

"Yes." Roslyn hesitated.

"What did he tell you when he came to see you?"

"How did you know he was here?"

"He told me he was going to talk to you. I'd been trying to get him to do that for a month now."

"Judy, what's been going on?"

A loud sputter shot along the phone line. "About six weeks ago, I bumped into Jim after work one night in town. I'd stayed late because I was meeting my husband for dinner. I had some time to kill and Jim invited me for a drink. We chatted about this and that for a while until he started asking me questions about some accounts. Finally he let out that money was missing from one of his discretionary accounts, and he couldn't find any paperwork in his files to back up the transfer of funds. When I asked him if he'd reported it to Ed, he said he wanted to do some investigating on his own. I suggested he talk to you. Obviously, he didn't."

"Why didn't you say anything to me?"

"Because I promised him I wouldn't tell anyone. Then I thought maybe he *had* talked to you and that…well…things hadn't gone well."

"What do you mean?"

"I knew you'd been dating him. After he came

back from his cruise, I noticed that things were a bit cooler between you two. I'm afraid I assumed that he'd spoken to you about the funds, and you'd reported it to Ed.''

"What?" Roslyn was horrified.

"That's the way it looked. Suddenly you were leaving for Iowa and then, practically the next day, an audit team comes in.''

"But Ed essentially ordered me to come here," Roslyn protested. "Then I was in the car accident.''

Judy's voice softened. "I know. I—I'm sorry I didn't call, but things have been so crazy here. Are you all right now?''

Roslyn took a moment to change the receiver to her other ear, wiping her sweaty palm on her T-shirt. "Yes, I'm fine now. And heading back to Chicago as soon as possible to get to the bottom of this.''

"There's no point now. Everyone thinks Jim ran off the road on purpose. Gossip has it that Jim knew he was about to be charged.''

"The police said it was an accident.''

"On a perfectly clear night?''

"Maybe he was tired. He'd driven all the way from Plainsville to Des Moines for the flight back, and I don't think he got much sleep here.''

"Jim wasn't the kind of person to commit suicide. And he wasn't the kind of person to embezzle," Judy said.

"Of course he wasn't! That's why the gossip makes no sense.''

"Well, I'll admit that I'm not buying the accident

story. Especially with everything that's been going on here the last few weeks.''

Roslyn rubbed the throbbing pulse point at her temple. ''What else has been going on, Judy? Fill me in. Please!''

Judy did. Afterward, Roslyn sat in the chair by the phone, staring vacantly about the room. Judy's vehement denial of any relationship with Jim made her feel guilty that she hadn't sprung to Judy's defense after Ed's suggestion about the two. But what preoccupied her all the rest of the day was Judy's statement that she'd been pressed to quit after Ed and the head of the audit team had threatened to charge her as an accessory to fraud. ''All because I photocopied a few papers for Jim,'' she'd said flatly.

Roslyn sighed and forced herself out of the chair. Sophie had left lunch and departed. They'd decided that since Roslyn could now fend for herself, Sophie would only come in for the mornings. It was a warm day, going into the second week of May. Lunch on the veranda with another of Ida Mae's journals sounded like a great way to spend an afternoon until she had to get ready for dinner with Jack.

When she was settled in the wicker rocking chair, Roslyn reached for the last journal she'd read to make sure she was reading them in order. The final entry was dated June 30, 1930. Ida Mae had been talking about her father's financial problems. Roslyn read the page again, pausing at the cryptic statement about Ida Mae's guilty feelings. She wondered if her aunt had done something to get back at her fiancé and sister.

Other than cut them off from Plainsville for the rest of their lives.

Placing the journal at her feet, she retrieved another from the wooden box and checked the date inside the cover. July, 1930. She carefully spread apart the leather-bound jacket and sank back into the rocker.

Papa looks deathly ill. I know he's worried about the bank's losses. I felt terrible last month when he came to me, his face ashen, and revealed that June and Richard had stolen my wedding dowry. He said he'd kept the bearer bonds in a strongbox inside his desk in his bedroom. When he went to fetch them, he discovered the box had gone missing. He searched the house, but he knew all the while who'd taken them. Only June and I knew where he kept the key to his desk drawer.

The sight of his crumpled face almost made me break down. I would have eventually, but then June started calling from Chicago. Trying to get us to come visit—to talk and mend fences, she told Mama. I couldn't believe her gall. After Papa came to me about the bonds, he wanted to confront her, but I rushed to stop him. He said I was a saint, and I hardly slept at all that night. If only he knew!

Roslyn stopped reading to take another bite from her sandwich. The despair and bitterness of the journal contrasted so sharply with the spring day that she had to blink a few times to come back to the present.

Bearer bonds gone missing. She wondered how much money was involved. Her grandparents certainly hadn't lived like wealthy people, although perhaps they'd spent the money on their house. Stealing a fiancé was bad enough, she thought, but taking money from your own family…

Roslyn paused before she resumed reading. Did she really want to know more contemptible things about the members of her family? On the other hand, she was curious about Ida's comment—*If only he knew.* Knew what?

The next entry was dated August 17, 1930. More than a month after the previous one. Roslyn sipped her iced tea and began to read.

I had my chance to confess and now it's too late. Telling Papa that I had taken the bonds myself wouldn't have prevented the stroke. His death is my punishment, in part. After Papa's telephone call to June, disinheriting her and forbidding her to return to Plainsville as long as he and Mama lived, Papa's health deteriorated even more. June didn't dare show up for the funeral, although she called. Sometimes in the dead of night, I remember how Junie and I used to whisper stories to one another. And I cry.

Roslyn let the journal fall onto her lap. So, Ida Mae stole the bonds intended for her own wedding dowry and contrived to make her sister appear the guilty person. Why? Obviously for revenge. Roslyn sighed and took another sip of iced tea, fortifying herself for the next entry, dated September 20, 1930.

They say that bad things happen in threes. Mama's fatal heart attack two weeks ago has left me holding all of the Petersen shares in the bank—not that they're worth very much anymore. For a moment I thought of the bearer bonds, but even fifty thousand dollars is a drop in the bucket. Besides, I could never bear to touch that money. It's tainted for me now.

June called several times after she heard of Mama's death. I can only assume that she's kept contact with someone here in Plainsville. Probably with Rachel. When I first learned that Rachel—my own bridal attendant!—had known all along about June and Richard, I decided not to give her the pressed glass dish that I'd bought and instead kept it for myself. When June called, I hung up. I'm thinking of having the telephone number changed, but perhaps, eventually, June will simply give up.

So her grandmother had made several attempts to plea for forgiveness. Had Ida Mae's persistent refusals etched the first bitter lines in grandma's face? Roslyn set the journal down onto the wicker table and stared pensively at the Iowa rose.

Its leaves had thickened around the canes that arched now in abundant cascades from the soil. She could see that as it bushed out, the rose would become the focal point of the garden. The tulips along its border were dying off, their leaves and stalks yellowing and drooping onto the soil. Roslyn could imagine how pretty the garden might look once colorful annuals were planted between the rose and the other plants. Maybe she'd buy some before heading back to Chicago—just to give herself a visual memory of the garden for summer in the city.

She stood up, restless, pumped with energy that had no outlet. She walked to the edge of the sidewalk, turned and surveyed the house and land around it. Her house, she thought. Her domain. Oddly, there was a great deal of satisfaction in saying those words. Certainly what she was looking at was much more impressive than her one-bedroom condo in Chicago. Or the narrow row house of her grandparents.

Roslyn thought back to her first glimpse of the house, shrouded in curtains of driving rain. Dismal, dark and cold had been her early impressions. Even when she'd left—en route to an accident—the carved wood-and-plaster moldings and quaint furnishings meant no more to her than props in a museum exhibit. Someone else's possessions rooted in someone else's past.

Yet now, less than a month later, she was beginning to view the house and all of its nooks and crannies as hers. As familiar as an old pair of slippers. She knew the precise step that creaked on the staircase, the kitchen cupboard that wouldn't close properly and which faucet in the second floor bathroom had to be turned extra hard to prevent dripping.

The grandfather clock that had once spooked her now gave comfort in the dead of night when she couldn't sleep. The continuous tick had somehow become a reassuring symbol of things simply going on. Which is what she needed to know during those restless nights when she was tormented by unanswered questions.

All this is mine, she thought, *if I want it.* And for the first time since arriving in Plainsville, she savored the idea. After Jim's death and the intrigue surrounding it, the urge to return to her former life had begun to wane. She was beginning to see that leaving Plainsville meant more than giving up the house and property. It also meant giving up Sophie—and Jack. Especially Jack.

Roslyn couldn't help but smile at the memory of the person she once was. That defensive, cynical woman was mellowing, and Roslyn liked the metamorphosis. Then she frowned. Would Jack continue to care for her if she assumed ownership of Ida Mae's house? Or would his own interest in the property conflict with his feelings for her?

Don't race ahead of yourself, Baines. Letting her suspicions take control had always been a weakness of hers. She wasn't going to let it jeopardize her relationship with Jack.

She headed back to the veranda, pausing once more in front of the Iowa rose. To stay, or not to stay. For now, she'd take life a day at a time. She decided to call Randall Taylor to find out if he knew anything about the bearer bonds. Then she'd bathe and dress for her dinner date with Jack. And enjoy the night.

"SORRY, MISS BAINES, but Miss Petersen gave up her safety deposit box many years ago and as I told you before, the only cash assets remaining after burial costs come to about thirty thousand. To my knowledge, there are no bearer bonds. And if there were any, I hope Miss Petersen would have kept them in a secure place. Those things are a rare commodity these days. Getting hold of them would be like finding a blank check. You wouldn't want them to fall into the wrong hands, that's for sure.''

"They must be somewhere," Roslyn said.

"Maybe she cashed them in years ago."

"Perhaps…" Roslyn answered. But not likely, she was thinking. Taking the bonds had been an act of revenge, not greed. And Ida Mae had written that she would never touch the "tainted" bonds.

"Well now, on another note. I know you've made a full recovery from your accident, more or less. And thank you for keeping me informed, by the way. How're things going with the insurance compensation? Any problems there? Has the case been resolved yet?"

Roslyn sighed. It had been a while since she'd thought of the accident, although letters and phone calls had been fielded back and forth between Plainsville and Des Moines since her return from the hospital. "I just received a letter advising me that all of my hospital costs plus the compensation for the rental car were being processed."

"You haven't changed your mind about litigation? The settlement you claimed doesn't account for loss of income, personal inconvenience and so forth."

Roslyn smiled. No wonder there were so many

lawyer jokes going around. Even though Randall wasn't her personal lawyer, his hunting instincts were as sharp as eagle claws. "No, Mr. Taylor, I'm not going that route. The truck driver died as a result of his injuries. I think his family has suffered enough. And frankly, I've no need for more money than what it took to cover my expenses."

"A unique sentiment these days, Miss Baines. Now, what have you decided about the house?"

Roslyn took a deep breath. She'd known the topic was going to surface, but still was waffling. "There are some complications at work and I'm not going to be able to make a decision at the moment. Could I have more time?"

"Of course, my dear. Naturally, I'd like to get the business over and done with but the taxes are paid up until the end of the year. I understand you're taking on the current maintenance expenses yourself."

"Yes, I appreciate your offer to have them deducted from the estate, but I wouldn't feel right doing that unless I knew for certain—"

"You were going to claim it?"

"Exactly. Anyhow, thank you very much for your help and I promise to call you as soon as possible." Roslyn sat in her chair a few more minutes after hanging up, wondering where her aunt had stored the bonds. As Randall Taylor had said, they were as good as cash in the bank to the person who found them.

WHICH IS WHAT she explained to Jack later that evening. They were sitting outside on a small but artfully designed patio in the narrow strip of land behind

Jack's office-cum-apartment. The unit was attached to the rear of the garden center, but had its own entry from a lane that passed behind the store.

The days were already getting longer and in spite of the hour, the sun was just beginning to slip beneath the horizon. Jack's living quarters faced west and he'd suggested they have wine and appetizers and enjoy the sunset.

Jack stretched his legs out across the top of a wicker ottoman, a match for the hunter-green patio furniture. Roslyn took a moment to watch the last sliver of crimson disappear. Almost on cue, a string of Japanese paper lanterns twinkled on, their multi-colored reflections bouncing off the glass sliding door leading into Jack's kitchen.

Roslyn gasped.

"Just like magic," Jack quipped. "Actually, they're on a timer. Part of an experiment for a customer who wants me to redesign her backyard."

"They're pretty."

He pursed his lips. "Too cute for me. At least I know how to set it up for her." He reached for the wine bottle. "More?"

"Not yet, thanks. I should eat more first, otherwise I might make a fool of myself."

Jack's eyes fixed on hers. "Can't have that," he murmured. "At least, not before you've tried my shrimp linguine."

Roslyn forced her eyes away. She'd been prattling ever since they'd settled on the patio, fighting the urge to fling herself at him.

"Anyway, as I was saying," she cleared her throat

nervously, aware of the suggestive grin on his face, "Ida Mae took the bonds to ensure that the split between my grandmother and the family would be permanent."

"Sounds pretty malevolent. I can't believe she'd do something like that."

"I've been thinking the same thing, although I never knew my aunt. Perhaps she intended to confess, but after her father had his fatal stroke, how could she? It would be tantamount to claiming responsibility for everything."

"Hardly her fault. Strokes happen—no one can predict them. Look at my father and how well he's recovered from his."

"But then her mother died so soon afterward. So whom would she confess to? June Rose and Richard? She'd vowed never to speak to them again. I mean, how can you get together as a family after all of that?"

"Good point. Okay, finish that last piece of Brie while I add the shrimp to the sauce."

Roslyn watched him unfold from the chair and head into the kitchen. Looking at a man after you've made love with him provided a whole new perspective, she decided. Knowing what waited beneath the khaki trousers and cotton Polo shirt doubled her anticipation. But past experience reminded her that this relationship still had several obstacles ahead.

Am I ready for all this? she asked herself, taking in the tiny domestic scene. The perfect garden surrounding the patio. Candles flickering from the table set inside. Music pulsing softly from some unseen CD player. Jack standing at the kitchen sink as he strained the linguine, steam wafting around him.

Is this what you want? In exchange for hard-won professional success? She looked away, reaching for her glass to finish her wine. Then he was standing in the opened door, a tousle of hair slicked against his forehead and an eager grin on his flushed face.

"Ready?" he asked.

She was on her feet, her doubts falling away from her like scraps of paper buffeted by the wind.

THEY FINISHED the linguine sometime between midnight and daybreak. Standing at the counter—Jack in boxer shorts and Roslyn in a borrowed shirt—and laughing as they spiraled pasta onto their forks directly from the ceramic bowl Jack had carried so formally to the table hours ago.

"No kidding," Roslyn said, "it tastes just as good as it did the first time."

He shook his head. "Not the same. And wait till you see the dessert. I hope it's still okay."

"I thought we had dessert." She grinned.

He dabbed the fleck of pasta from the corner of her mouth and gently took the fork from her hand. Pulling her toward him, he murmured, "Maybe we did. Shall we see if *it* tastes as good the second time around?"

Roslyn pressed her face into the warm dampness of his chest, inhaling a faint hint of talcum powder and the musky scent of sex. She kissed the ridge defining his pectoral muscles and flicked her tongue against one dark-brown nipple. He shuddered and clutched her tighter.

"Ahh! If you keep doing that I'll—"

She leaned her head back to smile up at him. "Drag me back into the bedroom?"

"Something like that." He kissed the end of her nose.

Roslyn stroked the other side of his chest, rubbing his erect nipple gently between her fingertips. "I can't pull myself away," she whispered, "but it's almost dawn."

Jack groaned, burying his face into the thick mass of her hair that he clutched in his hands. Roslyn carefully extricated herself just as those hands began to stray below the nape of her neck.

"Can we put a closed sign on your shop door?" she asked.

His laugh was regretful. "This is one time I wish I didn't live behind the store."

Roslyn placed a hand on the counter to steady herself. "I guess that means I should get dressed."

"As it is, I'm sure some neighbor will see us drive up to your place in my van."

"With its logo in full glory."

"You said it. Not much goes unnoticed in Plainsville."

"Well, it's not all bad," she murmured, absently touching his forearm as he held on to her shoulder. "Beats the anonymity of big cities like Chicago."

"You wouldn't have said that a month ago."

She glanced up at him, surprised by his observation. "I suppose I wouldn't have, would I? But then, I'm not even the same person I was a month ago."

He stared thoughtfully down at her, as if assessing

the accuracy of her remark. "No, and you're even more beautiful than the first time I saw you, standing half-naked in Ida Mae's guest room."

"I was in my nightie!"

"I rest my case," he said, drawing her to him for a last kiss. When he finally released her, he whispered, "Some nightie."

Later, as he drove her through the quiet streets of Plainsville, Jack said, "We have some serious talking to do, Rosie my love. The store closes at five today and I'll be on your doorstep fifteen minutes later. Okay?"

Roslyn stared at him. "My father used to call me that," she said.

"Rosie?"

She nodded, her eyes still fixed on his.

"Do you mind?"

"No," she murmured. "I—I kind of like it."

He leaned across the gear shift to kiss her. "Sweet Rosie," he breathed against her mouth. "My sweet Iowa Rosie."

TOO ENERGIZED to consider sleep, Roslyn made a pot of coffee and sat in her own kitchen contemplating Jack's parting remark about a serious talk. It had to come, of course. She wished she could shake the dread building inside her, knowing she simply wasn't able to say to Jack—unequivocally—that yes, she'd make Aunt Ida's home her own and stay in Plainsville. Because there were too many other questions clamoring for attention at the same time. Like, does that mean you and I...?

Too many ifs were involved. Reluctant to deal with any of them, Roslyn decided to tackle some spring cleaning, a task so atypical of her that when Sophie caught her at it two hours later, she could only gape in amazement.

''Restless night?'' the housekeeper asked, which brought a deep flush to Roslyn's face.

She pushed more vigorously on the vacuum cleaner, shoving it beneath the living room sofa while Sophie observed with interest. The machine coughed and sputtered. When Roslyn pulled it out, she saw that something had caught in it. Something red. She let the handle drop and plucked a square of plastic from the bristled mouth of the cleaner.

It was a floppy computer disk, labeled J. Naismith.

CHAPTER THIRTEEN

"What's that?" Sophie leaned over Roslyn's shoulder.

"A floppy disk. For a computer," she continued at the question in Sophie's face.

"Yours?"

"No. It belonged to Jim Naismith."

"How do you suppose it got under the sofa?"

"Well, that's where Jim spent the night. Must've fallen out of a pocket or something."

"Or maybe he hid it there and forgot to tell you."

Roslyn turned to look at Sophie. "What a strange idea! What makes you think that?"

Sophie's large shoulders lifted. "Don't know. Most likely you're right, though, and it fell."

Roslyn tucked the disk into the breast pocket of her shirt. "I guess. Strange that he'd have brought it. Unless he planned to show me something on it and changed his mind." She thought back to that night and how disinterested she must have appeared to Jim. Maybe—like Judy—Jim had concluded that Roslyn sided with Ed.

"Something wrong?"

"Hmm? No, just wishing I'd seen this earlier—before Jim went back to Chicago."

Sophie bustled about, packing up the vacuum cleaner. "Well, no point fretting about it now. If it had been so important, he'd have remembered to take it with him."

Maybe. Unless, as Sophie suggested, he left it here on purpose to keep it safe and intended to tell me later—but didn't get the chance. The thought propelled Roslyn upstairs to her laptop. But as she'd expected, the password request came up on the screen. Roslyn stared at the screen a moment longer until she remembered Judy. Jim might have entrusted his password with her.

But the automated voice of an operator informed Roslyn that Judy's number had been changed to the unlisted directory. Roslyn held on to the receiver a moment longer, stunned by the information. She'd just been talking to Judy only yesterday. Why hadn't she mentioned she was getting an unlisted number? Unless the decision to do so happened very suddenly. But why?

Impulsively, and knowing she was making a pest of herself at work, she dialed Ed Saunders's office number.

"Yes, he just got in. I'll put you right through," informed his secretary.

Ed's voice boomed jauntily across the line. After enquiring about Roslyn's convalescence, he said, "I'm afraid I've got some bad news for you, my dear. It's about Jim Naismith."

"I know, Ed. The Plainsville sheriff came by Sunday night to tell me."

There was a brief silence. "How so?"

"Well, uh, Jim was here the night before and—"

"Good Lord! What was he doing *there?*"

"He came to see me about…about—"

"Not about the inquiry, I hope?" he interrupted again.

"Well, not exactly," she lied, wondering why she was feeling so defensive.

"Surely not a social call?"

"Uh…not exactly…"

"Roslyn my girl, what the hell is going on? Was he there to visit or to tell you something?"

"Does it matter?"

"Certainly does! To the investigation and to you. Come on, let's have it."

So Roslyn gave him an edited version of Jim's visit, implying that he'd come to proclaim his innocence.

Ed blustered. "I'm afraid he was trying to set you up, Roslyn. I told him that he should contact a lawyer because he was about to be charged."

"When?"

"Can't recall exactly. Maybe Friday."

"I—I thought you were in the Caribbean on Friday."

"Yes, yes. Before I left. Naismith was a fool. He ought to have heeded my advice."

Roslyn paused, reflecting how Ed was more concerned about making his point about Jim than expressing sympathy for his death. She realized suddenly Ed was talking again.

"I asked you if he referred to the inquiry directly."

"Huh? Sorry, Ed, I was thinking about something else. Not really. No. He was just very upset."

"And he came all the way to Plainsville to tell you that? He must have been on the edge, that's for sure."

"What do you mean?"

Ed lowered his voice. "Word here is that he went off the road purposely."

"That's ridiculous!"

"Well, these things happen. Unfortunately, he might have been thinking about what I'd said and realized his career was about to go up in flames."

Roslyn didn't want to speculate with Ed on the cause of Jim's death. "I tried to call Judy a few minutes ago but—"

"Her number's unlisted."

"You know already?"

"What do you mean, already?"

"Well, I just called her yesterday and she still had the same number."

There was a pause. "Personnel called her this morning and found that out." Then, in a sharper voice, he demanded, "Why did you call Judy?"

Roslyn felt herself being drawn into the old office gossip routine. Everyone wanting to know who was talking to whom and why. Suddenly she had no stomach for it, although it was a habit she'd indulged in herself many times.

"When I talked to your secretary last week, she mentioned that Judy had quit. I just called to find out how she was doing and so on."

"You know why she quit, don't you?"

"Uh...no, not really," she lied again, curious to hear Ed's version.

"Judy didn't tell you?"

Roslyn saw her lie swell. Too late to back out now, she thought. "No, I just got her answering machine."

A loud exhalation of breath filtered down the line. "I regret to say that my earlier warnings to you about Judy and her involvement with Naismith were right on, Roslyn. I caught her photocopying parts of my own files, and she admitted she'd been helping Naismith. When she broke down in my office, I felt sorry for her and gave her the choice of resigning or facing charges with Jim. Naturally, she took the former and was deeply grateful to me for it."

Roslyn closed her eyes.

"Are you still there?" he asked after a moment.

"Yes," she murmured. "Then I assume you don't have Judy's new number."

"Not yet and if she contacts you, let me know at once! I'll inform the investigating team."

"Isn't it over now that Jim's dead?"

From the change in his voice, the question must have startled him. "Well, more or less, I suppose. But there are still a few loose ends to tie up. For our own records."

"I see." It was all too depressing to discuss, Roslyn thought. Jim was dead and people were still gossiping about him.

"So, my dear, when will you be coming back to work?"

It was Roslyn's turn to be taken aback. "I—I'm

not sure, Ed. Would you mind terribly if I took another week?''

''Not at all. You know the new office is still on hold until all our financial problems are settled?''

''Yes. And I appreciate the extra time. Oh, and there's one more thing. I don't suppose you have any record of Jim's computer password, now that...well, now that his files have been taken over by someone else?''

''Of course. We got his password the day the inquiry kicked in and Jim was put on suspended duties. Why do you ask?''

''Well, he left a disk here by mistake and I thought I'd pop it into my laptop to see if it was important.''

''What kind of disk?''

''Nothing, Ed. It was probably in his jacket pocket and fell out by mistake.''

''If it's an office disk, then we'll need to pass it on to the police. Can you courier it to me right away?''

''If you give me the password, I'll see if—''

''I don't have the password here. It's in Personnel in his file. A lot easier just to send the disk back.''

''Sure, although if I'm coming back in a week I could bring it with me.''

''Since the inquiry is still on, send it as soon as possible. Okay?''

''Sure, Ed.'' After Roslyn hung up, she replayed the conversation again in her mind. Ed had been understandably upset about the disk and the inquiry. Maybe he suspected others at the office of being involved in the fraud, as well. She just hoped that the circle of suspicion didn't include her.

Wandering aimlessly down the hall, she spied Sophie making lunch in the kitchen. The door behind the main staircase and across from the kitchen led to the basement. A good place, Roslyn suddenly thought, to hide a metal strongbox.

Wafts of moldy air billowed out from the door when she opened it. She ran her hand across the wall until she found a light switch and cautiously descended. Standing at the foot of the stairs, she realized that Ida Mae had truly been a pack rat.

Roslyn wandered in and out of the various piles of things, checking for anything that resembled a metal box. But the magnitude of the collection overwhelmed her, and she knew she couldn't possibly search thoroughly unless she and someone else physically moved all of the stuff. An impossible job.

And for what? she asked herself. She'd be better off reading through the rest of the journals for a possible clue about where Ida Mae had hidden the bonds. Though it was unlikely Roslyn would accomplish that task in the week she had left. She headed back up the stairs, reaching the top just as Sophie appeared in the doorway.

"Goodness!" Sophie exclaimed, clutching a hand to her ample bosom. "I wondered why that door was open. What in heaven's name were you doing down there?"

"It's a long story," Roslyn began.

"Good. I'll hear it over lunch."

"I KNOW ONE THING," Sophie announced after Roslyn had finished her story. "I doubt those bonds would be hidden in the basement. Don't you think she'd want to check on them once in a while? See if they were all right? And I know that in the twenty-five years I worked for Miss Ida, she never once stepped foot in the basement. Didn't need to, seeing as how the laundry room was set up out on the back porch there."

"Maybe they're hidden upstairs somewhere."

"Where? I went through the whole house after she died. I had to sort through her bills and papers for Mr. Taylor, in case there were any outstanding accounts."

"You never looked in the wooden box that Henry Jensen gave her."

"At the time I didn't know where she'd put the key. Didn't find it myself till weeks after her death. Besides, did you find any bonds in the box?"

"No," Roslyn mumbled. She pushed aside her plate and downed the last dregs of iced tea. "Well, they have to be here somewhere. Maybe in the attic."

Sophie looked skeptical. "Maybe. But there again, Miss Ida never went up to the third floor."

"Why would she have to check on them? She wrote that they were stored in a metal strongbox. They'd be safe for years."

Sophie shrugged. "Just seems like something Miss Ida would've done, knowing her. She was always just a bit anxious about things. Never really trusting that things could be all right without her watching over them, so to speak."

Which sounded like someone Roslyn knew all too well.

"What time is your doctor's appointment this afternoon?"

"I completely forgot about that! I think two o'clock. Should I call a cab?"

"It's a beautiful spring day. Warming up nicely. I think you could walk to his office in fifteen minutes or so—it's right next to the hospital. Remember?"

"Yes, the nurse showed me when I was discharged. Actually, a walk around Plainsville is just what I need."

"I agree—check out the place before you buy your ticket back to Chicago."

Roslyn nodded, distracted by the comment. Decision time was looming closer than ever. "Guess I'll have to go back soon anyway," she laughed, "now that it's getting warmer. The few things I brought with me in late April have had their run, even with the use of Ida's washing machine. I'll have to go home just for a change of clothing."

"There are nice stores here in Plainsville," Sophie hinted.

Half an hour later, Roslyn was walking along the sidewalk into the center of town. Main Street bustled with midday traffic and shoppers. Jostled several times on the sidewalk, Roslyn almost felt as though she were back in Chicago. The comparison made her laugh. *I've been away from the big city too long if this seems hectic to me.* She turned off Main at Columbus and saw Saint Mary's hospital a couple of blocks ahead.

The sight resurrected memories of the accident and her stay there. The events of the weeks since had fortunately overshadowed that time. *Funny how I thought my stay in Plainsville would be boring.* But that was before she'd found the journals and learned about the rift in her family. Before Jim's death and the turmoil at the office. Before she'd gotten to know Jack.

No, she mused, walking up to the clinic across from the hospital, *my visit here hasn't been dull in the least.*

SHE MADE A detour on the way home, pausing in front of J.J.'s Landscaping and Garden Center. She was tempted to drop in to see Jack, but changed her mind. The parking lot was packed and he'd be busy. Another reason he wouldn't want to leave Plainsville. No, if she and Jack were going to stay together, she'd be the one giving up her home.

Sophie had already left for the day when Roslyn pushed open the screen door at the back porch. Leaving doors unlocked was another Plainsville custom she'd adopted. She poured herself a glass of iced tea and wandered through the cool, shaded rooms on the ground floor.

Restless, she climbed the stairs to retrieve the box of journals, stopping long enough for a superficial search of the closets for a metal box, and then took the journals into her bedroom. Lying across the bed, she found the place she'd left off yesterday, where Ida Mae had written about her mother's heart attack.

The next entry was dated December 18, 1930.

Interesting news via Henry this morning. He informed me that he'd heard through the town grapevine that June was pregnant. He urged me to forgive and forget. I told him he was a fool to think I was ready to do such a thing. Pregnant! Having the baby I always wanted. It isn't fair.

Roslyn closed the journal. It was depressing to read such bitterness, no matter how justified. She picked up the two remaining journals, leafing through them to find out how long Ida Mae had recorded her life story. The date of the last entry was four days after Roslyn's mother died.

A sad day today. All my family has gone now, except for a grand-niece I shall likely never see. I spent so many years thinking of June's daughter and saving the little notes she wrote. How I wish now I'd taken pen to paper and responded to just one of Lucille's notes. Too late. Can hate become a habit? If so, it's one I've excelled at.

All the people I could once call family are dead—except for Roslyn. A pretty name—I suppose a version of Rose, after June Rose. Or maybe a tribute to the Iowa rose, which June and Lucille never had a chance to enjoy. I've been doing some serious thinking lately. For years I thought I'd leave this place to young Jack. He's a dear sweet boy and I love him like my own. And I know how much he loves this house.

But I haven't had a good night's sleep since reading Lucille's obituary. What can I do to make amends to my family? Perhaps this Roslyn

would be untainted by the whole Petersen bad
blood and be willing to see this place. To grow
to love the rose and Plainsville as I do. Perhaps
then I can make up in a small way for the un-
happiness I let destroy my family.

And there the journal ended. Roslyn lay her head
down on the bed and thought about Ida Mae and June
Rose. Born on the same day with identical faces.
What different lives they'd led. Ida Mae's journal explained a lot of the silent inflexibility Roslyn had seen
in her grandmother. Yet her daughter had continued
the effort to mend the family. If only her mother had
spoken to her about the rift. Too late now for all of
them, Roslyn thought. *But maybe not for me.*

JACK OPENED a beer while Roslyn finished her account of Ida Mae's journal entry.

"Hard to believe someone as tiny as Ida Mae could
have so much hate in her. And to be honest, as I've
said before, you'd never know she was carrying such
a monster grudge."

"People can be deceiving," Roslyn murmured. She
reclined against the back of the wicker rocking chair.

They were sitting on the veranda enjoying the
breezes that were whisking away the day's heat. On
impulse, Jack had picked up containers of Chinese
food and a six-pack on the way over.

They'd reached the end of the meal without mentioning Roslyn's imminent departure. All day Jack
had been trying to come up with some counterargu-
ments. Once Lenny had caught him moving his lips

and had teased him about talking to himself. Now here he was, sitting beside her, the evening air carrying all the promises of summer, and he was scared. Scared of losing her.

"More noodles?" she asked suddenly.

He closed his eyes. "Couldn't take another forkful."

"Chopstickful."

"Speak for yourself. You're a lot more adept with them than I."

"Years of practice," she said and reached over to spear the last pot-sticker. "There's a great Thai place a few blocks from my condo. Every Friday night I indulged."

"I," he was thinking. Not "we." Focus on that. "Do you miss it?"

She turned to look at him. "The Thai restaurant?"

"That, and your condo. The whole Chicago scene."

"Well, I don't know what you mean by the word *scene*. You mean my life there? My job and the people I work with?"

He sat upright, letting the front legs of the chair thud onto the cement floor of the veranda. She had this knack of turning the most innocent comment or question into a Spanish Inquisition. "I guess I meant your whole life there, yeah."

"At times, of course. Other times, I realize I haven't thought about work for days. I—I suppose what I really miss is having a goal."

"A goal?"

"When I'm at work, I know what's going to happen every day, more or less. Within the structure of that framework—and trust me, in my job it's not as dull as I'm making it sound—there are incredible highs, lows and totally unpredictable events. That's what I like about the trading and investing field. Here—'' she waved a hand at the lawn in front of them—''in Plainsville, life seems to be always the same. And that's relaxing.'' Seeing him frown, she rushed to add, ''but I feel as though I'm drifting. Just bobbing along this great wide river, bumping into rocks or floating into shore and back out again. No purpose and no destination in sight.''

He let the air slowly squeeze out of him. Okay, buddy, time to get serious here, he told himself. But how and where to start? After a long moment, just when he thought she was about to get up and go inside for something, he blurted, ''Maybe you feel that way because things are still unresolved.''

She fixed her eyes on his, narrowing them as if to sharpen their focus. ''Unresolved?''

Damn, he thought. Wasn't there some kind of bad TV show about conversing in this manner? ''You know, making a decision about staying in Plainsville.''

She sank back into her chair, turning to gaze out to the lawn again. ''Ohhh,'' was all she said.

His mind raced, trying to interpret the emotion behind that drawn-out ''Oh.'' ''I—I just want you to know that, whatever you decide to do, I'll accept.''

Her head swivelled back to him, the sharpness in her eyes erupting into something else.

''You'll *accept* it?''

She was doing it again. Lobbing every question back at him. Confusion flowed through him. "Just that I guess I have a vested interest in your ultimate decision and I don't want to influence you one way or another. In case—" he turned away from her eyes, which were reproachful now "—one of us is sorry later."

She stood up then, setting her palms onto the cement surface of the balustrade and leaning over it. He watched her staring out across the garden and lawn. Stupidly, he reminded himself to pick up some annuals for her to plant around the edges. He forced his mind back to the conversation. If it could be called that, he thought.

"I hoped we could come to some kind of decision tonight about...about whether or not you'd be staying on."

"And keeping the house," she murmured, her back still to him.

"Of course."

"Anything else?" she asked.

Jack rubbed his forehead nervously. He had a sense of the ground giving way beneath him. What else? he wondered. The house—staying here—of course, the money that went with it all, and the rest of the property. The rose. *What else?*

"Well," he knew he was blustering but couldn't stop himself, "and everything that goes with it. You know—the works. It'll all be yours if you stay."

She swung round then. He pulled his head back, startled by the expression on her face. Had she been crying?

But her voice was frighteningly calm. "The works? I guess that's one way of putting it. I realize what the estate entails, Jack. I also know I have to make a decision about it soon. As a matter of fact, I told Ed I'd be back in a week's time."

He felt his heart rate speed up at that news flash. He opened his mouth to say something—anything— but she interrupted him.

"The thing is, there's a whole part of this decision that hasn't been raised at all. At least, not by you. And that is my life in Chicago. My condo, my friends and my career. What about all of that?" She leaned toward him.

He stood up. "I haven't forgotten any of that, Roslyn. That's what I meant when I said I didn't want to influence you. I know what you'd be giving up. And, as I said, I've got a vested interest in your decision."

"I need to know exactly, what is the nature of your *vested* interest?"

He stared at her, trapped by the quiet tone of her voice and the leading expression in her eyes. She wanted him to say something more specific. The dim glow of understanding began to seep into his brain. *Not here, not yet.* Jack couldn't tear his eyes away from her and he couldn't speak, either. *Not here, not yet* blared away inside him like some kind of perverse mantra. Finally he said, "As a beneficiary, too, of course I have a vested interest in your decision. And—"

Before he could finish, she spun away toward the door, opening it with amazing speed and pausing only long enough to give him one last withering look. "It's late, Jack. I've got a lot of thinking to do and I guess it'll have to be done alone. Good night.'' The door closed behind her.

Jack wiped the sweat from his brow with the back of his hand. There was a large, hurtful knot in the bottom of his throat. Not because of her, but because he'd known what she'd wanted to hear. And he hadn't been able to say the words.

CHAPTER FOURTEEN

SHE DIDN'T SLEEP. Sometime in the dead of night she got up and carried the last two journals back to bed with her. At daybreak, she finished reading. She struggled from the bed and peered blearily out her bedroom window to view the sunrise. The metallic taste in her mouth came, not from her insomnia, but from the wastefulness of Ida Mae's life. A life devoted to nursing resentment.

The bittersweet surprise inside the last journal had been a manila envelope stuffed with all the notes and cards June and Lucille had sent to Ida Mae throughout the years. Changing her will may have been Ida's attempt to redeem some of those lost years, but her effort came too late.

Roslyn thought of the love that was passionate enough for June Rose to betray her twin and her parents. What had become of it? She suspected that the hard years afterward had eroded much of it. Had her grandmother ever regretted the elopement? Or her grandfather? She'd never know.

Roslyn headed into the bathroom to shower. She stared at herself in the mirror above the sink. *How much of your grandmother do you have in you? Will you risk all for love? Or are you going to let the man you love slip away because you feel hurt?* But there were no answers in her reflection. She stepped into the tub and pulled the shower curtains closed.

When she emerged, refreshed, Roslyn was still pondering the question. Again, she marveled at how much she'd changed since coming to Plainsville. Weeks ago, she'd have viewed her life in Chicago as exciting, always changing. Yet looking back, she saw how her life in the city had been governed by work and routine. The highs and lows she'd talked about with Jack had nothing to do with the caring, passionate woman inside her.

These weeks in Plainsville and meeting Jack had revealed that woman. Knowing that person now, Roslyn couldn't bear to think how returning to Chicago would erase the part of herself she had just discovered. She swiped at the foggy mirror with her towel and decided that she would face Jack and ask for some answers.

Last night she'd waited desperately for him to give a sign that there was a reason beyond the house for her to stay in Plainsville. *Just say it. Say what I want to hear.* Instead he'd stumbled about, saying everything but the simple words, *I love you. I want to spend the rest of my life with you.*

She stood before the mirror a few seconds longer. Every inch of her skin seemed to glow just at the memory of Jack's touch. Thinking of Jack's hands on her, the way he exulted in making love, made her skin prickle with desire. In spite of his protestations of recent inexperience, he was a wonderful lover.

She flashed herself a goofy grin. *Not that you're*

an icon of expertise yourself, Baines. But now wasn't the time to daydream about being in Jack's arms again. At least, not if she wanted to be up and dressed by the time Sophie appeared. Roslyn padded into the bedroom to search for something to wear. The day was gearing up for heat and all she had were jeans and her short black wool miniskirt.

A hasty search through kitchen drawers turned up a sharp pair of scissors. Roslyn skipped back upstairs to convert her denims into cutoffs. She was drinking her second cup of coffee when Sophie let herself in through the back porch door.

"You been shopping?" Plastic bag in hand, Sophie stopped inside the doorway.

"No. Just a deft hand with the scissors."

Sophie raised an eyebrow. "Those looked like expensive jeans."

"Better than sweating all day. How is it out there?"

"Hot, as you said." She made for the kitchen counter to unload the plastic bag. "I didn't do a lot of shopping this morning because I wasn't sure how much longer you'd be staying." She turned away from the counter to face Roslyn.

No beating around the bush for Sophie, Roslyn thought. "I...uh, well I told my boss yesterday that I'd like another week."

"Another week! For what?"

Roslyn squirmed in her chair. "I guess to...you know...make a decision and then sign whatever official papers I have to sign and make whatever arrangements I need to make."

Sophie yanked out a chair. Her face was a blend of disgust and pity. "Roslyn, honey, let me be frank with you. Seein' as how I'm old enough to be your mother, I guess I can get away with it."

Roslyn really didn't want this talk to be happening but felt helpless against the pull of Sophie.

"This is how I see it," the housekeeper began. "When you first came here, you weren't interested at all. We could all see that. Plainsville wasn't going to be part of your future. You left, had the accident and came back. Somewhere in those next few days you changed. No, no. Hear me out. At least, you started to change. You began to unwind and relax. You got to know all of us—especially Jack." She paused.

Roslyn flushed, but kept her eyes on Sophie.

"Now, I'm not too sure how things are going with that, but even an old lady like me can figure some things out. And I hear things."

"What kind of things?"

Sophie shrugged. "This is Plainsville. What more do I need to say? But you should know, they're kind things. People here like you, even though you've only met a few. I know you'd be welcome here."

"Sophie—"

"Okay, I'm almost finished. What I'm trying to tell you is that at first I wanted you to go back to Chicago so Jack could have this house. He spent a lot of time here as a kid and again when he came back to stay. I thought he deserved the house. And as I said, you didn't seem to care."

"But I do care!" Roslyn protested.

"I know. I'm getting to that part. Hold your

horses!'' Sophie patted her brow with a folded tissue. ''Heavens! It's already too hot. All right, where was I?'' She put up a hand before Roslyn could speak. ''Okay. Then you started reading all about the family you never knew and learned all this stuff—how Miss Ida Mae had been deceived by her sister and all. It was a shock but it was part of learning about your family. The good and the bad. That's the thing. There's always a mix, right?''

Roslyn nodded.

''I think knowing what you know now, you won't be able to walk away from Plainsville and act as though it doesn't exist. You coulda done that at the very beginning, but not now. Of course, you have to consider your career and all your friends in Chicago. That's going to be real difficult for you.''

All my friends in Chicago? Roslyn knew she could count them and still have fingers left on one hand.

''To be honest, I think you already know in your heart what you want to do,'' Sophie said. ''I think you just don't have the courage to go with it.'' She leaned across the table, sticking her florid face nose to nose with Roslyn. ''I say, go with your heart, girl, and forget all that analyzing nonsense. What if this and what if that.''

''But Jack—''

Sophie leaned back into her chair and waved a dismissive hand. ''Jack's a grown-up. He's been through a lot already. He can stand up to anything.''

Maybe so, Roslyn thought, but can I?

''If you want my advice—''

Roslyn smiled. She was going to get it anyway. "Yes?" she prompted.

"Walk around town some more this week. See what you'll be leaving behind."

Roslyn nodded. A walk around town might just give her some answers. Of course, a walk wouldn't solve her dilemma with Jack. For that, she needed to speak to the man, himself.

SHE WALKED FOR an hour around the property behind and to the side of Ida Mae's house. She revisited the place above the river gorge where she and Jack had walked the day they met. Now the trees were in full bloom and wildflowers speckled the landscape. Tall grasses plumed out from the banks of the river. Roslyn could almost picture children swimming or fishing there, filling the river valley with shouts and laughter. As a child growing up in Chicago, she'd done all of her swimming at chlorinated, public pools.

She tramped back toward the house through fields of dried cornstalks and compact ridges littered with the stubs of last year's crops. Another person who depended on her decision was the farmer who leased these fields. *Add him to the list.* The weight of that impending decision settled more heavily on her shoulders.

She paused to pick a handful of long stems twined with tiny pink petals. Instead of returning to the house, Roslyn took a more direct route from the fields to the road, stepping onto the pavement just beyond the stop sign that marked the town limit. The Goshen

Road. She turned to face east—and Chicago. *One more week.*

Roslyn kept walking, forgetful of the bunch of wildflowers, aiming for the center of town. As Sophie had said, a person could get through and around Plainsville on foot in a little more than half an hour. With time to stop for a hello here and there. *Maybe a hello to Jack.*

When Roslyn arrived at the entrance to J.J.'s Landscaping and Garden Center, the rolled-up cotton shirt she was wearing was sticking to her skin. Sophie had lent her an old pair of sneakers abandoned by one of her nephews and they'd begun to rub against her bare heels. She was ready to leap into the river, if it wasn't so far behind her.

The parking lot was filled with cars again. Not bad for a little past noon on a Wednesday, she thought. But the third week of May was approaching, and Jack had told her that that was his busiest time, when people began to dig up their gardens and plant the first annuals.

She hesitated a few feet outside the main door. The grunginess of her appearance registered even more when she noticed various customers in crisp shorts and chinos. She stared down at her bunch of flowers, wilting rapidly in the midday heat. Now wasn't the time to drop in on Jack. She headed back to the main sidewalk. She crossed the parking lot on a diagonal and had almost reached the end of the gravel lot when a female voice followed by a deep baritone caught her attention. She turned her head to see Jack helping a woman load a station wagon with flats of annuals.

The woman was chatting merrily, pausing every now and then to gaze up smilingly at Jack or pat him on the forearm. Roslyn couldn't hear what they were saying because of street traffic, but Jack's beaming face indicated he was enjoying the conversation. She watched him hold open the driver door for the woman, leaning in after he'd closed it to continue talking. They laughed heartily at something together and Roslyn felt an irrational stab of envy.

Of course other women would find Jack attractive and charming. *Why should that bother you?* she asked herself. But it did. When the woman's car revved into action, Roslyn moved quickly to reach the sidewalk before Jack turned around to see her. On the walk home, she pictured the scene again and again. *When you leave this town,* she reminded herself, *he will find someone else. It's inevitable.*

She promised herself a tall lemonade—maybe with the last airline bottle of bourbon tossed in—when she got home just to take her mind off everything. Seeing Jack from a distance. How handsome and funny he was and how other women thought so, too. Wanting him. Especially that.

The ache of wanting him sucked the last reserves of energy from her so that by the time she reached the back porch she could hardly drag herself up the few wooden stairs. Sophie had left the screen door unlocked as usual and Roslyn pushed it with the last ounce of strength in her. She sagged into a chair, letting the coolness of the shady kitchen wash over her. When she could breathe like a normal person again, she headed for the fridge and the lemonade.

She stopped midway. Sniffed the air curiously. Cigarette smoke. She inhaled deeper, to be sure. The acrid odor was even stronger nearer the hall. She followed it, going from room to room on the ground floor. Scanning the tabletops, Roslyn found no evidence of ashes or butts. But someone had definitely been smoking in the house.

Perhaps Sophie had had a visitor. Someone who smoked. That was the explanation Roslyn settled for, although she knew she wouldn't be really satisfied until she saw Sophie the next day.

THE PHONE CALL came about seven, but it wasn't the call Roslyn had been expecting. She'd finished the rest of the shrimp salad Sophie had made for lunch, eating inside at the kitchen table because the veranda was too hot. She rinsed her dishes and wandered into the living room to see if the sun was still pouring in through the bay window.

She was standing beside the telephone when it rang, and jumped. Jack? Her hand hesitated above the receiver. What tone of voice would she present to him? Lighthearted and casual? Quiet? Forgiving? Perhaps inviting, she thought dreamily. But when she answered, her voice echoed disappointment. Not Jack.

"Miss Baines?"

"Speaking."

"Evening, ma'am. Mac Christensen here. Hope I'm not bothering you and I want to say right off that this call isn't a bad-news call, in case you're thinking it's number three."

"Number three?"

"You know…bad things are supposed to come in threes."

"Oh, right."

"I wonder if I could ask you a couple of quick ones about Mr. Naismith. I just had a fax from the Chicago police asking me to verify a few things for them."

"Is there some kind of investigation into the accident?"

"Maybe. Apparently a witness has come forward to say that another car might have been responsible for Naismith's going off the road that night."

"Oh, no!"

"Yep! Anyhow, they know that Naismith had left his own car at O'Hare and had picked it up on his return. He rented a car in Des Moines to drive to Plainsville."

"That's right," she murmured.

"What the police want to know is, did he mention to you what his plans were after getting back to Chicago?"

"Uh, no, he didn't. Not at all. He left early in the morning—or maybe it was the middle of the night. All I know is that he was gone when I woke up the next morning."

There was a slight pause which Roslyn quickly filled, blurting out, "He slept on the sofa in the living room, and when I came down to make coffee, he'd already gone."

"Hmm. So he never said that he was going to be meeting someone or going into the office or anything like that?"

"No, nothing. Can you tell me how this fits in with someone forcing him off the expressway?"

"Well," he drawled, "not sure that it does fit in. They figure it happened on his way home, however—"

"He left here in the morning but the accident occurred at night," she interrupted.

"Right you are. His flight landed at O'Hare about five so there's a gap of a few hours where Naismith's presence isn't accounted for. We're just trying to account for that time. Not to worry, ma'am, just routine. I'll let you know if anything turns up. Will you be staying on in Plainsville much longer?"

Roslyn closed her eyes and made a rapid count to ten. "Another few days, at least."

"Okeydoke. Thanks again."

She replaced the receiver and sat down in Ida Mae's armchair. The suggestion that Jim had been run off the road was too awful to ponder. Her mind raced with a dozen questions all beginning with "What if…" All along she'd believed his death had been an accident, while others assumed it was related to the investigation. Now she didn't know what to think. Could Jim really have been framed? If so, then perhaps his death was connected to whatever was going on. And if that was the case, the floppy disk he left behind might well be a lot more important than Roslyn had imagined.

She clicked off the table lamp and sat a moment longer, staring out at the dark garden. The moon was almost full and illuminated the front lawn, spotlighting the rosebush. It was covered in leaves now and its long canes shot out from it in a thick, bushy fountain. Soon buds would form.

She thought again of Ida Mae, watching the rosebush year after year from this very chair. And when she was no longer well enough to come downstairs, she'd sat in her great sleigh bed looking down at it from the second floor. Aunt Ida must have been obsessed with that rosebush. Never wanting it out of her sight.

Roslyn mulled over that thought late into the night. Then she had an idea why her aunt had spent all those years watching the Iowa rose.

CHAPTER FIFTEEN

"I JUST HOPE you know what you're doing."

Roslyn glanced up from where she knelt. Sophie was standing on the sidewalk, frowning at the pile of soil heaped next to the rosebush.

Sophie muttered something, proceeded onto the veranda and closed the door behind her. Roslyn shoved the trowel back into the earth. She'd been up since daybreak, digging in a tight circle around the rosebush. She'd worked carefully, sensing she might damage the plant if she dug too closely. In spite of her assurance to Sophie, Roslyn wasn't certain of her success. How much of the garden would she have to dig up before proving—or disproving—her theory?

She scarcely glanced up when Sophie emerged from the house almost an hour later, set a mug of coffee onto the veranda balustrade and, without saying a word, bustled back into the house. Roslyn felt a twinge of guilt, knowing Sophie didn't like to be left in the dark about things. She took a break to drink the coffee, burning her tongue in the rush to finish it and return to work.

When the moat around the rosebush was complete, Roslyn sank back onto her heels to think. If she was right, she needed to look at this from Ida Mae's point of view. Ida Mae would have had to work quickly, digging a hole deep enough and cleaning up her mess after. If she never wanted what she was hiding to be found, she'd have to bury it close to the rose but far enough away that it wouldn't easily be discovered. Hadn't she mentioned in her journals something about relatives asking for cuttings from the rose?

Roslyn's eyes circled the garden, searching for a possible place. Near to the rose, but not actually within range of its branches or roots. But how far down or out did the roots extend? She wished she knew more about plants. She wished Jack were there.

Digging was hard labor and her shade was disappearing as the sun began to stretch over the rooftop onto the front lawn. Her mind raced, trying to see the garden through Ida Mae's eyes. The rosebush had always been in full view, even from inside the house. Jack had cut back the withered tulip stems and leaves from the border. He'd mentioned that Ida Mae hadn't wanted him to plant annuals there. She'd wanted the rosebush to have lots of room.

Maybe there was another reason why she didn't want him digging between the rosebush and the garden's edge, Roslyn thought. She got up and walked up onto the veranda, vaguely aware of muted voices from inside the house. Sophie, she figured, was on the telephone. Roslyn hovered on the top step, reenacting the scene from Ida Mae's perspective.

It's the middle of night. Ida Mae tiptoes carefully down the steps and walks toward the rosebush. Stops at the edge of the garden and looks toward the house. It's in total darkness, everyone sleeping soundly. She

*hesitates to step into the garden itself. The damp earth
will ruin her slippers and she'll have to dispose of
them. If she removes them, her feet will get dirty and
leave a trail throughout the house. Easier and better
to just squat right here at the edge, in front of the
rosebush. Can't dig too deep, because there's not
enough time.*

Roslyn worked silently. Just as Sophie stuck her
head out the door to ask Roslyn if she wanted lunch,
the trowel struck something hard and unmoving.
Heedless of Sophie, she dug faster, clearing a rectangular patch to expose a metallic surface.

"Sophie!" she cried. "It's here."

The older woman watched from the top step as
Roslyn dug around the box and was able to lever it
out with the trowel blade. The surfaces of the box
were mottled with rust spots and pitted. Roslyn
scraped the lumps of dirt away and carried the box
onto the veranda.

"Good heavens!" was all Sophie could say.

Roslyn set the box onto the wicker table. A small
rusty padlock dangled from the hinged lock. "I'll
never find the key," she murmured.

"Looks like you could just rip off that old thing,"
said Sophie. "Hit it with the trowel. If that doesn't
work, we'll get a hammer from the shed."

The hammer did the trick. Afterward, Roslyn carried the box into the kitchen and placed it onto the
table. She was almost afraid to open it, in case she
was wrong.

"Go ahead," Sophie urged. She settled into a chair

with all the anticipation of a child waiting for a slice of birthday cake.

Roslyn wondered if her own face was as flushed with excitement. Using the tip of the trowel to pry it open, she raised the lid. Inside there was a leather-wrapped bundle which Roslyn carefully withdrew. The leather was actually a sack and once Roslyn had unfolded it, she loosened the thong drawstring, poked her fingers inside and took out a wad of papers that were stuck together as if someone had pressed them with an iron.

"I think moisture has gotten in," Roslyn said as she carefully tried to pry the papers apart.

"Maybe steam will loosen them," Sophie suggested.

"Maybe." Roslyn worked at the first layer of paper, unravelling it enough to see that her hunch had been a good one.

"Are they the bonds you were telling me about?"

Roslyn raised her head. "They are," she whispered.

"Seems strange to be looking at them, knowing the last person to see them was Miss Ida Mae so many years ago."

Roslyn pulled off the outer layer of paper. She'd only seen textbook reproductions of bearer bonds this old. The amount was for ten thousand dollars. Wordlessly, she showed the bond to Sophie.

"How many are there?"

"Going by my aunt's journal, I'd say five."

"A nice sum of money," Sophie said.

"Especially for those days. No wonder my great-grandfather had a stroke after he realized they'd been taken.''

"Why do you suppose he just didn't demand that June give them back?''

Roslyn shrugged. "I don't know. I've a feeling Ida Mae had something to do with that. It sounds as if she really took charge after my grandmother ran off.''

"Sad to think so much pain is attached to those bonds.''

Roslyn began to tuck the papers back into the leather bag. "I don't think I'll try to separate the rest until I get some expert advice about how to do it safely. For now, I should store these in a safe place. Maybe I'll put them in the old desk in the living room.''

As Roslyn was leaving the kitchen, Sophie asked, "None of my business I know, but what will you do with the bonds, Roslyn?''

Roslyn paused. "They belong to the estate and whoever inherits it.'' Then she left the room, not daring to look at Sophie's face.

IF JACK HAD BEEN ABLE TO, he'd have delegated someone else to stay until the end of business hours. He kept looking at the clock, urging the hour hand to move faster. If it weren't for the blasted irrigation pipe, he'd have seen Roslyn last night and...

And what? he asked himself. Asked her to marry you so you could have her *and* the house? That question and more plagued him throughout the day. He made his closing-up rounds early in order to race out of the parking lot after the last customer had departed.

But to test him further, the last customer was Mac Christensen. And Mac liked to chat.

Jack waited by the door, biting his lower lip while Mac debated between pansies and impatiens.

"Thing is," Mac was saying, "I can't remember which one Patsy wanted and then she'll accuse me of not listening."

"Take them both and return what you don't want."

Mac swung round to look at Jack. "Am I keeping you from something?"

Jack shrugged.

Mac cocked an eyebrow. "Guess it's been a long day for you." He made his choice, paid the cashier and bent to pick up the flats. As he brushed past Jack out the door, Mac said, "I was talking to your friend yesterday. Roslyn Baines."

Jack caught the glint in his eye.

"She mention it to you?" Mac asked.

Jack knew Mac was dangling a baited hook but lunged for it anyway. "I haven't seen her for a couple of days," he mumbled. But he followed Mac out into the parking lot, knowing the talk would continue.

"I had a call from the guys in Chicago. Seems like that Naismith fellow's death might not have been an accident."

"What do you mean?"

Mac stopped at the rear of his Jeep, passing the flat of annuals to Jack while he got out his keys. "There's a witness—somebody who'd been following a few yards behind—who says that it looked deliberate."

"Did they get a plate number?"

"No, but a good description of the car. And some paint scrapings."

Jack leaned over to set the flowers inside the Jeep. Mac closed the door but made no effort to move. Then he said, "Reason I called Miss Baines was to ask if Naismith had mentioned his plans to her. There's a big time gap between his arrival at O'Hare and when he got hit by the car."

"What did she say?"

"Nothing. Least, she said he hadn't told her about going anywhere or meeting anyone."

"Did she tell you about the fraud inquiry?"

Mac narrowed his eyes. "What fraud inquiry?"

"Apparently Naismith was being audited for possible embezzlement of funds at work."

"Oh yeah?"

Mac's voice sounded casual, but Jack read keen interest in all his body signals. "You should contact the Chicago police and tell them, in case they don't already know."

"Will do, though they probably know. They've interviewed his boss and some other people at the office."

"Maybe they don't know that Naismith felt he was being framed. That's why he went to see Roslyn."

"And if he was being framed, maybe he met with the person he suspected?"

"And was pushed off the highway."

Mac pursed his lips. "Yep," he said, "that's a possible scenario. Guess I should call them back. Just in case." He opened the Jeep door and started to climb in. "Why'd you suppose Miss Baines didn't mention all that from the beginning?"

Jack felt his face heat up. "Who knows?" he answered lamely.

"Maybe she thought she was protecting him."

"Maybe."

Jack stared into his friend's face a few seconds longer before averting his eyes. He waved as the Jeep pulled out of the lot and then jogged toward the store. Twenty minutes later, he was sitting in the pickup at the foot of Roslyn's drive.

Funny, he thought, how he'd automatically begun to think of it as her place now, rather than Ida Mae's. He waited a few more seconds, then coasted up to the house and got out of the truck. Waiting at the front door for Roslyn to answer, he thought maybe a screen door would be great for the coming summer. One of those reproductions of older models. Then caught himself sharply.

Not your door, buddy. Not now. Maybe not ever.
He jumped when her face appeared on the other side of the etched glass. The door groaned as it opened. She looked tired, was his first observation.

"Hi, Jack," she said. "Do you want to sit out here or in the kitchen? It might be cooler inside." The veranda was bathed with sunlight.

"You know, Ida Mae always talked about putting a deck out back to get the cooler air at the end of the day. She never seemed to get around to it." He stopped, aware that he was babbling and also of the quick frown that appeared on her face. Did she think he was making plans for the place?

Roslyn turned and headed toward the kitchen. Jack followed, feeling a bit like a chastened pup. All he could focus on was the rhythmic and completely unconscious sexiness of her walk. He didn't have to try hard to conjure up the look and feel of the smooth, taut flesh underneath her denim shorts. Or the sweep of her long neck, exposed now that her tumble of hair had been knotted up into a frizzled lump at the back of her head. He imagined his lips moving along that curve and down onto other fleshier curves below. His arms prickled with goose bumps.

"A beer?" she asked, opening the refrigerator and reaching inside.

"Great." He exhaled a mouthful of air and rubbed at his arms.

"You're not cold?" she asked.

She was standing inches away, handing him the frosty can of ale and all he wanted to do was set it down and take her into his arms. But he didn't.

"No, no," he protested. "Thanks for the beer."

"There's something I want to show you," she said, abruptly spinning out of the room and returning before he'd flipped the aluminum tab off the can. She was carrying a dented, rusty metal box which she placed in the center of the table as if it were a sacred offering.

"Remember I told you that my aunt had hidden the bearer bonds her father had bought for her wedding present? Well, I've been racking my brain trying to figure out where she'd have put them. Then I thought of the Iowa rose and how she was always taking care of it and looking at it and so on."

Jack sensed he wasn't catching on as quickly as he should, so intent was he on every movement she made.

She glanced up at him as she took a leather-bound package from the box. "Remember?" she repeated.

"Uh, yes, yes. And you're absolutely right about how she was always fretting about the rosebush. Did you—?"

"Dig it up? Not the bush, but I guessed where she might have placed the bonds. And I found this box!"

"The bonds?"

"All fifty thousand dollars' worth."

"God," he murmured, watching as she carefully extracted one of the papers from the leather sack. "That's a lot of money."

"Even more so for those days," she added.

"What will you do with them?" he blurted, hating himself for the question as soon as it had popped out.

"Hand them over to Randall Taylor, of course. Isn't he the executor?"

Her voice was sharp. What had he expected her to do with them? was the angry and unspoken question that rattled around the room. He tried to make amends. "Of course. I just meant in the short term. To keep them safe."

"The oak desk, I suppose."

"Maybe you should put them away right now," he suggested, thinking ahead to the evening and possible distractions. She packed them up and left the kitchen. He sat down and sipped his beer. There was a nice steady breeze coming in through the screen door at the back porch. The sun porch, Ida Mae used to call it. Though she seldom sunned herself in it. Now he could understand why she'd never got around to having him build that deck. She wouldn't be able to see the rose from there.

A deck would definitely be the thing for summer, he mused. Take advantage of the shade and the cooling breezes from the river to the north, beyond the cornfields. He wiped a hand across his face. *Get out of your fantasy world, bud, and deal with the very pressing matters at hand.*

When she came back into the room he blurted her name at the same time as she said his. They both tittered, watching one another carefully. "Go ahead," he said.

"No, you," she whispered and he felt the lump in his throat double in size.

She walked slowly around his chair to get to the sink and washed her hands. "The leather leaves some kind of oily residue," she explained, brushing behind him once more to take the chair at the end of the table. Next to him. Her flowery scent packed the air around him, making it hard to breathe. That is, breathe and concentrate at the same time.

He knew he ought to get to the point right away. That's what he'd resolved to do and he suspected, what she wanted him to do. She was waiting for him to offer her a reason to stay in Plainsville. A reason beyond the house, the estate and now, the bearer bonds.

His stomach lurched. *The bearer bonds.* Great timing for a proposal, he realized. *Marry me—so I can then have access to all the things you've been left in the will. All the things I believed so long that I would come to own. Oh, and by the way, I actually do love you.* He could almost hear her silent rebuke. *Yeah, right.*

Instead, he said, ''Mac Christensen mentioned that he'd spoken to you about Naismith's accident and how it might've been deliberate.''

She stared down at the table. A deep stain surged up her neck and into her cheeks. He bet that if he tilted her head his way, he'd see tears. He fought the impulse to lean over and clutch her to him. Suddenly he wasn't certain anymore if the tears were for Naismith himself or for the way he might have died. Or maybe she felt responsible in some way, though he couldn't imagine why. Unless she knew more about this fraud thing than she'd let on. Jack bit his tongue, silencing the ugly thought.

''I hope you don't mind,'' he continued, ''I told Mac about the fraud inquiry and he was going to talk to the police in Chicago.''

He winced when she raised her head, the fire in her eyes blinding him.

''I'm sure the police already know about the investigation. Everyone in the office knew.''

''Yeah, but what about his claim that he was being framed?''

She frowned. ''Tough to prove,'' she murmured. ''Jim was the only person with access to his accounts.''

''Didn't you say he'd left behind a floppy disk?''

''Yes, but I couldn't open it without his password.''

"Still…" He gave up, feeling her drift further and further away. Except for the glimmer in her eyes, she seemed almost resigned. He played with the rim of his empty beer can, wanting the silence to evaporate along with all of his inhibitions. Wanting her to whisper his name and lightly touch his arm. Then he'd wrap her into himself and tell her how much he wanted her. Needed her. Loved her.

Abruptly, she plunked her beer can onto the table, pushed her chair back and strode over to the door leading out to the porch. "When I get back to Chicago," she was saying, "all of that will be sorted out."

So, she's made her decision. Jack swallowed back the bile that had risen into his throat. He pushed his own chair back and stood up. Raising a palm toward her, he said, "I need to do some thinking, Roslyn. Please—don't make any plane reservations until I get a chance to see you tomorrow."

"What's going to be different tomorrow?" she asked.

And he stood there, speechless, until she breezed past him and left the room.

CHAPTER SIXTEEN

SHE DIDN'T HEAR Jack leave, only the rumble of the pickup as it reversed out the drive. Several times she'd started to the door to flag him down.

And for what? To beg him to say those magic words? That he loved her? Wanted to marry her? She was disgusted at herself for contemplating such a scene. She'd known the man about four weeks. They'd become friends, then lovers. He'd murmured many wonderful things to her as they'd made love. And likewise. Yet neither of them had uttered the word *love* aloud. There had to be a reason for that.

Roslyn had expected him to make clear his intentions. She smiled at the notion. *As if I were the parent and he the courting suitor.* Still, he'd disappointed her, rambling on about Jim Naismith until she'd wanted to scream. As if she wasn't feeling bad enough about Jim's death.

Why hadn't she listened to him that night? Or at least encouraged him to go to the police. Roslyn realized that she'd set aside her life in Chicago to let Plainsville and those in it, both past and present, take over. But not anymore. She had an idea. Judy's best friend at the office, Andrea, worked in Personnel. Although it was after hours, Roslyn called and left a message, asking Andrea to have Judy contact her as soon as possible. It was an emergency.

Roslyn sat in the armchair a while longer. She was far too restless to read or resume sorting out the photograph albums and collection of letters, journals and cards in Ida Mae's cartons. All of that could be left for the lonely winter months ahead in Chicago.

Impulsively, she decided to make another call. Ed was probably steaming because she hadn't yet sent Jim's disk to him. Although it was unlikely she'd catch him at home, she thought it would be prudent to advise him that she—and the disk—would be arriving in the next few days.

When his answering service picked up, Roslyn left her message, adding that she hoped to get Jim's password in the next twenty-four hours and, if there was anything on the disk that was crucial to the inquiry, she'd courier it to the office immediately.

Having tidied up all the office loose ends, Roslyn decided to walk into town to have the dinner she hadn't had with Jack. She grabbed some cash from her wallet, tucked it into her cutoff jeans and closed the screen door off the kitchen. She'd be back before dark, she reasoned, and didn't bother turning on the porch light.

It was almost seven and most of the shops were closed. Roslyn enjoyed a salad and quiche at Laverne's, all the while staring through the picture window in the hope of spotting Jack. When she could no longer put off leaving, she paid and made a quick tour of the center of Plainsville. Fifteen minutes later, she decided to return home through the back streets. Perhaps she'd find Sophie's house and pop in for a visit.

Although she'd never been to Sophie's home, she knew the address and, after a bit of backtracking, eventually ended up outside a small aluminum-sided bungalow at the end of a crescent. The house was in darkness. Sophie and her sister obviously hadn't returned from Des Moines. Just as Roslyn reached the corner of the crescent, a bicycle whizzed round from the cross street, almost knocking her over. She shouted, but the cyclist didn't stop. Now that, she thought angrily, was right out of Chicago.

She reached the intersection near Jack's place and, after a second's debate about strolling by Jack's place, continued home. Plainsville's imitation gaslights flickered on as the sun slipped beneath the rolling hills beyond the town. Nighttime sounds took over. A sense of well-being flowed through Roslyn.

She sighed and trudged up the drive, struck again by the walk's reminders of what she'd be leaving behind. Roslyn hesitated at the back door. She took a deep breath, inhaling slowly. Floating in the night air was the unmistakable scent of tobacco.

She opened the screen door as noisily as possible, reached in her arm to click on the back porch light and waited. No echo of running footsteps. Stepping inside, she paused again. Silence. She tiptoed across the linoleum floor to the light switch and illuminated the kitchen. The odor of cigarettes wasn't as strong in here. Perhaps the mystery smoker had lit up outside, on the porch.

She wished she'd remembered to tell Sophie about

the last incident, but in the excitement of finding the bonds, she'd completely forgotten about the scent of smoke in the house. Now it had happened again.

Roslyn moved cautiously from room to room, turning on all the lights, scanning shelves and opening drawers. Everything appeared in its place, even the metal strongbox in the oak desk. Roslyn considered calling the sheriff, but nothing seemed to be missing. Not wanting to appear paranoid, she rejected the idea of calling Jack. Instead, she went up to bed, leaving on the exterior house lights.

The night was long. Even reading late failed to make her drowsy and she finally gave up, switching off the lamp and resigning herself to tossing and turning. Sometime before daybreak, Roslyn thought of the metal box. She hadn't looked inside to check the bonds. That realization nagged at her until she got up and padded downstairs, determined to set her mind at ease so she could catch at least an hour or two of sleep.

The box was empty.

AS ROSLYN EXPECTED, Sophie's reaction was one of disbelief. But when Roslyn mentioned the cigarette smoke as a postscript, adding that this was the second occurrence, Sophie's face reddened.

"Why didn't you say anything to me about the smoke?"

"I completely forgot, Sophie. It happened the night before I started digging for the box. Once I found the bonds..."

Sophie started to empty the dishwasher, banging

cupboards as she put away the clean dishes. Abruptly, she stopped and turned to look at Roslyn. Her eyes were watering. "I hope you don't think I took those bonds, Roslyn."

"It never occurred to me, Sophie! You've got to believe that. I'm only telling you because I'm not sure what to do first. Should I call Mac Christensen?"

"I—I can't be telling you what to do. Those bonds are worth a lot of money. This is serious." She shook her head. "Real serious." She looked away and hesitated, before continuing. "I hate to ask this, but I have a hunch. Would you mind holding off calling Mac for a while? I need about an hour or so."

Roslyn was struck by the distress in the woman's voice. "Of course, Sophie." She helped her to the front door. "Are you sure you can drive?"

"Heavens, yes. Made it all the way to Des Moines and back last night, didn't I?"

"How'd the trip go? I went for a walk by your place but it was in darkness."

"It was?" She frowned, then her face lit up. "The good news is that my sister had a job interview and she feels it went real well."

"That's great, Sophie. Anyway, you have a good rest and don't worry about a thing." Roslyn waited out on the porch while Sophie climbed into the beat-up car she drove and waved goodbye.

I need to talk to Jack, Roslyn thought. She knew he hadn't taken the bonds but she needed his advice. And she was worried about Sophie. Maybe Jack knew what was troubling the older woman.

HE WASN'T AT THE STORE. She'd arrived, breathless from the unaccustomed jogging, and had asked at the counter when she failed to see him.

"He's taken the day off," the clerk had said, while ringing up an order for a customer.

"Is he sick?"

"I don't know," was the indifferent reply.

Roslyn stood, hands on hips, at the edge of the parking lot. Then she started to jog along the pavement toward the rear of the garden center, beyond the greenhouses toward Jack's place. She rounded the corner of the second greenhouse and saw a narrow flagstone walkway leading toward the fenced backyard. She approached the gate built into the high fence, grasped the wrought iron handle and pushed it open.

Jack was standing in the middle of the yard beneath a tree, pulling on the end of a long rope. He turned sharply when the gate swung open and let go of the rope. Something fell out of the tree, but Roslyn hardly noticed. She couldn't take her eyes off Jack, his bare chest glistening in the sunlight, the waist of his faded jeans drooping low enough to reveal the line of downy black hair that extended below his navel.

"Roslyn!"

Her eyes traveled upward to safer territory. The surge of pleasure in his face gave her courage. "Jack, something's come up and...and I need to talk to you."

Wariness fell over his features then. He turned aside to retrieve a wooden container from the ground. "Just taking down my bird feeder," he explained.

"Stay there. I'll be right with you." Setting the feeder on the patio table, he disappeared through the open glass sliding door leading to his kitchen. Seconds later he returned, wearing a short-sleeved cotton shirt which he was tucking into his jeans.

"You look like you've run all the way here," he commented, eyes flicking over her. "What's up?"

Her throat felt swollen and parched. "Last night I walked into town for dinner and after, well, I just went for a long walk."

He raised an eyebrow at that, but she kept on. "When I got home, I noticed a strong smell of cigarette smoke. It had happened once before," she paused at his frown, explaining, "a couple of days ago. Just the smell. Nothing had been taken from the house…that time."

"Maybe you should sit down," he said, pulling out a chair for her. He stood with his feet apart, thumbs hooked into the belt loops of his jeans. "Okay," he said slowly, "so this has happened once before but you've never mentioned it."

"It didn't seem important, until last night. When I noticed the smoke again, I went through the whole house but everything was in place."

"The bonds?" His voice was sharp.

"The box was in the desk. But this morning when I looked inside, they weren't there."

"The bonds are *gone?*"

She nodded.

"You call Mac?"

"No—"

"Why not?"

She stared down at her hands clenched in her lap.
"I wanted to talk to you first. Then Sophie."

"Sophie didn't take them."

"I never thought she had. I just…I don't know…
I told her about them before I had a chance to call
Mac."

"But then you came right over here."

"Yes. Because I wanted to see you." She moistened her lips. "Could I have a drink of water?"

The narrowing in his eyes shifted slightly. "Sure."
He vanished into the house and came out seconds
later, carrying a frosted glass of water.

Roslyn took a mouthful of water. Some of it trick-
led down her chin and she watched dumbly while
Jack leaned over to wipe it away with the end of his
thumb.

"Better?" he asked.

She looked away, focusing on the glass of water as
she took another sip. Then she raised her face to
Jack's. "I know Sophie would never have taken them.
Besides, she and her sister were in Des Moines last
night."

The guarded expression blinkered his face again.
She knew instantly that she ought to have included
him in that statement, too. "And I know you had
nothing to do with the theft, either," she quickly
added.

Jack's lower lip curled. "Thanks for the vote of
confidence." His voice sounded bitter. He pushed his
chair away from the table and walked over to the rope
that had been attached to the bird feeder. Slowly, he
began to loop it around his hand.

Frustrated, Roslyn wanted to hurl the rope from his hands and haul him back to the table. "We have to talk," she insisted. "I just need to know—what do you think I should do?"

"About the bonds? Call Mac."

"Something's also come up about Jim and I think—"

"I think you should call Mac first and then we can get together and talk later—about when you're going back to Chicago and…and other things." He dropped the rope onto the table and stood, arms folded, looking down at her. "We've been through this before, Roslyn." Then, in a softer voice, he added, "I can't make the decision for you."

"You're still not getting it, Jack." She went on, seeing the confusion in his face. "I mean, it's not only my decision. You do have a part in all of this, like it or not. Tell me. What do *you* want?"

"What I want isn't the issue, Roslyn. You're the person giving up things here. Not me. My life isn't going to change with your decision."

She stood up then. His words thundered in her ears. She scarcely noticed him reach out his hands as she backed away.

"I didn't mean that the way it sounded," he was saying but all she could hear were the words *my life isn't going to change* pounding at her as she ran toward the gate and the lane beyond.

CHAPTER SEVENTEEN

ROSLYN RAN ALL THE WAY. Cramping in her lower abdomen froze her to the bottom porch step for a moment. She wiped the sweat dripping down her face with her forearm and, clenching the wooden railing, hauled herself up one step at a time.

Standing at the kitchen sink, she tossed a handful of water from the faucet onto her face, then held her palm against the back of her neck until her body temperature started to lower. She drank more water before taking the Plainsville directory down from the top of the refrigerator where Sophie kept it. In less than five minutes she knew precisely when and where the next bus departed for Des Moines. The next step—booking an air connection from there to Chicago—took longer. But by the time Roslyn trudged upstairs to shower and pack, she knew she'd be leaving Plainsville at four o'clock that afternoon.

You'd be proud of me, Jack, she was thinking as she reached the second floor landing, *I've finally made a decision.*

Packing didn't take long when your original luggage had consisted of clothes for two or three days. She checked the time again. Not quite eleven. The day—and the fear of changing her mind—loomed ahead. There were phone calls to make and one in particular, she couldn't postpone. Roslyn headed downstairs to the kitchen to call Sophie.

Another woman answered the phone, her voice reedy and distracted. "Sophie's not here," she'd said so quietly Roslyn had to press the receiver closer to hear.

"Please ask her to call Roslyn Baines when she gets in. It's urgent."

The woman scarcely waited for her to finish before hanging up. Must be Sophie's sister, Roslyn thought. Then she called Ed at the office to find out if he'd received last night's message.

"Mr. Saunders has left for the weekend," his secretary announced.

Roslyn repeated basically the same message and replaced the receiver. She wondered if Ed had already booked a courier to pick up the disk. The other possibility, she hated to think, was that he was en route to Plainsville to pick it up himself. She knew he was the type of person who'd do anything to get what he wanted.

She puttered about the kitchen. Her stomach heaved at the idea of lunch, although a cursory check of the refrigerator revealed lots of options, thanks to Sophie.

She'd made that plan, too, as she was calling airlines. The clerk had asked if it was a return ticket or one-way and Roslyn's hesitation was long enough for the clerk to suggest an open-end return. Roslyn had to admit that the clerk had made the decision for her. She'd have to come back anyway, she reasoned, to get Ida Mae's journals and other things. To say good-bye to Sophie. To see the Iowa rose in bloom.

Already feeling better, Roslyn took an apple from the fruit bowl and went out the back door to walk to the ravine and woods. She wanted a detailed mental picture of as much of the property as she could. *Small but pleasing comfort,* she thought, *when I'm sitting on my tiny condo balcony.*

SHE'D REMEMBERED to wear her watch. A good thing, she realized, because the walk to the ravine had been so fabulous that she'd been tempted to inspect the whole property. The heat over the past few days had dried up the soil enough to make walking easy.

She squinted at her watch. Almost two. Time to go back, take another shower, change and leave Plainsville. Something she'd been trying to do for a few weeks now, she told herself, recollecting that first time and the accident that followed. It all seemed so long ago. She wasn't the same person anymore. That's what had hurt the most in the scene with Jack. His cool remark that his own life wouldn't change if she left or stayed. Roslyn refused to believe he actually meant that. Her own life, she knew, had altered beyond measure.

When she reached the back porch, she could hear the telephone ringing inside the kitchen. She trotted up the steps and shoved open the screen door, rushing to answer.

"Roslyn! You sound all out of breath."

She pulled a chair closer to the counter and the

phone. "I am. Been getting more exercise today than I've had in weeks. How are you, Judy?"

"Good. I was glad to get your message."

"I found Jim's disk, but can't access it."

"So he left it there after all. He told me how he planned to set it up. But after the accident, I wasn't sure you had the disk. When I didn't hear from you, I thought maybe he'd changed his mind."

"Why didn't you ask me when I talked to you before?"

There was a long pause before Judy's voice drifted across the line. "Sorry, Roslyn, but Jim made it clear that if he thought you'd gone over to the other side, he wasn't going to leave the disk."

"What other side?"

"Jim told you that he thought someone at the office was framing him. He wanted to see you in person."

"Kind of like a test." The words tasted bitter in Roslyn's mouth.

"Yes, I suppose. Look, Roslyn, none of this was my idea. I'm only telling you what Jim planned."

Roslyn closed her eyes. Well, she thought, at least Jim had given her a second chance by leaving behind the disk, even if she hadn't exactly aced the test.

"Why did you change your number so suddenly?"

"Things were getting scary here—some silent phone calls and so on."

"Did you report them to the police?"

"Of course. But I was too afraid to tell them everything. They advised me to change my number."

"Listen, Judy, I'm returning to Chicago later today and bringing the disk with me. But I need the password, because Ed's been pressuring me to hand it over so the audit team can check it before they pass it on to the police."

"Just send it straight to the police. Ed's a creep. No kidding, Roslyn—I could tell you stories—"

"I know about his womanizing, Judy, but that's got nothing to do with the inquiry. Legally that information belongs to the firm and he's got a right to look at it first."

Judy gave Roslyn the password and agreed to meet her later on in the weekend.

Roslyn headed upstairs. Two-thirty. Still time to take a peek at Jim's file before showering. The laptop was sitting on the floor next to the bed and the open suitcase lay on top. She carried the computer to Ida Mae's childhood desk and set it up. Then she retrieved the disk from one of the inner pockets of the suitcase and loaded it into the computer. While she waited for the menu to display, Roslyn pulled her sweaty T-shirt off and tossed it onto the suitcase. She unbuttoned her shorts and was about to unzip them when the password prompt came up on the screen.

Sitting at the small chair tucked under the desk, Roslyn typed in the words *Fantasy Island.* Typical of Jim's sense of humor, she'd thought when Judy had given it to her. He'd used the same phrase when he'd urged Roslyn to accompany him to the Caribbean.

"We'll pretend we're on Fantasy Island," he'd said, "and are shipwrecked. No more ringing phones."

Roslyn brushed away the tears at the corners of her eyes. This wasn't the moment to get sentimental about Jim. Helping him clear his name when she got back to work was the best course. When she pressed the Enter button, the screen rolled into life.

More than a dozen individual files appeared. Roslyn peered around at her travel clock—two forty-five. Not much time left for reading and showering. She chose one file at random, labeled The X-Files. Another of Jim's jokes, no doubt.

Just as it flashed onto the screen, Roslyn heard a creaking noise in the hall outside her bedroom. She froze, hand poised above the computer mouse. Must be my imagination. She highlighted the first item in the file's index and clicked twice. The noise—there it was again. She stopped, craning her head toward the door.

"Sophie?"

No answer. Not that she expected one. Sophie wasn't the type to tiptoe along a hallway. Another sound. This time, something clinking against metal. Roslyn shot out of the chair toward the doorway. And came face-to-face with a man.

She screamed, raising her arms in front of her as he pushed her backward into the room with enough force to send her sprawling across the top of the bed and the suitcase. Roslyn cried out as the edges of the suitcase cut into her back.

Ed Saunders leaned over her, his face red and swollen with anger. "You should follow instructions, Roslyn."

"I don't understand…" Roslyn gasped.

"No? Well, I see you've successfully accessed Naismith's files." He was staring over her at the monitor. "And actually, that's a good thing for me. It gives me a way to link you with Naismith after all. Judy gave you the password?"

Roslyn glared at him.

"I figured you were talking to Judy just now. Another stroke of luck for me. Now, I suggest you get off the bed and put something on. Not that you aren't tempting, but I wisely decided years ago to leave you alone. You were far too valuable to the firm to end up leaving because of my extracurricular activities."

"Judy said you were a creep," she blurted.

"Did she?" He laughed.

He extended a hand to help her up off the bed, but Roslyn brushed it aside. She reached blindly for the T-shirt and pulled it on as quickly as she could. Her skin crawled at the sight of Ed watching her.

"Pack up the laptop and give me the disk."

She handed it over. "You can leave now. You've got what you wanted."

"Such naiveté! You're part of the picture now, Roslyn my love. When the police interview me, as they did after Naismith's death, I'll look sad and tell them how despondent you've been since your lover's fatal car crash. And, of course, how worried you'd been about the discovery of your involvement."

"You've got no proof to back up a crazy story like that."

"But I will have, when I get at your files and play with them a bit."

"No one can access my files but me and I'll never give you my password."

"I don't need to force it from you." He smirked at the notion. "I already have it."

"How?"

"Several months ago I paid a social call to Bruce McIntyre's wife. I took some wine and flowers and we had ourselves a pleasant afternoon. I told her that I wanted to ensure the passwords were still sealed in Bruce's safe and the trusting soul got the key and showed me the envelope, all nicely wrapped. I invented some reason for her to leave the room and was able to get an impression of the key. A couple of weeks later, I paid another visit. This time I slipped a little something into her wine so she'd fall asleep. It was quite simple to lift the wax seal on the envelope. The thing had dried out years ago. I had enough time to copy everyone's password and still leave Mrs. McIntyre snoring peacefully on the sofa."

"You're disgusting," Roslyn muttered.

"Resourceful, I'd say. Come on, my dear. Get up and finish your packing. Were you heading back to Chicago, by any chance?"

"Yes."

"Wonderful! We'll travel together—part way, at least."

"How did you get here so quickly?"

"Flew to Des Moines and rented a car. The same thing Naismith did."

"How do you know what he did?"

Ed shrugged. "Had a chat with him that fateful night," he replied matter-of-factly. "He called me from the airport as soon as he got into Chicago and said he wanted to talk. A foolish mistake on his part.

However, we met in a bar and I heard all his evidence. He even handed over a copy of that disk you had. A bit too trusting, your Jim Naismith. Though not foolish enough to tell me there was another copy.''

"You followed him from the airport, didn't you?''

"Indeed. I still hadn't worked out what I was going to do. I just knew that he wasn't going to live. I saw my chance and I went for it. Like today. I tried to convince you to send the disk, but you insisted on ignoring me. Your problem now, my dear.''

"Stop calling me that,'' she cried, though she instantly feared irritating him. She needed to stall, get more time. For what? she asked herself. The cavalry? The Plainsville sheriff, who doesn't even know you're in trouble?

"Tell me why, Ed,'' she said, turning away from clicking shut the laptop case. "And how it all worked. The fraud.''

"The why stems from an addiction to gambling and a luxurious life-style. The rest wasn't difficult, once I had the passwords. I set up a dummy fund and slowly began to transfer money into it. I started with Jim's discretionary accounts because I knew the likelihood of questions would be minimal. And it was going very well, until about two months ago. Unfortunately, one of Jim's clients questioned her account. That led to Jim's discovery of the transfer of money. I think at first Jim thought he'd made the transactions himself and forgotten. Eventually, however, he put most of it together. Too bad for him.''

"How've you managed to keep this from the other associates? Or are they in on it with you?''

"No, they're not. I set up my own fake fund, moving the money through an account in the Caymans. I even made up an entire file of phony paperwork to match the computer transactions and once I had the passwords, could access Tony's files, too, and log in the fund, there."

"And it all hinged on the fact that no one had access to the computer passwords."

He smiled broadly. "Yes! A wonderful, outdated custom that I once tried to persuade Bruce to abandon. Now I'm quite happy he didn't." He closed the lid on Roslyn's suitcase. "Time to go. You take the suitcase and I'll take the laptop."

"What makes you think I'll do anything you tell me to?"

He chuckled, shaking his head. "You're an innocent in many ways, Roslyn. That's what I've always liked in you. Along with your intelligence and your drive. We might have made an incredible team."

"In your dreams."

"True," he agreed. "I guess this might help persuade you to follow instructions." He withdrew a revolver from his suit coat pocket.

Roslyn's eyes widened. She'd never seen a real gun up close. The expression in his face told her he wouldn't hesitate using it.

"I've already crossed the line from fraud to murder. Pick up your suitcase."

She did. He followed behind, making sure the end of the gun was close enough to bunt against her back whenever she slowed on the stairs. When they reached the ground floor, the screen door creaked open and slammed shut. Roslyn stopped, hardly daring to breathe. The barrel of the gun jammed against the center of her spine.

A voice rang out from the kitchen. "Roslyn? You here?"

It was Sophie. Roslyn's heart thudded painfully against her chest.

Ed's breath puffed into her ear. "Get rid of her."

She wet her lips and swallowed. "Sophie? I'm coming into the kitchen. Stay there."

"Okay, set the suitcase down gently and go to her," whispered Ed. "I'm right behind. I'll wait outside the door, in the hall. If you indicate anything to her, if she doesn't leave *immediately,* I'll shoot you both. I'll ransack the place and police will think it was a burglary."

Roslyn thought at once of the bonds. Ed's scenario could work, simply because there'd already been one theft here. She nodded, eased the suitcase onto the floor and noisily walked down the rest of the hall into the kitchen.

"Sophie! What is it?" she asked.

Sophie was standing just inside the screen door. She pulled back her head and narrowed her eyes at Roslyn's greeting.

Too loud and blustery, Roslyn guessed. She swallowed again. "I called your place."

Sophie nodded. "My sister told me." She glanced at the table, noticing the envelope with her name on it. "You leaving?"

Roslyn felt her face redden. "Yes, that's why I called. I'm glad you dropped by so I could give you this.'' She swept up the envelope and held it out to the other woman.

"You wouldn't have left before I got back to you about the bonds, surely?'' Sophie's eyes flicked from Roslyn's trembling hand to her face. She ignored the envelope Roslyn was holding.

"No, but...but take this anyway. Actually, I've been on the phone.''

Sophie glanced at the telephone.

"The extension in the living room,'' Roslyn rushed to add.

"Oh, yeah?'' She fixed her eyes on Roslyn a long uncomfortable moment, then opened up the canvas bag she was clutching. "Here, I've brought you something.'' She held out the leather sack with the bearer bonds.

Roslyn gulped. She put the envelope down and held on to the table edge, steadying herself.

"I want you to know how very bad I feel about this, Roslyn.'' Sophie kept shaking her head. Her eyes brimmed with tears. "That day you found the box, when you'n me were talking about it here in the kitchen, well...my nephew, Frankie, was standing just outside on the porch. He'd been here earlier that morning, looking for me, and hung around the back porch. Eavesdropping.'' She paused, shaking her head sadly. "He came once before—the other night. That's why you smelled the cigarette smoke.''

Roslyn started to speak, but Sophie held up a palm. "No, no, let me finish while I've got my nerve up. As I was sayin', the day he dropped by to ask me for some money he heard everything you said and last night he came by on his bike. When he saw you leave, he just walked in the back door and helped himself. I can't tell you how sorry and ashamed I am.''

Roslyn's head reeled. She knew Ed was standing in the hall, gun poised. She had to get rid of Sophie. But now this. How much longer would Ed give her?

''Sophie, don't worry about it. You take that bag with you to Mac right now. He'll know what to do.''

Sophie stared at Roslyn as if she'd lost her mind. ''But that's why I came here, Roslyn. So Mac wouldn't have to know. See, Jack came by this morning.''

Roslyn weaved against the table.

''You okay? You look like you're going to faint. Maybe you had too much sun today.''

''I'm okay, really. Go ahead—but, please, be quick. I've got an important call on the line.''

Sophie frowned. ''Whyn't you just pick up the receiver there and tell them to call back?''

Roslyn shook her head. ''No, no. Just tell me.''

Sophie looked at the telephone again, then back to Roslyn. ''See, Frankie was so desperate to move to Des Moines. Anyway, my sister's beside herself with worry. If Frankie gets picked up for this, he'll be sent to the state prison. Jack came to see me about a few things—he'll discuss that with you later—and then he and I talked. He said if you hadn't already called Mac you might be willing to—''

''Drop the matter? Sophie, of course. Whatever I can do.''

Sophie turned her head toward the hallway. ''What's that? You hear something?''

"Just the house settling. Okay, Sophie. I'll talk to you about it later. Right now, you take the bonds to Jack."

Sophie frowned. "Why to Jack? You keep them." She extended her arm, trying to push the leather sack at Roslyn.

"I don't want them, Sophie. Now, here—" she pushed the envelope with letter and check into Sophie's bag "—take the bonds to Jack right now. Hear me? I've got to go." Then she pivoted Sophie around toward the door and, kicking it open with her foot, hustled the older woman out onto the back porch. Impulsively, she ducked her head down to kiss Sophie on the cheek.

"I'll never forget you, Sophie," she whispered and closed both doors behind her, leaving Sophie gaping mutely through the curtained window.

"Don't even think about it," uttered Ed from somewhere behind Roslyn. "Move away from the door and back into the hall. When she's gone, we'll be on our way."

Roslyn did as he ordered. She knew he wouldn't hesitate to hurt her—or Sophie. She backed toward the hall and stood there, huddled with him as if they were both hiding from a monster.

Except he's right here, beside me.

Sophie's car chugged noisily down the drive. Ed grabbed Roslyn's arm and pushed her ahead of him, through the hall to the front door. He ducked his head to see through a clear corner of the etched window, then turned back to Roslyn.

"Terrific performance, Roslyn. Now, pick up your

suitcase. I think it's wiser to leave by the back door. That's the way I came in, since you left it so conveniently open for me."

"Where's your car? It can't be in the drive or Sophie would've said something."

"Just a few yards down the road, toward the town limits. A quaint town, by the way. Especially if its citizens can so blithely leave doors unlocked. I'm surprised you didn't decide to stay and claim your inheritance. It seems a beautiful old home. However," he tittered, "too late to change your mind now. Come along."

Roslyn stooped to grasp the suitcase handle. Ed motioned with the gun, pointing it to the kitchen. "Move."

She set the case down to fumble at the doors. Her hands shook so badly she had to make two attempts.

"Stop wasting time!" Ed hissed. He shoved the gun against the small of her back, pushing her out the door and onto the porch landing.

She cried out, trying to reach around to rub the place with her hand. He knocked the suitcase aside, tossing it over the railing onto the ground. Then he grabbed her by the elbow, twisting her arm up behind her back. She grunted in pain.

"Get going!" he shouted.

"Not while you're twisting my arm like that."

He released her. "Okay. Let's do this as calmly as possible without attracting neighborly attention."

Roslyn gripped the railing, afraid that her legs would give out from under her and she'd slide to the bottom. When she set one foot tentatively onto the ground, she thought she saw something at the corner of her field of vision.

"Go pick up the suitcase," Ed ordered.

She moved to her right, toward the case, and was bending over it when she heard a dull thud from behind. She spun around, clasping her hands in front of her as if in prayer.

Ed was lying facedown on the grass. Jack stood behind him, clenching a garden spade.

CHAPTER EIGHTEEN

"GOOD THING YOU forgot to put the spade away," Jack said. He let it drop and rushed to gather Roslyn in his arms. He ducked his face into the swirl of hair about her head.

When he came up for air, he said, "I've been standing under that porch for the last couple of minutes afraid to breathe."

She clutched him, still too shocked to speak. Finally, she lifted her head. "How did you know?"

"Just a fluke. After you left this morning, I went over to Sophie's and had a long talk. I'll get to that later. While I was there, she confided that she suspected Frankie had taken the bonds. She asked me to confront him with her, but he was out. We drove all over town before we finally tracked him down. The kid was scared, so he didn't hesitate to hand them over."

There was a moan from behind. Ed was trying to sit up. Roslyn clasped a hand to her mouth.

Jack held up his hand. "It's all right. I gave him a good whack right on the back of the knees. He may be conscious, but he's not going anywhere."

"His gun—"

"Right." Jack sprinted over to where the gun had

flown when Ed fell. He picked it up and pointed it at Ed. "The police are on their way, buddy. Just relax and consider what more I'd like to do with you." Then, he asked Roslyn, "Who is he, anyway?"

"My boss, Ed Saunders. The person responsible for Jim's death. And much, much more."

"Your *boss?* Geez!" Jack walked backward to Roslyn, keeping the gun fixed on Ed. "When Sophie came rushing out of the house, she was raving about how strangely you were behaving. I remembered seeing the tail end of a car down past the stop sign as I pulled into your drive. So I told Sophie to get Mac. By the time I got to the bottom of the stairs, I heard him shouting at you inside the kitchen. That's when I spotted the garden spade under the porch."

Roslyn shuddered, thinking how it might have been if Jack had bounded up to the kitchen instead. She reached up to kiss him on the cheek. He squeezed her with one arm, keeping the other trained on Ed. "As I said," he murmured huskily, "if you hadn't left that spade there...." He stopped, at a loss for words, clutching her tightly against him.

They were still locked together when the wail of Mac's cruiser drifted down the street. It was accompanied by pained howling from Ed as he attempted to get to his feet. As soon as Mac rounded the corner of the house, gun drawn, he took control. Checking that Roslyn was uninjured, he asked her to call an ambulance for Ed. She was happy to oblige, eager to escape Ed's moans.

Sophie arrived behind the ambulance and, once the horror of what had happened subsided, began to make tea and sandwiches. After the ambulance pulled out of the drive, the two men joined Sophie and Roslyn in the kitchen.

Roslyn dropped the spoon she was stirring her tea with and ran to Jack. His arms swept her up, crushing her to him in an embrace so close Roslyn heard only muted clinkings of cups and saucers as Sophie and Mac moved quietly about the kitchen. She buried her face into Jack's shirt, basking in the soothing pats of his hands and the hushed words he whispered into her hair. Especially the ones he brushed against her ear after kissing it gently.

"I love you so much, Rosie. So very much."

And she knew then all the decisions had miraculously been made for her.

IT WASN'T UNTIL Mac had departed, with Sophie following swiftly on his heels, that Roslyn looked at the time.

"I'm supposed to take the four o'clock bus to Des Moines!"

"I don't think you made it," Jack said.

She laughed, but had caught the dismay in his face and the disbelief in his eyes. "No. I guess I should call the airline and—"

"Cancel?"

"I was going to say reschedule." She looked at him and couldn't say any more.

"Don't go, Rosie," he murmured.

"I have to, Jack. There are too many things to finish up." She uttered a nervous laugh. "I have— *had*—a whole life there. I can't simply walk away from it."

"Sure you can. You can do whatever you want."

"There are other people to consider, too."

"People like me," he said. "And Sophie."

"Of course. Heavens, you and Sophie mean more to me than you'll ever know."

"Tell me now. If it's the last thing you do before leaving, tell me how much we mean to you."

"I—I don't know where to start. When I first came to Plainsville, I never expected to stay more than a few days. And I'm still here!" She laughed, glancing across the table at him. But his eyes were serious, intent on her face. Waiting for her.

Roslyn felt unexpectedly self-conscious. She'd never been good at expressing her inner feelings. "All the things that have happened here have changed me in ways I can't even articulate. Not yet. I just know that before I came, I was like a…a piece of cork on an ocean. Unconnected to anyone. Learning about my family has made me see my life in such a different way. I know one thing. I'm not going to turn a deaf ear to love when it knocks at *my* door.

"Like Ida Mae," she explained at the quizzical look he gave her. "Sure, I accept that she was crushed by my grandparents' betrayal of her trust. But then she spurned the truly genuine love of a man who spent the whole rest of his life being her friend when I'm sure what he really wanted to be was—"

"Her lover."

Roslyn locked eyes with Jack. "Yes," she murmured. "Her lover. And to think she could have had such a better life if only she'd accepted Henry when she had the chance." She took a deep breath. "Jack," she said, her voice cracking hoarsely, "I'm not going to be like Ida Mae. I'm going to take my chance when it comes."

He held out a hand to her and Roslyn slipped out of her chair, moving to his side of the table. He pulled her onto his lap. He cupped her chin in his hands and looked long and hard into her face. "Promise," he whispered huskily. "Promise you'll come back. I love you, Roslyn. If you don't come back to Plainsville to be with me, my life'll be worth nothing."

Roslyn lifted her head at the hard certainty in his voice. She smiled, but felt the tears brim in her eyes. She stretched her neck to kiss the lobe of his ear, then his cheek.

"I'll come back," she promised. Tucking her head back into the safe harbor of his neck and shoulders, she whispered once more, "I'll come back soon."

JACK GLANCED UP from the cash register to the door. He'd asked Lenny to lock up on his way out, but the bell signaled another customer had just entered. He bit back the "We're closed" comment on the tip of his tongue as Mac Christensen walked toward him.

"Closing early today?" Mac asked when he reached the counter.

"Yeah. Why? Did you finally remember whether Patsy wanted pansies or impatiens?"

"Ha ha." But a grin split Mac's face. "Thought I'd pop round to tell you that Saunders's trial for Naismith's murder's been set for late July. Hope that's not going to interfere with the Jensen family picnic?"

Jack rubbed the crease along his forehead. He

hoped not, too. ''The picnic's set for the week after Fourth of July celebrations, so as not to conflict.''

''Good. Then it shouldn't conflict with the trial, either.'' He hesitated, keeping his gaze fixed on Jack. ''Heard from Roslyn lately?''

Jack scowled. Seemed like everyone he knew had been tiptoeing around that question for days now. ''She's only been gone two weeks,'' he grumbled. ''Geez.''

''Easy, friend. Just asking. Guess the police in Chicago will have to decide about the charges against Saunders from this end. Plus there's a little matter of murder to be dealt with.''

''Guess everyone'll have to get in line,'' Jack muttered.

''You said it.'' Mac drummed his fingertips on the counter.

Obviously, he had more to say. Jack took the day's receipts out of the till. He hoped Mac wasn't bringing him bad news.

What he didn't have the nerve to admit to his friend was that he hadn't heard from Roslyn for almost a week now. The last time they'd talked, she'd been revved up about all the goings-on at the office. Partway through the conversation, he'd begun to feel a little drumroll of anxiety beat its way up into his throat. She'd sounded just a tad too excited about the place.

When he'd tried to pin her down about her return to Plainsville, she'd been frustratingly vague. Talk of arrangements, phone calls here and there, subletting her condo and so on. After the first few items on her list he couldn't hear over the pounding in his ears. He was certain life in Chicago was making a claim on her again and the thought terrified him. He'd even begun making arrangements to head for Chicago himself. But then she promised to be in Plainsville to see the Iowa rose in bloom.

When she'd asked him for a ballpark time on when that would happen, he'd quickly blurted, "Tomorrow." She'd just laughed.

He closed the cash register drawer with more strength than he'd intended. Mac's fingers froze on the countertop.

"Feeling a bit anxious?" Mac asked.

"About what, Mac? I'm just trying to finish here. What is it you came in for, anyway?"

The grin widened. "Told you, the trial date and all." Then Mac frowned. "Oh, I also saw Sophie this afternoon. Coming out of the grocery store. Seems like her sister and the kids are making a new start in Des Moines."

Jack nodded. "Yeah. Her sister got a job there and Frankie's going back to school. Some special program for kids at risk."

"That's great. Just what Sophie needed—get that worry off her mind. I actually was surprised to see her carrying so many groceries. She said she'd been asked to do some shopping." Mac waited a beat. "For Roslyn."

Jack gripped the counter's edge. He could feel his mouth moving but nothing was coming out.

Mac laughed. He playfully punched Jack's shoulder. "I shouldn't be such a low-down rat, should I?

Have to tell you though, I was a bit alarmed to see some lights on at Ida Mae's barely half an hour ago.''

Jack handed Mac the cash bag.

''What's this? What are you doing?''

''Close up, Mac. Take the money home with you. I know it'll be safe.''

''Wait! I haven't got to the good part—''

But Jack was already running across the parking lot to his truck.

ROSLYN WAS SITTING on the veranda when the red pickup roared into the drive. She smiled. She'd seen Mac's cruiser prowl by the house twenty minutes ago and figured Jack would be here soon enough.

But as cool as she tried to be, nothing could have kept her on the chair once he climbed out of the driver's side. She met him halfway, on the flagstone path leading from the drive to the central sidewalk.

He didn't say a word, just pulled her into his arms, pressing her into his trembling frame so hard she thought she might disappear. Finally he loosened his grip, stepping back just enough to look down at her. He gently knuckled away the tears at the corners of her eyes and lowered his mouth to hers. The kiss was as sweet as every dream she'd had about it for the past two weeks. And just as breathtaking.

She had to pull away for air. ''I've been out of practice,'' she laughed.

''Why didn't you call again?''

The smile on his face hadn't budged so she knew he wasn't upset. ''I was going to,'' she explained. ''But I didn't know for sure until this morning that I was free to leave. My new tenant signed a sublease agreement and I figured, heck! Why stay in Chicago another twenty-four hours.''

He laughed then, clutching her to him. ''I'm afraid I'll wake up and find myself in the middle of another daydream.''

''Is that how you've spent the last two weeks?'' she teased.

''More or less.''

''God you look wonderful,'' she murmured.

''And you.''

They strolled along the path toward the house. Roslyn suddenly stopped. ''Is the rose in bloom? I didn't notice.''

Jack pointed to the rosebush, covered with buds that were on the verge of splitting open. ''Any day,'' he said. ''Maybe tomorrow.''

Roslyn stared at the plant. ''Maybe I'll stay up all night to wait for it.''

He laughed, pulling her into his side. ''I wouldn't do that. Besides, what if you're disappointed? It's only a rosebush.''

She craned her face to his. ''No, it isn't. It's my history. And my future.''

Jack kissed her again. When his mouth left hers, Roslyn tugged on his arm. ''Come on.''

He followed her onto the veranda. ''You were obviously expecting someone,'' he said, staring at the table set with candles, champagne and a plate of tempting appetizers.

''Of course, I was, silly.'' She placed a glass in his hand and poured some sparkling wine into it. ''You.''

"You didn't call when you got back."

"No need." She poured her own and set the bottle down on the table. "Plainsville grapevine," she said, smiling up at him.

"Roslyn, I—"

She held a finger to his lips. "Shhh. Bear with me, love. I want to make a toast. It's a long one, so be prepared. And take that worried look off your face."

Roslyn raised her glass. "Here's to the family I never knew I had. Here's to the family I once had. And my father, because he'll soon be visiting Plainsville." She giggled suddenly. "Wait, Jack. Don't touch. If you do that, I won't be able to finish. Please!"

"Go on," he whispered.

"Here's to the family I hope to have—in Plainsville."

Jack moved forward and gently took the glass from her hand. "Keep talking," he murmured. "I'm not sure where you're going with this, but it sounds good to me." He set the glass down and wrapped his arms around her.

Roslyn tilted her head back to look at him. "Jack," she whispered, "I called Randall Taylor yesterday."

"And?"

"And I told him I couldn't possibly take this house—"

He inhaled sharply, but said nothing, keeping his eyes on hers.

"Unless you promised to live in it with me every day for—"

"The rest of our lives," he finished. "Of course, my sweet Iowa Rosie."

▼ SILHOUETTE®
SUPERROMANCE™

AVAILABLE FROM 16TH APRIL 2004

BECAUSE OF THE BABY Anne Haven

Nine Months Later

When Melissa Lopez and Kyle Davenport give in to their secret attraction, Melissa becomes pregnant and their baby needs two parents. A wedding seems like the best solution…but will they be able to risk love?

LOST BUT NOT FORGOTTEN
Roz Denny Fox

Mitch Valetti knows the silver urn he found by the side of the road contains the precious memory of a life. But who does it belong to…? And who is the stranger in town, beautiful Gillian Stevens, hiding from?

CHILD OF HER DREAMS Joan Kilby

When Dr Ben Matthews meets supermodel Geena Hanson, it's a case of opposites attracting—he thinks she's shallow and she thinks he doesn't take her seriously. But *something* sets the passion simmering…

WONDERS NEVER CEASE Debra Salonen

Count on a Cop

Clever ambitious journalist Jill Martin isn't officer Ben Jacobs' usual type. But his canine partner Czar seems to approve of her—and soon Ben finds he can't fault Czar's judgement.

In Trinity Harbour, a little trouble breathes
new life into an old love. . .

On sale 16th April 2004

*Available at most branches of WH Smith,
Tesco, Martins, Borders, Eason, Sainsbury's
and all good paperback bookshops.*

0504/047/SH74

2 FREE

books and a surprise gift!

We would like to take this opportunity to thank you for reading this Silhouette® book by offering you the chance to take TWO more specially selected titles from the Superromance™ series absolutely FREE! We're also making this offer to introduce you to the benefits of the Reader Service™—

* ★ FREE home delivery
* ★ FREE gifts and competitions
* ★ FREE monthly Newsletter
* ★ Exclusive Reader Service offers
* ★ Books available before they're in the shops

Accepting these FREE books and gift places you under no obligation to buy, you may cancel at any time, even after receiving your free shipment. Simply complete your details below and return the entire page to the address below. *You don't even need a stamp!*

YES! Please send me 2 free Superromance books and a surprise gift. I understand that unless you hear from me, I will receive 4 superb new titles every month for just £3.59 each, postage and packing free. I am under no obligation to purchase any books and may cancel my subscription at any time. The free books and gift will be mine to keep in any case.

U4ZED

Ms/Mrs/Miss/Mr ....Initials...............................
BLOCK CAPITALS PLEASE

Surname ....

Address ....

....

....Postcode................................

Send this whole page to:
UK: FREEPOST CN81, Croydon, CR9 3WZ
EIRE: PO Box 4546, Kilcock, County Kildare (stamp required)

Offer valid in UK and Eire only and not available to current Reader Service subscribers to this series. We reserve the right to refuse an application and applicants must be aged 18 years or over. Only one application per household. Terms and prices subject to change without notice. Offer expires 31st July 2004. As a result of this application, you may receive offers from Harlequin Mills & Boon and other carefully selected companies. If you would prefer not to share in this opportunity please write to The Data Manager, PO Box 676, Richmond, TW9 1WU.